THE MONKEY HOUSE

Also by John Fullerton

The Soviet Occupation of Afghanistan

The
MONKEY HOUSE
John Fullerton

LONDON NEW YORK SYDNEY TORONTO

This edition published 1996
by BCA
by arrangement with Bantam Press

First reprint 1996

CN 5828

Printed in England by Clays Ltd, St Ives plc

To the memory of Rory Peck.

DAY ONE

1

'No-one knows what he can't do until he tries.'
ANON

ROSSO WAS ALIVE AND ASHAMED OF IT.

The policeman could do nothing about the sense of elation he felt at being alive when others were dead, or the shame that followed.

I live, others die.

It was a high like no other, better than amphetamines, even sex. Whenever it happened he wanted to laugh, hug people, throw a party, drink too much and get laid. It was like living at the speed of light while others crawled around in slow motion, as if underwater.

I am never so alive as when others die, he told himself. The sensation was brief, something akin to shock, but the shame which followed on its heels remained like a stain: I don't deserve to live any more than they do and they are dead.

He told himself the exhilaration at having survived countless incidents was entirely natural, an animal thing, an involuntary squirt of adrenalin mainlined into the bloodstream, a narcotic hit at the illusory conquest of death. It never failed, any more than the cold, teeth-chattering funk that preceded it or the self-disgust that followed.

It was only a step from there to atrocity. It was out of a desire to defeat fear of death that some men who survived in battle mutilated the bodies of their enemies. It was why they took trophies – a fingertip, ear or testicles – why they sometimes ate a portion of their foes' remains or left a calling card, such as an ace of spades, in the victim's mouth.

More than once he saw survivors clowning with the enemy dead, lying down among them, sticking lit cigarettes between their cold lips, propping them upright, shaking their stiff, bloodied hands, talking to them and finding the whole thing uproariously, hysterically funny.

It's not personal, he told himself.

Rosso could not afford to let it get personal. If he believed every artillery shell, anti-aircraft round and sniper's bullet were directed at him, he would not be able to get out of bed each morning, let alone cope with the job in hand.

Much better, he said to himself as he climbed out of the minibus into the snow, to imagine that you're simply a blade of grass and some asshole in a silly hat and check pants with a club is trying for a hole in one all the way down the fairway.

The travellers stood on the icy airfield, the snow whipped up by the wind flailing at their legs. They stamped their feet and beat their hands together. Rosso counted five apart from himself. They put their bags in a neat row under the wing of the huge plane that towered above them and then they stood back in a semicircle and seemed to inspect one another, shifting from one foot to the other and swinging their arms about as if engaged in a tribal ritual. Faces muffled in scarves and woollen hats, bodies bulging in puffer jackets, hands flapping in mittens. Anonymous, sexless. Rosso almost burst out laughing at the sight. Not a word was said. Their voices would have been torn from their mouths and shredded by the gusts of wind in any case. Rosso saw that the plane's engines – like huge silvery seedpods suspended from the wings – were still protected by orange plastic covers. There was no sign of life on board. The doors were shut. Even the cockpit canopy appeared to have a shutter across it. He turned slowly and could hardly make out the airport control tower or the terminal. The buildings were obscured by the horsetails of snow hissing across the runways. There were no other planes taking off or landing. The wind moaned about the lone and immobile Russian aircraft, rising to a shriek where it pushed past innumerable rivets in its metal skin. The snow whispered like blown sand, the millions of tiny pellets of ice pattering and crackling against their clothing, stinging hands and faces.

Someone kicked open the door in the side of the plane above Rosso's head. The policeman moved backwards and, craning his neck, looked up. A crewman pushed out an aluminium ladder and started to climb down. The flimsy device shook at every step the Russian took. Once on the ice the crewman turned and looked at Rosso, as if sizing him up, finally jerking his head at the ladder. Rosso did not hesitate. He picked up his bag, hoisted it onto his shoulder and climbed.

Fifty-three minutes later the plane – a massive, noisy and uncomfortable contraption called an Ilyushin-76, chartered from the Russians by the International Committee of the Red Cross – was about to drop from 14,000 feet to a few hundred in four minutes, a steep spiral to evade ground fire. Rosso, standing in the cockpit behind the copilot, was told by a crewman to bend his knees and get a grip on the fuselage as the nose dipped and twisted sharply. It felt to Rosso like a roller-coaster, only a roller-coaster was scary in a delicious sort of way, because you knew you were safe at a fairground. Here you knew nothing of the sort. Every part of the metal flying machine seemed to be howling in protest. It was a wonder the huge wings weren't torn off. He could see them rocking and trembling. The passengers' luggage was doing its best to escape the netting securing it to the deck. Rosso's stomach went into his throat and he found himself gazing up instead of down at the crests of the snow-crusted hills around the city as they zigzagged towards the runway, standing on one wing, the horizon slipping to the vertical and back again the other way.

Any moment there would be the heart-stopping bellyflop, the scream of brakes, the roar of reversed engines and the sudden silence as crew and passengers held their breath and listened for incoming from Serb lines.

If the odds were infinitesimal, then how come so many people got hit? No, he told himself, riding on his toes, this is no time for asking questions of that nature. Not in this flying coffin. Be a modest blade of grass instead.

Their papers checked and their pathetic bundles searched by UN police, the six tired, dispirited Bosnians were led out to the yard behind the terminal, waiting patiently in the mud to board a French armoured troop carrier for the run through a Serb checkpoint 800 metres from the French bunker at the airport entrance. It was a half-hourly shuttle service. Always the Serbs – wearing paramilitary blue uniforms and carrying automatic weapons – demanded to check the passengers, and so far at least the UN soldiers had always denied them the pleasure. Rosso could always hear their voices raised through the quarter-inch of steel behind his head. It was just a matter of time before the Cetniks decided to force the issue by using crowbars on the hatches. There were a thousand and one ways for the separatists to turn the screw and they knew them all. The detective hoped he wasn't travelling when it happened.

He sat near the rear of the Panhard and glimpsed the wreck of the city's lone Bosnian T-55 tank in the ditch, red with rust and its 105mm gun pointed impotently at a bruised grey sky, the muzzle choked with ice.

You didn't have to come back, Rosso told himself.

That tank made his heart sink every time he saw it. It stood for everything that had gone wrong: the false hopes, the clutching at straws, the ease with which the Serbs had bottled them up in this ghetto of a city.

Squinting through the peep-hole set in the rear doors, Rosso mentally ticked off each stage in their journey. There were the gutted houses lining the route, the windows and doors like empty eye sockets in fleshless skulls, each a potential firing point for a sniper. Moslems to the left, Serbs to the right. Here was the worst: he could hear the gears shift, the whine of the engine change as the troop carrier began to ascend the flyover at the western entrance to the city, frequently mortared and where both sides played chicken with UN patrols by firing rocket-propelled grenades at them. Rosso tensed for the impact, the final explosion that would tear them all apart. Think blades of grass. Think little white balls.

Think lucky.

The policeman worried about his car. That was the next and final stretch since leaving Zagreb that morning. To cope, Rosso mentally divided his journeys into stages, taking them one at a time. It was never wise to think too far ahead. He had left the squat Yugo outside the UN headquarters at the city's telecommunications building. It was in no man's land, but parked sufficiently close to the coils of razor wire to deter thieves, or so he hoped. Also it had a huge Bosnian coat of arms on the bonnet – the shield with the fleur-de-lis and the bar sinister – and above it the number 600: once the city's emergency services number. Once, because there were no emergency services worthy of the name any more and because the telephones worked at best intermittently, but most of the time not at all. Rosso was never really sure if the official badge emblazoned on the car would attract villains or repel them.

Nearly there and still alive. The first Bosnian army checkpoint lay ahead. He could see it in his mind's eye.

Welcome to Sarajevo.

Welcome home.

*   *   *

'Car coming,' said Mahmud. The burly fighter wore a battered trilby, a war-surplus, West German combat jacket and several layers of clothing beneath that. It was not surprising that he made no effort to get up. He held a one-shot glass of schnapps, full to the brim and he watched the clear liquid carefully lest it escape, car or no car. His bolt-action rifle was propped up against the side of the corrugated iron lean-to.

'It's your turn,' said his companion, a tall youth with a pinched expression exaggerated by hollow cheeks and stubble. When Zoran spoke it was obvious he had lost his front teeth. He was blowing on his fingers and stamping his feet. The skin, tight over his prominent cheek-bones, was a startling pink.

'It fuckin' ain't.'

'It'll cost you a smoke.'

'Here, fuckwit.' Mahmud tossed over a packet of twenty. 'Take one. One, mind!'

The boy, in jeans and bomber jacket with a Bosnian army badge crudely sewn on to the shoulder, lit up, threw the pack back, slung his weapon over his shoulder and shuffled outside. Zoran wore a black woollen cap, pulled down over his ears. His feet felt numb and he tried to wriggle his toes to get the blood moving in his damp boots. He had stuffed them with newspaper, but far from giving warmth all the paper had succeeded in doing was to restrict the circulation of blood to his feet. He saw a beige Yugo approach, parting the crowd of people trudging through the snow. The sentry checked that he had a round in the breech of his obsolescent Czech machine-pistol and extended the folding butt.

'Looks like our top cop,' he called over his shoulder.

At that his companion threw the schnapps down his throat, smacked his lips and heaved himself up. He looked round, patting his jacket, then hurriedly shoved his hands into one pocket after another until he found what he was looking for. He opened a fist, revealing a stub of pencil and a scrap of paper. His actions were hurried. He cast a furtive eye at the entrance, as if fearful that he would be observed. He bent, scribbled something, pausing at one point to lick the end of the pencil and turning his head to one side as if in deep thought. Finished at last, he rolled the note up into a tiny ball and pushed both it and the pencil back into a trouser pocket. Panting with the effort, he joined the other militiaman in the open, cradling the Mannlicher hunting rifle in his arms.

'Maybe he's got some coffee for us,' Mahmud said.

'Lucky bugger. Dunno why he bothers to come back.'

'It'll be a woman. Why else?'

Rosso drove with care, tapping the horn sparingly, almost apologetically, to forge a path through pedestrians searching for food, water and firewood. The crowd parted with painful reluctance, as if the walkers were unwilling to use more energy than was absolutely necessary.

He hunched forward, peering through a windscreen smeared with ice, both hands clenched on the wheel. He had no chains, and he could feel the little hatchback slipping on the layer of fresh, dry snow. The city was silent, the low mist obscuring the view of the gunners perched in the surrounding hills. On a clear day you could see the sun glint on their gun barrels, and they could see the moustache on a man's upper lip, even the colour of a woman's eyes, through their telescopic sights. People would sprint or hobble as fast as they could from one corner to the next, a contorted smile on their faces in the effort to at once mask the terror they felt and disguise the indignity of being compelled to run. Running for one's life became as routine as running for a bus in any other city. Most made it, some never did.

Today, despite the subzero temperature, everyone seemed to be out, taking advantage of the lull.

Rosso found these quiet periods disturbing. He could feel the fear like physical nausea, a nugget in his stomach, expand into his chest.

A silent scream of panic rose inside him.

He knew the calm to be deceptive, a lie and always shortlived. The price was always too high: more dead, people cut down queueing in front of a water-pipe or soup-kitchen. The Cetniks dug into the hillsides sought to lure people out of their chilly homes before lobbing a salvo of 152mm shells into a throng of civilians. It usually happened mid-morning. There would be a pause and just as ambulances arrived, the Serbs would loose off more rounds.

Rosso took to the backstreets, hugging the industrial sector. Many pedestrians were heading for a sawmill where there was a regular hand-out of bread. Although Rosso had one of the few cars and the petrol to keep it going, no-one spared him so much as a glance. They were moving in the same direction as the policeman, but were too intent on their mission, on not falling and breaking their brittle bones, to move quickly out of his way. If they were resentful, they did not waste effort expressing it. They carried 'perhaps bags' or tugged children's sleds in the hope of finding something, anything, to alleviate hunger and cold. They were thin, their faces blank, eyes unfocused. Rosso left this tide of ragged humanity and turned onto the main drag – he always knew how dangerous a place was by the number of people about and there no-one at all could be seen – save for one old man digging up the roots of a tree in the centre island. Only his head could be observed, bobbing up and down above the highway known as Sniper's Alley.

It was as if Rosso had stumbled into a world of scarecrows. I will look like them again very soon, he said to himself. A few months' living on scraps, no bathing, shaving with a blunt blade in cold water and wearing the same unwashed clothes. The same resigned stare, the soft-shoe shuffle through the snow to an empty market.

Patriotism meant nothing to the starving.

Perhaps that was part of the problem, Rosso thought. People were not starving, not really, they were simply malnourished, losing their vitality and health too slowly to die out of hand and not fast enough to take some desperate measure to alleviate their plight by an act of supreme will. Their passivity alarmed Rosso. As their teeth fell out, their skin developed ulcerous rashes and diarrhoea became routine, their ability to adapt, their acceptance of their lot

16

– including diversion of UN food on a huge scale to front-line units and the black market – was their very undoing. Had he fallen into the same trap, dreaming of an end to it all when there was none?

When he opened his door, Rosso could smell the soldiers at the checkpoint – the not altogether unpleasant smell of damp clothes, unwashed bodies, cigarette smoke and schnapps on their breath. They shivered in the icy wind; like half-starved young dog foxes eyeing a chicken, furtively drooling from the mouth.

He wondered if he looked well fed, and if they could smell his English mother's soap on his skin from the hot bath he had had that very morning at her home in Zagreb. He felt like a cartoonist's missionary in the cannibals' cooking pot.

They stared at his papers blankly, then asked respectfully for coffee, cigarettes: the currency of survival. Rosso always brought extra for the checkpoints, but he insisted the fighters paid the going rate. Otherwise, they would get greedy. He would be regarded as an easy mark and stripped of everything. On the other hand, by providing them with luxuries he was putting them in his debt. It made getting through checkpoints a lot easier.

He produced receipts for the 500-gram bag of coffee and a carton of cheap, Croatian-made cigarettes, showed them to the soldiers and waited while they muttered to each other and reluctantly dug the almost useless dinars out of their pockets.

They searched his vehicle carelessly, without interest.

Mahmud managed to push himself into the rear of the little car, his large buttocks protruding as he rummaged about behind the seats. He stopped suddenly, paused and then extricated himself. Red-faced and wheezing, he stood upright. Zoran handed him his rifle. He took it absently. They both stared at the gleaming metallic bottles on the floor behind the seats, looking questioningly at the detective and exchanged glances.

'Oxygen,' Rosso said helpfully, so they did not have to lose face by appearing ignorant or impolite by asking.

'Ah,' said Zoran, nodding. As if to say 'Of course, naturally. Think nothing of it.' And he stamped his frozen feet again and looked away, down the road. He wanted to get back to the lean-to and out of the wind. He had his cigarettes now.

'For the hospital,' Rosso said to Mahmud. He said it quietly, easily; he knew it could lead to unpleasantness.

'Wha'?'

'For premature babies, mothers in labour, the wounded—'

That was enough for Mahmud; enough talk of babies and women. He had a suspicious nature, he thought the worse of people if he could. Yet all talk of women and babies had him flustered and the policeman had spoken so calmly, so equably that further inquiries would only reveal his own ignorance of medical matters and all things female. Rosso was no stranger, besides, he was a senior police officer. Deference was his due.

It was the way things were. In the old days, one glance from Rosso would have been enough. They would have waved him through, never entertained the notion of searching his car. Now his authority was gone, or at least his official rank carried little weight. All that was left was the stamp of authority on his face, the way he carried himself, the tone of voice. Rosso knew how to obey orders, and he expected to be obeyed. It showed. But the badge, the rank, the office of superintendent – well, he had to admit they were not what they once were.

Mahmud grunted and slammed the door viciously, looking embarrassed, and then started apologizing for having treated the car door roughly. It was his clumsiness more than anything else. He opened it again. After all, they had not finished their search. There was the stuff in the front.

For his part, Rosso thought he had said too much, been too laboured in his explanation, the words tumbling out over one another in their haste, as if he had something to hide. He had: guilt – both particular and general. As for the particular kind, it was not the guilt of a smuggler, but of a man who has, for a few days at least, lived a normal life, shed the constant risk of a violent death, left behind the gradual humiliation of the effects of a bad diet and no way to clean either the body or the shabby clothes left on his back. Instead he had lived in the very lap of luxury (though he had hated every moment of it and perversely counted the days to his return) while others shivered, hungered, saw hope fade and died. He was alive, and who could say he deserved to be?

Guilt in general was Rosso's cross. It was what made him such a good detective, a diviner of men's secrets. He felt himself apart, living as one who expects to be found out at the very next moment. Rosso did not believe in original sin. He had lived it all his life. It gave him a peculiar empathy with the men and women he had to interrogate from time to time. He understood them better than they did themselves. As for common criminals, never for a moment did he believe himself superior; indeed, for much of the time they had his genuine sympathy.

The soldiers glanced cursorily at Rosso's bag on the front passenger seat. The policeman unzipped it for them; it was not locked. They made no comment on the bottle of perfume and the make-up he had bought in Zagreb. Rosso had laid these items on top for the very reason that they should deter a more rigorous search. Mahmud stared at the fat, fancy bottle with its amber liquid and the pink, plastic make-up bag until Zoran nudged him roughly, as if telling him not to pry into another's affairs.

There was a bottle of vodka, a few cigarettes.

Rosso felt Mahmud next to him. It felt as if the bulky Moslem was pushing him. For a moment Rosso was irritated, annoyed at Mahmud's clumsiness. But then his right hand was grabbed, his wrist held firmly. Something was pushed into his palm, his own fingers forcibly curled around whatever it was and in a moment Mahmud had moved away from him again.

Zoran appeared to have noticed nothing.

'No Scotch, chief?' Mahmud cried in mock surprise, his humour restored to him. Zoran grinned, then covered his gap-toothed mouth with his fingerless mitten. Simple, decent men in their way, Rosso thought. But there were no doubt simple, decent men up in those hills. Simple, decent men could do, and did, the most terrible things.

*   *   *

19

There was a commotion down the road, the way Rosso had come, the sound of car horns blaring continuously, like sirens. Mahmud and Zoran stepped back. Mahmud put his hand on the superintendent's arm.

'Watch out!'

The three men stared at the approaching cavalcade.

There were three cars, moving at surprising speed through the crowd from the south-west – the way Rosso had come – and making little allowance for the shabby tide of humanity. First came a silver grey Mercedes, luxuriously sleek, its headlights on. Two men had their heads and shoulders out of the rear windows, Kalashnikov rifles pointed skywards.

Behind the Merc and slightly to each side were the two chase cars, black Opels packed with gunmen, weighed down so much that the exhausts almost scraped the surface of the ice. The gunmen held the doors ajar, ready to spring out and beat some poor unfortunate if he or she did not move out of the way fast enough. They shouted and waved their guns.

Rosso turned away. He felt ashamed that people could be subjected to this display of intimidation; that this arrogance was being flaunted in this place and at this time. He felt personal shame, too, that he of all people, one of the most senior police officers left in the capital, simply stood by.

On the sides of the escort cars were painted yellow moons, each with the black outline of a wolf, head thrown back, baying: the emblem of the so-called Special Forces. They were special all right, Rosso thought, but not in the manner of America's celebrated Green Berets or Germany's crack Grenzschutsgruppe-9 anti-hijack force. Luka's boys were street fighters, thugs who had taken advantage of the siege to adopt the trappings of official sanction but more than ever saw themselves as beyond the law.

'Luka,' said Mahmud, as if anyone needed telling.

'Good man,' said Zoran, raising a hand in salute.

'I fuck your mother and sister,' Mahmud said in an almost

conversational voice – lest he be heard by the gunmen leaning from the cars – and he contented himself with a sullen glare in their direction.

'Fuck your God,' retorted Zoran. Then he laughed and clapped Mahmud on the shoulder. The Moslem ignored the insult. It was commonplace. Zoran was his mate, anyhow. A curse meant nothing, reduced to insignificance by repetition in a city still largely secular, multiconfessional in outlook.

All it meant was that they disagreed about Luka's place in the order of things.

The convoy surged past. Mud and melted snow spurted up from the potholed road. The heavily laden Opels bounced up and down as they went by. The passing gunmen gazed blankly at the checkpoint and its comically dressed guardians. They did not return Zoran's wave. They wore black woollen caps like commandos, Rosso saw, part of the dressing-up men indulge in when they set about creating the myth of their own narcissistic invincibility.

Rosso bent slightly, hands on knees, and looked carefully at the Mercedes. He was sure he could see, just for an instant, Luka at the wheel. He was staring straight ahead, sitting up straight, head high, that long jaw jutting forward. The detective wasn't searching for Luka. He was looking for Tanja and he felt relieved when he failed to see his god-daughter sitting next to him.

What would she have said if she had been sitting there and seen Rosso standing in the snow at the side of the road? Would she have urged Luka to have stopped, right there, and offered him a lift home? Or would she have hesitated, as so many people do, until the moment passed and then rationalized out her failure to stop? Just one of life's innumerable little betrayals of someone we love, until they accumulate into indifference, or worse? Was she ashamed of her adoptive family already? Had the cars and guns gone to her head? Were the tales of glory too good to resist in a climate of despair?

Would he have accepted a lift?

But she wasn't there, so it didn't matter.

'Always in a bloody rush,' grumbled Zoran. His admiration for Luka slightly dented by the fact that his trousers were liberally sprayed with a new layer of Sarajevo's glutinous mud.

Rosso had lost a bottle of whisky to the Polish police officer who had searched his bag at the airport – the price of letting him through with the oxygen. The police contingent at the airport was huge, unnecessarily so, and seemed to comprise every nationality under the sun. All the officers seemed to do was stand around and wait for a genuine civilian, a local, someone like Rosso, so they could order him about, demand papers, wave rules in his face – their rules, not his – and filch cigarettes and whisky. And he, the city's most senior detective, one of three deputies reporting to the interior minister himself. It was humiliating.

Anyhow, what was the point of bringing home expensive foreign booze to an alcoholic wife who'd distil it from boot polish if she had to? When he thought of Sabina, his heart sank. She was a responsibility that hung heavily on his mind simply because no solution presented itself. It was like an incurable disease. Alcoholism wasn't incurable, of course, but the state of mind that brought it about apparently was. His thoughts turned instead to Tanja, their godchild. Rosso was anxious about her too. She was nineteen, a refugee. Since the Rossos had taken her under their wing – they had no children of their own – Tanja had qualified as a paramedic and had recently formed something of a friendship with Luka. He was always going off to the front line for a taste of the action and taking her with him. It was a taste the police officer would never acquire and he wished Tanja would stay well away – from both Luka and front lines. At first it had seemed a useful way to find out more about the man. Indeed, Rosso had encouraged her, had put her information to good use, but now Rosso feared his god-daughter was developing a genuine attachment to the man people called, not without irony, the Robin Hood of Sarajevo. He had used her; was she now using him? Were all families like this? They felt so much

22

and had so much to say to one another and yet were so tongue-tied and inhibited in expressing the things that really mattered. What mattered now was tenderness. Like food placed before a man with a full belly, love had been taken for granted, used carelessly in times of peace. Now Rosso felt it well up in him. Tears came to his eyes. He wiped them away with the back of his hand. You sentimental old fool, he told himself. You're not even drunk.

Just afraid, and that was nothing new.

'It was a woman, all right,' said Mahmud, waddling back to his seat in the lean-to and collapsing onto it with a sigh.

'How do you know?'

'Didn't you see that big bottle of perfume?'

'He could be planning to sell it.'

'Bollocks. If he wanted to deal on the black market he would have brought more smokes and coffee. No, he's cunt-struck, poor fellow.'

Mahmud, a former nightclub bouncer and amateur weightlifter, took a swig from the bottle and sat down. 'He's come back for a little boom-boom.' He made a pumping motion with his right fist. 'Boom-boom,' he said again.

'You're a cynic.'

'No, just wise as to the way the world works.'

'He's probably married with three kids.'

'Well, if he is, that bottle isn't for the wife.'

'We'll never know,' said the boy, disappointed by his companion's jaded view of humanity and bored by all the talk. Zoran was a countryman, his mother a Hercegovinan Croat and proud of it. All this chatter was the habit of idle Moslem townsfolk. A lot of good it did them.

'This war is full of people doing the right things for the wrong reasons and the wrong things for the right reasons,' Mahmud said importantly. 'The cop is one of them.'

'I wouldn't drink too much of that if I were you. It's turning you into a philosopher.'

As if to emphasize his contempt for philosophers, Zoran hawked spittle up from his throat and spat into the snow.

Mahmud was unmoved. He picked up the bottle again.

'Fuck off, will you?'

2

'Man is a social animal who detests his fellow man.'
DELACROIX

.

THE PRIDE OF SARAJEVO'S POLICE FORCE WAS IN A SORRY STATE, ITS
big glass doors peppered with shot and shell splinters and held
together with brown-paper strips. A large chain and padlock
proclaimed the main entrance to the headquarters temporarily
shut, though anyone brave or foolish enough to try that way in
could have crawled through the gaping holes – provided, of course,
that they managed to get that far. Instead, Rosso held his breath
and hurled his car across a pavement to the rear of the building,
shot across an exposed alley, hauled on the handbrake to execute
a slalom around two scarred cherry trees and finally plunged into
the darkness of a subterranean garage.

He climbed internal stairs to the detectives' offices on the third
floor. The stainless-steel lifts stood idle, their automatic doors
jammed half open. Out of breath, the detective threaded his way

through nests of desks to his glass box of an office. It had his name on the door: Rosso, Superintendent. He could see the files piled three feet high and spilling out of his in-tray. He snapped open a drawer in his unprepossessing metal desk, tossing in his badge, spare ammunition clip and gun, and kicked it shut. He took off his coat, hung it behind the door and flung his jacket over the back of his swivel chair. The detective removed his pullover and started rolling up his sleeves. Then, remembering there was no heating, he rolled them down again and did up the buttons on the cuffs. He looked across the room at the coffee machine. It had not worked for three years and when it had it produced anaemic Western dishwater. God, what wouldn't he do for a decent cup of fresh Turkish coffee, the real thing this time, flavoured with cardamom and accompanied by a sandwich of cheesy *kajmak* or, even better, *raznjici*, chunks of veal, cooked over charcoal. How wonderful to eat something so fattening, so tasty – the kind of food Sabina had always been telling him would give him a heart attack. A heart attack! He should be so lucky. There were plenty of heart attacks, but they weren't caused by overeating. The detective sat down, smiling to himself at the thought, pulling the first files towards him.

Rosso's cubby-hole spoke volumes about the man, yet said little at the same time. There was nothing whatsoever personal to distinguish it from a hundred others in similar government buildings across the city – no framed, autographed portraits of the rich, famous or powerful, no snapshots of wife and children, no sporting trophies, diplomas or signed football from a favourite city team. Nothing reflected any ambition, any desire for status, any endearing hobby. There were files, more files and still more files, stacked from floor to ceiling, tied neatly with tape. Every other part of the office was crammed with police directories, reference books on forensic science, textbooks on pathology, manuals on handguns and booklets on drug abuse. In one corner a personal computer with a cracked screen sat crookedly on a grey filing cabinet, covered with dust. There was just enough room for the incumbent to sit at his desk and for one other to squeeze in and

26

sit carefully, perilously close to pillars of books and folders, that a wrong move with elbow or foot could bring crashing down upon the visitor's head. This was the office, it seemed to say, of a man who keeps work and his private life separate, who eschews the symbols of a moderately successful career.

Beyond Rosso's self-effacing workspace the open-plan office was empty, the phones silent. He glanced at his watch: not yet nine. Rosso barely registered the rumble and rattle of gunfire. The bank of electronic clocks that was supposed to display the hour in Zagreb, Belgrade, Vienna, London and Moscow was dark. Time itself seemed to have stopped, leaving Sarajevo suspended in international limbo. The network of overhead tubes that used suction to propel little cartridges with urgent messages from one section to another, controlled from the aptly named Tube Room in the basement, had been silent for months. Rosso had grown fond of the weird popping sound they made as they hurtled around, carrying news of human nature's excesses. It was like having an upside-down model railway attached to the ceiling. The Tube Room's entire complement of eight had been marched off into the Army in one go and their office turned into a holding cell and nicknamed, for reasons that escaped Rosso, The Tank. Ranks of computers stared out blankly, their green screens filmed with dirt, their printers useless without ribbons.

The detectives' offices covered the whole floor. It was an impressive sight, once. The blinds were intact down Rosso's side, but on the southern flank of the building the windows were broken, most of them, and several desks and chairs lay jumbled up in a confused pile, like a forgotten bonfire no-one had remembered to set alight. The pot plants, once luxuriant things redolent of exotic, far-away tropical places with shiny, rubbery leaves, had long since shrivelled and died for lack of water. The venetian blinds were lopsided, holed, or dangled out of the gaping windows. No-one sat there any more – it was too exposed to enemy fire and anyway, there were more desks and chairs than staff. On that far side there were scorch marks on the walls, burnt patches in a carpet soaked with melted snow and littered with broken glass, while, from the ceiling, wires dangled like the ends of some monster tarantula's nest. The smart, 1970s look – all smoked glass, chrome, leather upholstery and bright Anatolian rugs, of which the police department had once been so very proud – and the careless disarray of war damage collided to create a dismal shabbiness, a sense of a world at odds with itself.

He looked away from the ruin, down at the desk in front of him and drew the files towards him, stretching out his arms and scooping them up. They were colour-coded and Rosso dealt with the buff ones first, the politically sensitive cases. The first folder contained a protest note, addressed to the presidency from the UN commander of Sarajevo, over the alleged failure to allow his men to retrieve evidence from the scene of a mortar attack in which four civilians had been killed. Security forces, it said, had refused UN troops access to the location, and had denied them physical evidence. Annotations, all classified, littered the margins. The vice-president, sensitive to foreign opinion, had scribbled in his tiny, crabbed academic's hand: 'This is having a negative impact among our friends.' Imamovic, the defence minister, added his own brusque dismissal: 'Nothing to do with the ministry.'

It was like an onion, Rosso thought, so many layers. These words are merely the skin. The government feared the United Nations had already compromised its sovereignty. As for the jottings, they represented the power play inside the presidency. The only man who really knew what had happened during the mortar attack was not mentioned, nor had he been invited to comment.

Luka.

Rosso sucked the end of his pen for a moment, then tore off a sheet of paper from a lined foolscap pad and scrawled a reply, to be forwarded to the UN civil affairs officer. It was a way of sidelining the affair, an exercise in buck-passing.

'Further to your . . . The Sarajevo Police Department regrets any restriction placed on UN officials, military or civil, in pursuit of their duties,' he wrote. 'But the Department points out that the area in which the attack occurred was, at the time, under the jurisdiction of the security authorities and cordoned off by militia in accordance with standing instructions and in the interests of national security as well as the prompt removal of wounded . . .' Rosso paused to inspect his handiwork, scratching the thinning hair at the crown of his head.

He scrabbled around in a drawer, looking for the official stamp and ink-pad. Then he threw the file in the out-tray.

Rosso riffled through the second buff envelope, pausing at a paper here, a memorandum there, the whole of it quite worn and discoloured, stapled together and comprising six months of correspondence between the police and the UN headquarters on the subject of black marketeering by the peacekeepers. Rosso began with an official note protesting against the sale by foreign troops of cigarettes and petrol to unlawful elements in the city and shook his head in part-admiration, part-despair at a UN rejoinder to the effect that it was the responsibility of local authorities to deal with organized crime. Rosso wrote a swift note in his blunt longhand: 'The Police Department will, with immediate effect, regard any infringement by UN personnel of the stringent regulations controlling the sale of food, alcohol, tobacco and fuel in Sarajevo as a contravention of Bosnian law and transgressors, local or foreign, will be dealt with under the Bosnian civil penal code . . .'

There was only one name that seemed to rise from these well-thumbed pages: Luka.

Forty minutes later, Rosso had reduced the pile in his in-tray to a foot of paper. He scribbled a comment to be attached to a report by the city's chief medical officer to the UN on the subject of venereal disease. He answered a query from the defence ministry on the reported theft of five Egyptian UN soldiers' personal weapons from their armoured personnel carrier, parked outside a mosque while the troops prayed inside. Rosso signed a note asking the United Nations Protection Force to prevent their men from importing narcotics into the city, composed another protest – carefully mixing what Rosso hoped was an element of diplomacy with firmness – at the UN soldiers' purchase of sexual favours from local women, and initialled a note from the interior ministry complaining of Luka's commandeering of government vehicles and petrol. He scanned and signed a report on the shooting of a UN soldier in civilian dress after curfew.

It was a game, Rosso told himself, and he had been saddled with a role in it because he was one of the very few senior officers left. Eventually it would be left to a sergeant from the traffic division, long after all traffic had finally vanished from the streets. These terms – ministry, department, division – represented mere shadows. It was all about saving face. It was about decline. It was about failure. Bit by bit, inch by inch and day by day, the presidency lost ground to the advancing ranks of professional bureaucrats under the blue flag. After all, it was they who delivered the food. Their planes and trucks provided the winterization materials – the plastic sheeting, the blankets. It was their diplomats and soldiers who negotiated a brief respite from the killing. Government was sliding under, yielding inexorably to pressure from superior Serb fire-power, the relentless weight of international bureaucracy and, finally, from men such as Luka.

Rosso, distaste written across his face at the thought, turned to the blue, criminal dossiers.

He glanced through them first: a teenage suicide, a double killing by a drunken off-duty soldier who found his girl in bed with the local butcher, sexual assault on a minor, armed robbery at the city's department store (an act of lunacy or stupidity, as there was nothing left on the shelves worth stealing), several reports of domestic violence and burglary, the odd case of extortion – the underside of urban life that Rosso understood. His bread and butter, so to speak. Even here, the siege had an impact. His forefinger traced the names of the perpetrators, the victims, the witnesses, the charges and the convictions. His lips moved as he counted, totting them up. Rape, relatively rare in Sarajevo before the war, was sharply up. Heroin addiction had gone through the roof. Every day, bodies were found; bound, shot through the head at close range and dumped in ditches or gutted buildings.

Rosso leant back, yawned. It was then that he remembered the incident at the checkpoint that morning – the ball of paper pushed into his hand by the gunman. Had he dropped it in the snow? Had it fallen? Rosso had only made the gesture of pocketing it so as not to appear discourteous.

It was still there. Rosso unfolded it, flattening it on the desk. It was grubby, a scrap torn from a newspaper. The message was written in crude capital letters. Rosso could hardly make them out. The pencil was faint, more scratches than lines.

NACELNIK. Supervisor. Woman murdered. Alipasino Polje, Block Nine, sixth floor. Mr Vasic knows but no-one come. Beware! Your friend.

There was only one woman Rosso knew of at Alipasino Polje, a neighbourhood to the south-west. It must be her.

'Boss!' A shout from the far side of the room, a clatter of doors opening, a rush of feet, voices all speaking at once.

There was no time to pull her file, but in his mind's eye he could see the woman's startled face, the light caught in her eyes by the police photographer, the black-and-white mugshot pinned to her file.

It must be her.

Sergeant Anil Salahuddin was her handler.

Had been.

Laughter and the hubbub of raised voices burst over him.

Rosso crumpled up the slip of paper.

Vasic rolled into view. He was a detective inspector, said by the department's wags to have won his fight against anorexia hands down during peacetime and who had now decided to take on the Serb siege single-handedly. He was, it was true, probably the only surviving fat man in Sarajevo. He was all that was left of the burglary squad, in fact, and he was indeed obese. His tie hung halfway down his bulging shirt and came to rest on a paunch that seemed to defy both gravity and the laws of anatomy. He could have stood a bottle of whisky on it. He wore a furry Tyrolean hat with a cockade of partridge feathers in the ribbon and set at a rakish angle on his head. Vasic did not bother to make his way between the desks and chairs. He simply bulldozed them aside as he made for Rosso's office, throwing open the door without bothering to knock.

Beyond Vasic's bulk, Rosso could see two detective sergeants, Boris Stanojevic and Anil Salahuddin, sole survivors of the homicide squad, in jeans and bomber jackets.

Did Anil know his snitch was dead?

Boris was half-Moslem, half-Serb. His wife was Croat. Anil was half-Croat, half-Moslem. His wife was Jewish. They were misfits in a world of old communists and new nationalist slogans. They lived an ideal that was long out of fashion. They belonged nowhere else but in Sarajevo. To be a Sarajevan was an attitude of mind, a way of life. If the city went, so would they and the dream of a secular, democratic Bosnia would die with them. Anil held a large bottle of brandy in one hand and his pistol in the other. Boris was searching for glasses, opening and shutting desk drawers with loud detonations as they crossed the office, like a pair of hooligans looking for trouble. Rosso cast a baleful eye in their direction.

The only reason they weren't in the military was because they had both failed the medical. Boris had lost a foot in the very first week of the war, Anil was missing four of the fingers on his right hand, lost during the war in Croatia.

'Good trip?' Vasic asked.

'It was OK,' said Rosso, still watching the two sergeants. 'How are things with you?'

'The same crap. Nothing changes except our ability to shovel it.'

Rosso needed to talk to Anil – alone – but he couldn't be seen talking to him with this creep hanging around.

The treble of female laughter and the sharp tapping of high-heeled shoes drifted up from the stairwell at the end of the room. The typists were turning up for work. Vasic kicked Rosso's door shut with the side of his foot.

His eyes, slightly protuberant and heavy-lidded, fell on the papers scattered across Rosso's desk. He was trying to read upside down but doing his best not to appear to do so.

'Hinko has done a bunk. That's why you've got all that shit on your plate. They say he's shacked up in some fancy Frankfurt hotel with his whore and a briefcase stuffed with marks.' Vasic sounded as much envious as scornful.

'Uh-huh.' Rosso was being patient.

They waited for a particularly loud – and close – series of three mortar impacts to die away. Neither flinched, but Rosso knew Vasic was counting off the seconds of each interval. Everyone did it. It was a way of trying to work out the range, the pattern, and most important of all, where the next one would land. Think little white balls. Think golf.

'So what's new?' Rosso asked.

Hidzovic had been the uniformed police commander and responsible for foreign liaison. It was a sinecure won by family connections and had nothing to do with practical policing.

Vasic shrugged. 'More drugs on the streets. More stiffs. More weapons. More tarts.'

'Nothing new then.'

Vasic picked his nose as he considered the question. His eyes seemed to vanish as he lowered his head – a gesture that meant Vasic was holding back, or wanted to blurt something out.

Vasic took his hat off, revealing a head entirely bald save for the bunches of hair on either side, just above the ears. He flicked imaginary dust off the brim of the hat, inspected it with a frown of concentration and flung it on Rosso's desk. He lowered himself into the only other chair in the office. It creaked ominously.

'No, nothing else,' said Vasic after a pause.

'What about the woman in New Town?'

'Woman?' Vasic sat upright as if he had been kicked.

'Yes, the woman. Murdered in New Town. Block Nine, sixth floor.' Rosso avoided eye contact, looked away with studied nonchalance.

Vasic touched his small brown toothbrush moustache with a forefinger. Got you, you son of a bitch.

'Of course. The Serb woman. I forgot all about her.'

Out of the corner of his eye Rosso could see Anil and Boris perched on a desk. Anil appeared to be rolling a huge joint. The loss of four fingers did not seem to pose any difficulty. Boris was drinking from the bottle, holding it by the neck and throwing his head back as if he meant to get seriously drunk very quickly. They were joined by Zlata, a secretary in a tight black miniskirt and famous for her ribald jokes. Two uniformed police officers, Taher and Salco, made their way over to them.

'A party?'

'Salco's birthday.'

'It's only just gone ten,' Rosso said.

Did Anil know? He had recruited her, run her. Rosso had authorized the informer's payments, the occasional *douceur* to keep her on side.

'It's no ordinary birthday. He's forty. That makes him too old for active duty,' Vasic was saying.

'As things stand.'

'As you say.'

Everyone had heard rumours that reservists up to and including fifty were about to be mobilized, including what was left of the civil police.

'You want me to speak to them?'

Rosso shook his head. At least they had turned up today.

'You know I really wasn't sure you'd come back,' Vasic said with a sly smile.

Rosso ignored the remark but he turned and looked steadily at the other man and this seemed to disconcert the inspector, who put thumb and forefinger up to the corners of his mouth, an instinctive attempt to hide his face.

'You were going to tell me about the murder?'

'Oh, yes. Look. You're busy. I'll—'

'Spit it out.'

Did Vasic know the woman?

'It was a rather unusual stiff.'

'How come you didn't remember it then?'

'A Cetnik bitch. She drowned.' He said it with satisfaction, almost smacking his lips. Shrugged.

'Drowned?'

'Yeah,' Vasic grinned, and started to shake with laughter.

'How do you mean?'

'She was found drowned in her bath.'

Vasic's face creased with mirth, little lines shot out from the corners of his eyes and mouth and joined together, turning his whole face into a series of ripples. His mouth opened and tears sprang into his eyes but no sound emerged. He trembled with silent laughter, making the chair creak.

Rosso passed a hand wearily over his face. Policemen like Vasic dealt with death and violence all their professional lives. Wearing out shoe leather on the streets toughened them, blunted their sensibilities, thickened their skin, gave them prejudices like callouses on the brain.

'Explain.'

Vasic cleared his throat, and shook himself free from his convulsive mirth.

'It must have taken her days if not weeks to get enough water in the bath and then she goes and drowns in it.'

'I don't find it funny. It's fucking tragic.'

Vasic wiped the corner of his eyes with the side of one of his plump hands and sniffed loudly.

'Well,' he said, shrugging. He was embarrassed. 'You're probably right, boss. But it did strike me as funny.'

Funny as in funny because she's a Serb. You asshole.

'It happened today?'

Vasic opened his hands upwards. 'Hell, I don't know, chief. She was found yesterday. I think.'

'You think? Where's the paperwork?'

Vasic shook his head.

'Who went to the scene?'

'It was reported by the local command.'

Some command: Mahmud.

'You mean we haven't sent anyone over?'

'No, chief.'

'Why not?' Rosso kept his anger in check, his voice even.

'Chief, it's fucking dangerous. For another thing—'

Rosso was out of his chair, dragging his pullover over his head, pushing his arms into the sleeves of his jacket, snatching up gun and badge. It was dangerous, of course. And Vasic was going to say they didn't have the cars, or the petrol, and it was unwise to send anyone on his own and there weren't enough officers to operate in pairs.

'Flat number?'

'Superintendent—'

Rosso felt the pure, cold stream that was anger flow through his limbs, kick start his brain.

'I asked you,' he said softly, 'for the apartment number.'

'All I know is Alipasino Polje. Block Nine.' Vasic recognized the signs of an imminent explosion of Rosso's famous temper.

'Let's go. My car.'

'Super, I think we'd be wiser to take mine.'

They passed the celebrating policemen. A glassy-eyed Anil held out the remains of the marijuana joint, pushing it almost into Rosso's face. Rosso could not help but inhale the heavy, sweet scent. If this is an act, Anil Salahuddin, then it's almost too good.

'C'mon, chief. Lighten up, man. It's great shit. Lebanese Gold.' Anil winked at him. A conspiratorial wink.

Rosso sidestepped the offering, pretended not to notice, and headed for the staircase.

'So this is what it has come to,' Vasic said once they were out of earshot. 'Your own men taking drugs, flouting the law, in front of your very eyes and in the detectives' room.'

Not that Rosso cared one way or another if someone smoked hashish in private. It was breaking the law, however, and Anil was supposed to uphold it. Rosso fought to subdue his temper – not at Anil, but directed at Vasic and the sneer in his voice, his effort to insinuate himself into Rosso's favour. Anil was a fine copper when all was said and done.

'Why your car?' Rosso asked as he and Vasic pounded down the steps to the basement. Rosso led, struggling into his overcoat at the same time.

'Everyone knows yours, chief. It attracts too much attention. We cops were never popular in that part of town as you know. Now everyone's got guns—'

'OK. You drive.'

'Chief, she's only a Serb. Probably slipped and fell. Weak from hunger and all that.' Vasic had to break into a run to keep up with Rosso. 'Let the military send us the papers. Let them handle it.' His voice seemed very loud in the basement.

Rosso didn't answer, but stood next to the battered BMW while Vasic struggled with his door. Only a Serb.

'Pathologist's report?'

'No pathologist, chief. No report.'

Rosso strapped himself in, lowered the window.

'Who was she?'

'A dentist, apparently. Serb, as I said. Widow.'

Wrong. Rosso could see the file in his mind's eye, handwritten, Anil's left-sloping hand full of loops. Divorced, not widowed.

The car's interior stank of stale cigarette smoke.

'Does she have a name?'

Vasic started the BMW. He shook his head.

'Sorry,' he said. 'They did say. I forget.'

Chrissake, Rosso thought. Either he doesn't think it important enough to write down or he is lying through his teeth.

They had to drive through town, past the presidency, along Sniper's Alley and then turn left, crossing the broad highway and moving south, uphill towards the cluster of high-rise apartments. It meant covering a lot of open, exposed ground.

It was not only his own life he was putting at risk, Rosso thought, but that of the inspector. Vasic was there because Rosso ordered it, because he was reluctant to refuse, because he was possibly too weak to admit his own fears, to argue more strongly that what Rosso was doing was irresponsible. Heroes are just people who are too frightened to say no.

'Who's the commander?'

'One of Luka's people. It's part of his sector.'

Both men stayed silent. Vasic drove as fast as he could, the German car – it had been abandoned in Sniper's Alley by a departing US television crew, only to be salvaged by Vasic – lurching from one side of the street to the other as Vasic tried to use the available cover as best he could.

The apartment blocks of Hranso, to their left, were swathed in smoke and dust.

'Looks like they've been hit today,' said Rosso.

Vasic shifted uneasily in the driver's seat.

'I don't like it,' he said

'No-one does.' What Rosso meant to say was that he did not feel any braver or better about it than Vasic, that he too knew what the risks were, that he too felt afraid. He wanted to turn back, also. His instincts were no different. He wanted to live. He would have liked to have told Vasic that, but he was the inspector's superior officer. He had to play his part. He must stay the course.

They were approaching the crossroads.

'Do you know something about this case that I don't?'

Vasic shook his head.

'Know what they call these apartments, the ones in Block Nine?' Vasic asked.

'Should I?'

'The Monkey House,' Vasic said. He smiled as he said it.

Rosso would have asked him what he meant, only there was a terrible ripping sound, an electric whiplash over their heads that almost stunned them. Rosso's ears rang and Vasic was huddled down as low as he could get behind the wheel. The car rocked from side to side, whether from Vasic's shaking or his deliberate attempts to evade the enemy's fire Rosso couldn't tell.

It was an anti-aircraft cannon.

Someone up there in the Serb lines was trying to kill them with it, pumping out streams of 20mm cannon shells that reverberated around the roofs and walls. One round from such a weapon would rip straight through the engine block and tear both men in half.

So much for little white golf balls.

'Block Nine,' said Vasic, pointing.

The buildings were very tall, in clusters, facing different ways in an attempt by the architects to give each apartment and balcony some privacy, and something of a view beyond the red slate, white plaster and brick of the neighbouring homes. They were elegant once, a housing development for lower- and middle-income groups, typically young families, but put up with some flair, an eye for neighbourhood, not the grey and regimented Stalinist Utopia of Belgrade.

On the ground floor there were pedestrian walkways and shopping malls, or what had been shops, their windows smashed, once-bright awnings stained and tattered, lampposts bent, patterned brick lanes torn and split and everywhere begrimed, overgrown with weeds. Rosso glimpsed naked mannequins in one boutique, their plastic pink bodies all leaning to one side, tumbled into one another like dominoes, some with their limbs torn off, the absurdly red lips, dead eyes and high cheekbones of their bald heads bloodlessly chipped, parodying the dead as they had once parodied life. There was something particularly obscene about the sight, something that harked

39

back to the unspeakable evils of another generation, another genocide.

Put. Put-put-put.

Bupppa. Buuupppp.

Zzzzzziiiiiiiiiing!

The buildings distorted the noise, deadening the detonations yet amplifying the sound of the projectiles' passage through the air above. The sounds were bounced up and down between the ground and the low cloud.

Rosso and Vasic crept forward, hugging the walls.

No-one was about. That was a bad sign.

3

'If you can keep your head while
all around you are losing theirs, then you have
misunderstood the situation.'
GRAFFITO

INSPECTOR VASIC INSISTED ON TALKING AS THEY CLIMBED, HIS
leather-soled shoes sliding and scraping on steps that had not
been swept for months. He quickly became very short of breath,
so much so that he had to stop every few steps, gulping for air,
and the further behind he was, the louder and more staccato his
voice became in the stairwell. The intervals, during which he leant
against the wall, were filled with the sound of his laboured panting,
then the slow shuffle of his feet would start again. Perhaps it was
the relief at being indoors, or at not being intercepted on the way
in by Luka's men, that made the inspector so talkative. The local
militiamen would have been preoccupied in any case by the skirmish
or whatever it was that was taking place on the other side of Block

41

Nine, to the south, across Nedarici to the government-held district of Dobrinja.

Rosso pulled a pencil torch from a pocket, and flashed it briefly on the name-plates.

'What did you say her name was?'

As if Rosso could forget.

'I didn't,' Vasic panted.

'She had a Serb name.'

'Right.'

It was the fifth floor. One more to go.

Vasic followed wearily, cursing under his breath.

Rosso swept his torch along the names again, his lips moving as he read: Dudic, Martic, Kusacs, Markova, Dusan Bukovac.

'Bukovac,' Rosso said out loud.

'That's it.'

'Sure?' Rosso was sure. He had to know if Vasic was.

'Sure I'm sure.'

Dusan must be the husband's first name.

'Flat 6B. OK, let's do it.' Rosso's voice was little more than a whisper, shooting puffs of steam into the dank air.

Vasic had his pistol out, the little Makarov, holding it against his thigh as they moved along the corridor.

Rosso flicked the torch on and off to check the number. Vasic stood to one side, his back to the wall, pistol held with both hands, pointing the muzzle down between his feet. He watched Rosso, who stood in front of the door.

Rosso rapped sharply on the door with his knuckles, three times, and stepped back.

'Police!' The shout was swallowed by the corridor.

They waited in the darkness. Rosso knocked again. Again, three times, but banging with the palm of his hand this time.

'I'll try the neighbours, shall I?'

Rosso did not reply. He had his torch out again and was examining the door. Someone had forced it, tearing into the frame with a crowbar or something similar and lifting the door off its hinges. The wood was torn and splintered opposite the lock and where the hinges would have been.

'Let's give it a shove,' said Rosso. 'You take that side.'

Rosso put his shoulder to it. Vasic moved closer. They were back to back, braced to push.

'One,' said Vasic. 'Two. Three.'

The door gave way easily. Rosso propped it open.

It was a small place, scrupulously clean. The front door opened into a tiny hall. There was a mirror on the wall, a mat on the floor and a polished woodblock floor led off down a corridor. Immediately to the left was the sitting-room and beyond it, a window and balcony.

The first thing Rosso noticed was dried mud on the polished floor, and imprints of boots. Rosso paused, staring. At least two people, he told himself. There was an old rule of thumb used by policemen – measure off a metre and a half of ground, ignore the heel and toe marks and count the number of full-sized footprints for an estimate of the number of people who have walked or run past.

Christ, that smell again.

We'll need a photographer, Rosso thought, stepping carefully over the mud and gesturing to Vasic to do the same. He reminded himself there were no police photographers; those who were not in the Army were working for the foreign press.

The sitting room was L-shaped. Rosso and Vasic moved across it cautiously, for the window and balcony stretched its entire length and anyone standing in the room was exposed from the waist up. The interior walls were cream, there was a matching loose cover on the sofa, a coffee table with an inlaid brass top covered by lacework, a floral vase, a framed print of an Orthodox saint and, piled high on an ironing board, carefully pressed bedlinen. The iron – the old-fashioned kind that was heated over a fire – stood at the end of the ironing-board. A cream, woolly rug completed the picture of softness, of simplicity.

A narrow bed was squeezed into an alcove, the bottom of the L, between the sitting-room and the tiny kitchen. The bed was made up neatly, Rosso noted, with hospital corners. The pillowcase and the sheets appeared to be clean, pressed even, and undisturbed. The bed had been placed there, Rosso realized, because at every angle whoever slept there was protected by a wall – out of the direct line of fire.

'Prob'ly still in the bath,' said Vasic.

The body was there if the smell was anything to go by. Death has a cloying, sweet stench. It is all-pervasive. There is nothing else like it. It cannot be masked by perfume, by flowers, by a handkerchief held over the face. It seeps under doors, through windows, into food and drink. If the source is close enough, the remains sufficiently decomposed, it will cling to a man's clothes, to his hair, and it can take days or weeks to wash the taste out of his mouth.

Rosso smelt it now. He could taste it on his tongue. He was no stranger to it. He led the way into the kitchen. There was barely enough room for both of them.

'Why don't you check it out,' Rosso said, referring to the bathroom. He wanted to be alone, alone to think, to look.

The metal sink was pristine. On the draining-board lay two cups, two saucers, two plates, two knives and forks, two teaspoons. A drying-up cloth, quite clean, had been neatly folded over the edge of the sink.

Had she had a visitor before she died? Someone she knew?

Was it Vasic himself, perhaps? Rosso told himself he had no grounds to suspect Vasic. All right, the inspector is not from homicide, not one of us. He's certainly fat. He's undoubtedly unpopular. A militiaman gives you a scrap of paper with his name on it. But that's not enough.

Rosso opened the cupboard above the sink and used his pen to probe the contents. A cup of rice in the bottom of a cellophane bag. Salt. A chipped saucer with perhaps three teaspoons of sugar. A tin of sweetened condensed milk. A twist of paper containing tea-leaves. A bag of lentils, perhaps half a kilo, and a quarter loaf of bread, so stale it was as hard as stone. The dry, crumbly skin from a clove of garlic and the murky dregs in the bottom of a bottle of cooking oil.

That was all, but it was enough for a thief, enough to kill for. The tiny fridge was empty. It was hard to recall when there had been sufficient electricity flowing into the city to power household gadgets other Europeans took for granted.

Rosso peered closely at the drainpipe, looked under the sink, carefully examined two plastic buckets and a coil of plastic piping, running his fingers along the edges and sniffing them. Chemicals, acidic – bleach, perhaps. He opened and shut drawers. Then he went out onto the balcony, ducking down and crawling unabashed on hands and knees, trying hard not to cut himself on the broken glass.

He was looking for bloodstains, for some sign that someone had tried to remove evidence of a struggle.

Vasic came into the sitting-room and watched the superintendent through the broken window.

'She's there,' he said.

Rosso got up and went back inside, glad to be out of the cold but preferring it to the stink of corruption.

'Bedroom first,' he said.

It was a pleasant place, he decided, with good natural light. It was almost too clean, though, even for a female occupant. It was more like a flat that is regularly serviced and rented out rather than a home. Rosso told himself that every home he had visited, including his own, had its dusty corners, its dirty clothes, its rags tossed carelessly into the bottom of a dark recess where no-one was expected to look.

'Too good to be true,' he said aloud to himself.

'What was that?'

'Nothing. Talking to myself.'

Rosso wanted to look at the bedroom. Vasic fidgeted in the corridor, his expression one of suppressed annoyance. There was a peculiar curl to his mouth, and Vasic appeared to be avoiding Rosso's eye.

It was a look that seemed to say it was all a waste of time and that Vasic wanted to get it over with. For his part, Rosso told himself the body wasn't going anywhere. Rationally, though, he knew it made more sense to examine the woman's remains first in case they were interrupted by neighbours, or worse, the local militia. But then murders were seldom rational, and the solution lay more in the emotional tangles of the lost life than in reason. Rosso often fell back on his instinct, his feel for what had happened. She was orderly, that much was clear. Very clean, almost obsessively so. There were few artefacts – few of the gee-gaws women seem to accumulate, from little cut-glass goldfish to china plates or twee pictures of romantic people and places. There were no fashion magazines, no pictures of a favourite niece or nephew, no jewellery box, no trays of make-up, not so much as a lipstick – nothing that in any way suggested vanity, an interest in family, in style, in looks.

If she had roots, they weren't here.

The bedroom was small, square and simply furnished like the rest of the home. There was a blue-edged Chinese rug, the space where the bed had been before it was moved to its safer position, a pine chest of drawers, a narrow wardrobe. No dressing-table, no pots of paint, hairbrushes and the like. No full-length mirror. No woman is comfortable living anywhere without a full-length mirror. Rosso used the end of his pencil torch to open the drawers. The clothes were neatly folded. There was nothing extravagant, no silk nightdresses or satin briefs. It was all sensible stuff, cotton most of it, ironed and laid out neatly. Rosso prodded around, trying to find a letter, a diary, something at any rate that gave him some personal insight into the life or lives that must have flowed in and out of the apartment.

There were three pairs of sensible shoes, all worn down at the heel, in the bottom of the wardrobe, two skirts, two winter dresses, two summer frocks, a pair of navy slacks, a green winter overcoat – all these on wire hangers and all size 10. Nothing new, all of it in fair condition, clean.

He glanced at the labels. He did not recognize the names. They were local, unremarkable, inexpensive.

A large alarm clock stood on the top of the chest of drawers. It was the kind that winds up and the hands had stopped at 2.20. Next to it lay a pile of books. Rosso picked them up, spine upwards and shook the pages in case a note or some other paper had been concealed there. Then he flipped through them, only to find they were all textbooks on dentistry. He put them back. There was a little face-powder, a new bar of soap still wrapped in cellophane, smelling of lavender. Otherwise, the room was as sexless as a convent.

'OK,' he said, squeezing past Vasic. 'Let's take a look.'

The woman lay face down in about eight inches of water.

God help me. Did we do this to you?

She was naked save for a camisole, a flimsy cotton garment that was rucked up under her arms and around her shoulders.

Her back, buttocks, much of her legs and feet, her shoulders, neck and the back of her head all protruded above the water-line. Rosso told himself people drowned in rain puddles if they were drunk enough. The smell was bad, even for someone as familiar as Rosso with the business of clearing up after the messily dead. It was his bad luck that the bathroom was the only room in the apartment with a window still intact. Anywhere else, and a fresh breeze would have provided some relief. It was a very small window, high up, with a pane of thick frosted glass. It looked out over an internal courtyard or shaft of some kind. The detective got down on his knees and searched the bath's edges and sides carefully with his eyes, keeping his hands well out of the way by sticking them in his jacket pockets. The smell of death was not the only odour. The victim – because that is what Rosso was now sure she was – had fought hard, but she knew she was losing. Her assailants were too powerful. The water was filthy, dark brown and impenetrable to Rosso's gaze. A nasty crust was forming along the water-line. The woman had bled profusely, presumably from somewhere on the front of her body or face. She had been struck or stabbed repeatedly in the bath – unless of course her killers had cleaned

47

up afterwards. There was blood on the sides of the bath, where she had apparently struggled, trying to prevent herself from being pushed down and held there. It was drying and going brown and hence indistinguishable from the excreta. There were streaks of blood where her fingers had been, clawing vainly at the enamel as she lost ground to her attacker or attackers. He estimated the woman at about 5 feet, 5 inches tall. Her brown hair, cut short, was streaked with grey. She was slim, with what had once been a good, trim figure – before the war. That was like saying before the beginning of time itself. Now she was skeletal.

Rosso made a mental note.

Weight: 17-20 kilos. Age: mid-thirties.

The skin was stretched over the bones. It reminded Rosso of pictures he had seen of the Nazi extermination camps, the appalling piles of dead. Images that made him retch, break into a sweat. She too was very pale, the skin like alabaster – for the dentist had been dead long enough for the body fluids to settle to her front. Rosso could nevertheless discern along the ridge of backbone a lesion or bruise, slightly discoloured, where the skin had been broken. It was about as long as a pencil and twice as wide. There were also blue-black splotches on the upper thighs each about the size of a 50 dinar coin.

There was no doubt in Rosso's mind there had been a struggle and that there was more than one assailant. He turned on his knees, and looked about him. There was broken glass under the wash-basin and a toothbrush, along with the toilet roll which had become soaked in bath-water, lay on the tiles. Vasic was right: it must have taken days to collect that much water in the bath. Rosso looked around again. A bloodied hand-towel lay in a corner against the side of the bath, as if someone had flung it aside after wiping the tiles with it.

'What do you reckon, chief?' Vasic held a handkerchief over his face, and his voice was muffled.

Rosso stood up.

'She's been dead a while. I'd say at a guess between thirty-six and seventy-two hours. More maybe, going by the smell.'

He wanted the whole place dusted for prints, the pathologist to look at the body before it was removed for a proper post-mortem, he wanted blood samples taken from the bath, and the gaps between the floor tiles scraped and sent to forensics. The reality was that none of these procedures was possible any longer. Forensics was all but shut down. It followed that in cases of this kind it was becoming increasingly difficult, if not impossible, to find the criminals and gain a conviction.

Rosso got down once more on his knees.

Rigor mortis had come and gone.

Only the wrist of the woman's right hand was visible. It was folded over, the main part under her face as if she had been holding it up to shield herself. The left was entirely under her. The hands should be bagged, samples taken from under her nails, a hair or two from her head.

That wouldn't happen, either.

'What do you think, Inspector?'

Vasic shrugged.

'I told you. She fell. Had a heart attack.'

'Come here. Take a look.'

Vasic didn't move. He looked sullen, angry. Rosso told himself it was because Vasic was afraid.

'Come on.' Rosso leant back, reached up and took Vasic by the arm, and pulled him towards the bath. 'Tell me you don't see bruising on the back. Tell me what you smell. Not just the start of decomposition. I smell shit. She lost control of her sphincter muscles. She was being strangled.'

'How can you be so sure?' The inspector's face was ashen.

'I'm not. But I can make an educated guess. There's a good deal of blood in there, too. Someone, or some people, struck her – maybe someplace else but most likely right here in the bathroom. In the bath. Maybe they thought she was dead and they would dump her in the bath to make it look like suicide, only she wasn't and she started to put up a fight when she realized she was going into the water. So she decided not to play possum after all. It was too late by then, you see. One assailant had his knee or foot in her back, forcing her down. He or his friend had their hands around her throat. Or a belt, or a rope. Or maybe they just broke her neck. We won't know until we get her out. They stabbed her. She bled heavily. But she knew what was happening and put up a fight. Perhaps she had blacked out but the water woke her as they threw her in the bath. You can see the streaks of blood there, on the side. Those are her fingers, scrabbling to get a grip on the sides of the bath as they forced her down into the water. We should get good prints.'

Rosso was thinking how he would want her lungs and stomach drained to see if she had died from drowning, or before she ingested the grisly mixture of water, faeces and blood.

'There's something else,' said Rosso.

Track marks, where she had injected herself, heroin probably – mainlined into the veins above the left ankle. There was no doubt now in Rosso's mind: this was Anil's informer all right, the woman whose face stared back at him from one of the files held at central registry.

'See that?' Rosso pointed at the bruised, punctured vein.

But Vasic went out onto the balcony and, regardless of the risks of exposing himself to any snipers lurking in the attics of neighbouring apartment blocks, threw up over the railing, vomiting noisily into the snow six floors down.

'Better?' asked Rosso when Vasic returned, wiping his face with his sleeve.

'Sure,' croaked Vasic.

Most police officers Rosso knew respected human life. He admired and even envied the younger ones for their innocence in the face of violent death. The difference was not that Rosso didn't respect life, or respected it less. He simply did not regard the body in the bath as being human, as belonging to anyone in particular. The woman, the occupant of the corpse, had long since departed for wherever it was that life went, if indeed it went anywhere at all. For Rosso, what was left behind was as impersonal as the damaged mannequins.

'Explains a lot,' said Vasic, 'her being an addict, I mean. Prob'ly OD'd, fell in the bath, struck her head, drowned. Those bruises and lesions are prob'ly old anyhow.'

Rosso said nothing, just looked up.

'We finished?' Vasic wanted to know.

'Very nearly. Tell me, who phoned this in?'

'Don't know, boss. Whoever it was didn't leave a name.'

'But it was the Army, right? Or Luka's boys? Let's make them our next call, shall we?'

Vasic scowled.

'Like I said, he didn't leave a name.'

'It was a he, not a she.'

'Yes.'

'Are you saying this was an anonymous tip-off? That it wasn't official?' Rosso asked.

'Right.'

'So we're the first people on the scene.'

'Could be.' Vasic seemed to tense.

'The door could have been forced by the killers, not by the military or neighbours,' Rosso ventured.

Vasic looked away. He said nothing.

'Who took the call?' Rosso stood.

Vasic was restless, shifting his considerable weight from one foot to the other.

'Can we get out of here?'

'Who took the call?' Rosso was insistent.

Vasic's voice cracked, blood rushed to his face.

'What are you trying to prove? That a Croat cop cares about a Cetnik cow who mainlined herself to junkie heaven and fell into her own stinking bath and drowned in her own shit?'

Vasic's voice rose.

'It sucks, Superintendent. I don't give a monkey's for this woman,

and I don't give a rat's arse for your efforts to atone for the past.'
Vasic raised a fist, shook it. 'Fuck you. I'm risking my neck here
just so you can prove to yourself you're not your father's brat.'

Vasic regretted those last words the moment they were uttered.
His fury subsided. He looked ashamed.

Yugoslavia was gone, old enmities resurfaced. Vasic had touched
on the unmentionable: Rosso's family, in particular his father's
collaboration with the Nazi regime set up in Zagreb during World
War II.

The notorious Ustashe.

Rosso had always had the gift of doing the unexpected. He
did something then that Vasic would never have anticipated.
There was no flash of temper, no hand on pistol grip. Vasic
would have felt better if his superior officer had threatened
him. Struck him, even. But Rosso simply smiled; a broad smile.
A congratulatory smile.

'Well, Inspector. You do surprise me.'

'Look, I didn't mean to insult you—'

'Course not.' Rosso was still smiling.

'It's just—'

'I know.'

Rosso was headed for the front door.

'Keys?'

Vasic looked confused.

'Your car keys.'

Vasic pulled them from a pocket.

Rosso held out a hand.

Vasic hesitated, then threw them over.

'I'm going to find a sawbones who'll take a look at this. I want
you to stay here.'

'Look—'

'Did you have any breakfast?'

'Yeah,' Vasic said. It was spread all over the snow six floors
down.

'Someone will relieve you. Don't leave the flat for whatever

52

reason. No-one is to enter. Got it? If you need to take a leak, do it over the balcony.'

'I do think you should leave this to the military. Let them clear it up.'

'You can put it in your report. In the meantime, keep your prints off the place and don't let anyone else in.'

The inspector nodded despite himself.

'If you do take a look around, we need positive ID. See if you can find a bag, a suitcase, a purse of some kind. Any papers. A driver's licence, a bus ticket. Anything.'

Rosso's steps faded quickly down the corridor.

Rosso's mind was so full of what had to be done that he entirely forgot the risks he was taking in driving back alone. He failed to tick off in his mind the landmarks along his chosen route. He did not break the trip up into stages, taking one at a time as if he were rationing his courage. He passed through one Army checkpoint in such a preoccupied state he scarcely remembered having done so. He certainly could not recall anything that was said, or the faces of the soldiers who had checked his papers. It was an oblivion that brought relief through single-mindedness of purpose. As for thoughts of Sabina and his anxiety about his god-daughter's romantic inclinations, they were mercifully driven into some recess of his mind.

It was indeed merciful. The detective was not the kind of man to reflect too deeply on his own motives. If he had, he might have realized that it was not merely duty that drove him to pursue the matter of an informer's death in a small, high-rise apartment, but because, to some degree at least, it allowed him, for a little while, to act normally. He could cease for a few hours the nerve-wracking contemplation of his own imminent death at the hands of the besiegers. He could stop worrying about his wife's mental and physical disintegration. He could avoid the issue of Tanja's involvement with the city's chief brigand, an involvement which he now regretted having encouraged at the start for his own selfish, professional reasons. Our capacity for self-deception is limitless; we create crises to escape. If there was indeed some escapism involved in Rosso's single-handed devotion to duty and his belief in the rule of law, then it was also because he could revert to doing what he was good at and hence what he enjoyed most: being a detective. He had a mission, something he had lost along the way to the nursery slopes of middle age, and somehow having it back made life, and the prospect of losing it, less important.

Little white golf balls could be put aside.

Rosso took the main drag all the way back, driving fast but without even considering the possibility of a safer route through the backstreets. He held a private discourse with himself. There was as yet no obvious motive for the murder – at least, not to anyone without access to the files or not involved in the investigation. To be a Serb in Sarajevo was not in itself a crime, a cause for retribution of this nature – not yet anyway. He would need to be seen to establish the woman's identity first, then question her neighbours, if there were any left. That was the way to go – to be seen to go. Of course he knew her name, had seen her file, had given his approval. The apartment was a safe house – the question was: ours, or theirs? It was at any rate important that he follow procedure: her colleagues must be interviewed – other dentists and medical professionals who would have known her. Rosso knew nothing of her family, if there was family. There were no family snapshots or portraits, at least none that he could find. He assumed her killer or killers had broken in, yet there was no sign of a struggle outside the bathroom – no blood, no disorder or indication of sexual assault. In fact, he needed proof that the body in the bath belonged to the occupier, the spouse of the Dusan Bukovac whose name appeared on the door. As things stood, it was an assumption that the body and dentist were one and the same: an informer with an expensive habit.

Had Vasic been right? Was Rosso's belief in upholding the law, in the job, nothing but a personal obsession, a drive to atone for his own father's past? Everyone knew who and what his father had been. Rosso was not a name that passed unnoticed, that prompted thoughts of science, medicine or the arts. Rosso had hoped that with the passing of the Tito regime, the collective memory of the events of 1941–5 would pass, but he knew, now that the old Yugoslavia was gone, it would never be.

The name Rosso would be neither forgotten nor forgiven.

There was no place for him under the red chequered shield of Croatia, but wherever he lived he remained his father's son. Nothing either of them could do would ever change that fact. What mattered was what Rosso did with his unwanted legacy.

Professor Misic wagged a scalpel at Rosso. It seemed to be both greeting and warning. Misic was tall with close-cropped grey hair. The half-moon spectacles that clung to the end of his prominent nose gave him a distinguished if somewhat distracted air. He wore a long green gown and cap with a white face mask. His hands and forearms were covered in thin latex gloves, also green. He stood in the nearest of six cubicles, each containing a hospital bed on which lay a woman. At least three that Rosso could see and hear were in labour, two of them making heavy weather of it too, judging by the moaning. Two midwives were moving from one to the next, counting contractions, reassuring their patients. They were stout, middle-aged women with a professional, no-nonsense air about them – the sergeant-majors of the medical world.

Misic turned away to his patient. Above both of them was a large, circular light, apparently powered by a hospital generator. The woman lay quite still. She too was covered in green, though the sheets had been gathered away from where the doctor was poised to make the first cut.

'It's you,' he said to Rosso. Then, addressing one of the nurses: 'Give him a mask.'

Rosso hesitated.

'Come on, you might learn something. Don't tell me our superintendent of police is squeamish.'

Once Rosso had allowed a white mask to be fixed over the lower part of his face, Misic stretched out his gloved hand and took hold of the detective's arm.

'Come along, now. No shirking. It's an interesting case.'

Rosso did not want to be there, but he needed Misic to attend to something much worse than this. This was a small price to pay. He offered no further resistance but found himself inside the operating room, standing next to Misic and looking down at the pale skin of the woman's abdomen.

'Heard the term ectopic? No? It means outside the womb. She's forty-four, married, and has been trying for a child for a long time. An old patient of mine, in fact. She's conceived all right, but in the Fallopian tubes. That's dangerous. Her abdomen has filled up with blood.'

Misic flourished the scalpel. He made the incision swiftly, a decisive, controlled gesture. Rosso stiffened.

'If we don't operate now, you see, she'll die.'

Misic's right hand dropped the scalpel, now blood bright on its glistening blade, into a white, kidney-shaped enamel basin. It was swiftly removed from Rosso's field of vision. First the doctor's fingers, then his entire hand, disappeared into the woman's abdomen. Misic kept talking as if this was the most normal thing, like slicing carrots on a kitchen chopping board, but to Rosso the words kept disappearing and reappearing as if there was something wrong with his hearing. There wasn't. It was just that what Rosso was seeing a few inches in front of his face seemed to blot out all other sensations.

The obstetrician began to scoop out blood. It looked thick, very dark – almost black – as if it wasn't very fresh or was even beginning to congeal. Some of it fell on the green sheets, so neatly rolled back from the incision. Globs of it splashed onto Misic's gown and drops spattered onto the floor at their feet. Rosso dared not look down in case he would be accused of trying to avoid the surgery or of being fussy about his clothes. Misic's gloves were shiny, slick with blood.

'Ironic, isn't it. So many people trying to kill us, and this woman damn near dies because she wants a baby.'

The hand slid in again. Rosso felt slightly dizzy. He could smell the blood. He had smelled blood that very morning. He told himself it was nothing. The human body contained eight pints. Losing one or two was manageable. Even a third.

'There are a lot of vital organs in the abdomen,' Misic said. 'It's a nasty place for things to go wrong. The chest cavity is far preferable. Not that we have a choice, eh?'

More blood.

'How's the family?'

'Fine,' Rosso replied.

Misic chatted on as he worked.

'Funny thing – there is an increase in pregnancies. Hard to figure out why. Cynics would say that without electricity people don't have much else to do except make babies. At the start of the war, abortions shot up. So did the number of premature births. Now it's as if people are getting used to the war, to living under sentence of death. Maybe it's a biological way of fighting back, getting even.'

Misic looked up, pointing with his chin at a small window at the far end of the room, just outside the last of the cubicles. Rosso could hear the rumble of guns coming from it.

'For one thing,' Misic said, 'no-one can get hold of condoms.' He smiled with his eyes.

'Course, the premature babies are the result of stress, fear, shock – and poor diet. They're nearly all underweight. That's because the mothers smoke so heavily.'

Rosso could not tear his eyes away from Misic's hand where it vanished inside the unconscious woman.

'Ha!' said Misic. 'Found something.' His right hand moved very slowly. Rosso tried to switch off. The way the sheets were arranged the patient didn't look like a person at all, but Rosso could not help imagining that this could be Sabina or Tanja. Rosso tried to think of the operation as an impersonal exercise, a lesson in surgery.

'Naturally,' said Misic, 'none of this would be necessary. I mean the open surgery. The war has put us all back years. In peace, I'd insert a miniature video camera, and there'd be a tiny puncture to drain the blood. She'd come in one day and go home the next.'

His hand moved again.

'There,' said Misic triumphantly. He held up a round object, moist and pink, about the size of one of those little golf balls Rosso thought about when he was afraid.

'Scalpel!' The nurse was there in an instant at his elbow.

Misic examined the object, turned it over, held it up in his bloodied left hand and then with a swift, stabbing movement of his right hand, punctured it with the instrument.

Clear liquid spurted down the front of his gown.

'Tumour,' said Misic. 'Must have been giving her some discomfort, though she never mentioned it. Nasty, but probably quite benign. Two birds with one stone, eh? With a laparoscopy we could have drained it, too, befo the war.'

Misic signalled to one of his assistants.

'We're finished,' the doctor said, gesturing to Rosso to move out of the cubicle.

'Clean her up, please,' Misic told the sister.

'Will she live?'

'Course she will. She'll be stitched up now. No children, I'm afraid, but she'll have a life. In a few weeks things will be as normal for her as they can be in this city.'

Misic spoke to one of the midwives, picked up a clipboard and flipped through the papers attached to it. Behind the obstetrician Rosso noticed five wizened little creatures, newborn babies, wrapped in woollen blankets and lying on a row of hot-water bottles. A nurse stood in one corner heating a large pan of water over a gas flame. Misic's fingers left bloody marks all over the papers he was looking at.

'Now, what can I do for you, Superintendent?'

'You know someone called Bukovac.'

Misic was pulling off his gloves. A nurse undid the draw-string of his face mask. Then she held a bowl of water under his hands. He was careful not to spill any. It was precious.

'Is that a question? Course I do,' he said, drying his hands on a towel. 'Zeljka. She's a dentist. Good one, too. A member of our medical committee, actually. A Serb like myself. Serbian, really. From Serbia proper.'

'Married?'

'Divorced. Never knew the husband, though I hear he's some-where around. A Croat.'

'When did you last see her?'

Misic rubbed his face.

'Let's see. A week ago, maybe ten days. Something like that. At our last meeting. What's all this about?'

'I've reason to believe she's dead. We've found a body and we think it's her. I want you to identify it.'

'Sniper?'

'I don't know the cause of death. Would you be good enough to examine the remains for us?'

'Surely it's obvious? A post-mortem – that's not my line of work.'

'I know that. But the only pathologist we have has his hands full. I want you to have a look and if you have time later, do your own post-mortem. I'd make it official.'

'Well, let's see, shall we?'

'I can take you over there now. I have a car outside. Of course if you're close friends with the deceased—'

The doctor hesitated, frowning.

'I've some oxygen for you. Brought it in from Zagreb this morning. It's in my car.'

The obstetrician's face cleared. He smiled.

'You have a deal, Superintendent.'

4

'We have to distrust each other.
It's our only defence against betrayal.'
TENNESSEE WILLIAMS, *CAT ON A HOT TIN ROOF*

IT WAS EARLY AFTERNOON BY THE TIME SUPERINTENDENT ROSSO
set out for New Town in his own car, Dr Misic beside him. A
mutinous, glassy-eyed Anil was dragged – literally – away from
a boisterous party at headquarters. Taher, from the uniformed
branch, drove Vasic's wreck, accompanied by the sergeant who
lolled in the back seat, muttering self-pitying curses under his
breath about how unfair the world, and Superintendent Rosso
in particular, was to detective sergeants. The little convoy sped
along Sniper's Alley without incident, Rosso's Yugo in the lead.
The snow had stopped falling, the wind had died away. The city
was bathed in a mixture of freezing mist and woodsmoke. It was
impossible to tell where the mist ended and the low-lying cloud
began. As for the morning crowds, they had dispersed to homes,

basements and refugee centres to face a subzero night as best they could.

Misic was pleased by the oxygen. His face broke into a broad grin when he saw the shiny bottles behind the front seat of Rosso's car. The committee would be grateful. It was an act that would not be forgotten. Rosso told him it was nothing, which both men knew certainly wasn't true.

There was firing, but the fog dulled the sound, turning it into a booming echo that suggested the shooting was everywhere but nowhere in particular. It seemed to follow them as Rosso drove steadily, carefully. At times he switched on the car headlights but never kept them on long enough for the gunmen in the hills to draw a bead on the source of the vaporous beams. The car itself quickly became warm with the occupants' body heat. The windows misted up and Misic would lean forward and vigorously rub the windscreen with the sleeve of his coat. Shut up in their metal and rubber capsule, moving through streets that appeared ghost-like, Rosso felt a sense of brotherly confidence, a comfortable feeling, grow between them.

'Can you see them?'

'Yes,' said Rosso, glancing at the rear-view mirror. 'Just.'

'Why do you do it, Superintendent?'

Rosso laughed. 'Helping the injured and the sick seems a natural enough thing to do, doesn't it?'

'I wasn't referring to the oxygen.'

'The dentist, you mean?'

Misic nodded. 'Yes,' he said. 'Bukovac.'

'It's my job.' Rosso took his eyes away from the road for a moment and glanced at the obstetrician.

'She's a Serbian.'

'So what? You're a Bosnian Serb aren't you, Doctor?'

'It's dangerous for someone like you.'

'Someone like me? What does that mean?'

'You're a senior government official. Why not leave it to one of your men? It might be wiser.'

'In what way?'

Misic shrugged.

'In what way?' Rosso repeated.

'Forget I said it.'

'Is it because I'm a Croat?'

'It has something to do with it.'

'Because of my name?'

'That too.'

They both fell silent. The doctor's honesty surprised them both. Rosso glanced up; Anil and Taher were right behind them now. The two cars were about to cross over and begin the ascent to New Town. Rosso could see the buildings, their upper floors hidden in mist.

How long would it be, he wondered, before Sarajevo fell victim to the sectarian plague that raged through the Balkans and threatened even Albania and Greece? There were no real ethnic differences – Serb, Moslem and Croat alike were Slavs, originally from beyond the Carpathians in the region now known as Poland. It was only religion, a partial sense of history and nationalist politicians on the make that gave these minorities a warped sense of grievance.

'Right now there's a lot at stake,' Misic said.

'Yes?'

'People say things are coming to a head.'

'People say a good deal,' said Rosso. 'Much of it bull. Things have been coming to a head ever since Tito fell off his perch, or perhaps ever since he climbed onto it.'

'The word is that the Croat militia at Kiseljak have let the Serbs through – between the Army's Third and Fifth corps.'

'So?'

'If it's true, Sarajevo could be next.'

'So we Croats are the villains of the piece?'

Misic hesitated before answering. 'Let's just say I'd keep a low profile if I were you.'

'And avoid the company of Serbs.' Rosso was smiling.

'What can you tell me about the dentist?'

Misic shrugged. 'Not much. She was divorced. No children that I know of, but then I could be wrong. She went to the clinic every day. Like a lot of people she didn't charge for her services, but patients had to find their own fillings. She struck me as the sensible, independent kind. Decent, yes. Not unattractive. She fretted a lot about the lack of anaesthetic. Terribly talkative, but I put that down to nerves.'

'Affairs? A boyfriend?' Rosso asked.

'I've no idea.'

'Was she in debt?'

'I don't know. She was poor. We're all poor.'

'Did she smoke?'

'Oh, yes. Chain-smoked. Awful. Stank of tobacco.' Misic screwed up his face in distaste.

There were no ashtrays or cigarette ends in the flat.

'How did she afford it?'

'God knows.'

'Any other bad habits?'

'If she did, she kept them to herself.'

'You weren't close then.'

'Me and – Bukovac?'

'Yes, that's what I asked. You and Bukovac.'

'No. Not at all.'

'But you both served on the same committee. You were both Serbs. You were both medical people. You must have had a lot in common. She drew up lists of what the hospitals wanted and gave them to the UN. You advised her. But you weren't close. Why not?'

'Correction. She was from Serbia. I'm a Bosnian Serb.'

Rosso took another tack.

'Was she a Party member in the old days?'

'I've no idea. Does it matter?'

The superintendent tried again.

'Forgive me for failing to make the distinction between Serbs and Serbians.' There was bitterness in Rosso's voice. 'I suppose that explains everything these days. Is the committee entirely composed of Serbs and Serbians?'

'Yes. That's the whole point: that we should make our contribution to the city's survival. Her job was to draw up the lists of supplies we needed and try and persuade the UN to include them in their relief convoys to the city.'

'But the committee's not above accepting help from the odd Croat.'

'That's right.' Misic smiled. 'The odd loyal Croat.'

'Even a cop who is the son of a notorious war criminal?'

Misic laughed. 'If it gets us the access we need . . .'

'How very broad-minded of you.'

Misic laughed again. It was more like a bark of derision.

'You didn't answer the question. Why didn't the pair of you hit it off?'

'I never said we didn't get on. What I said was—'

'What you said was that despite being bosom pals of the medical world, impoverished members of the same so-called ethnic community, idealistic members of a humanitarian committee dedicated to showing how nice Serbs (and Serbians) really are, you weren't close. You didn't get your leg over. You didn't confide in one another. You didn't even get rat-faced together. Why the hell not? She turn you down, Doctor?'

Misic shook his head.

'Ever go to her place?'

'No.'

'Did she ever go to yours?'

'No!'

'Isn't that a little odd?'

'I don't see why.'

'No?'

'You're all the same,' Misic said.

'Know others of my trade, do you?'

'No, thank God.'

'What was it you said about Bukovac and anaesthetic?'

64

'If you've ever watched someone like me operate on a child without anaesthetic you'll know what I mean. Got any kids yourself?' He knew Rosso didn't.

'No.'

'It's our biggest single problem – along with antibiotics to keep infection at bay. Bukovac drew up the lists and quantities of what we needed.'

'What do you use? For the pain, I mean.'

'Anything we can get. Morphine, usually. It's better in some cases than in others. There are side-effects.'

'It's an opium derivative?'

'Yes.'

'And heroin?'

'That's morphine, or sulphate of morphine.'

'Is there any difference?'

The professor did not have time to answer. They were there. The daylight was fading, giving way to that strange twilight that is neither day nor night but somewhere in between; the grey, dismal purgatory of winter.

An argument was underway by the time Rosso reached the entrance to the flats. Two young men with AK-47s barred the way. They wore close-fitting black overalls, black boots and home-made body armour – steel plates fitted into cotton sleeves and sewn together by hand. The gunmen were careful to stand just inside the doorway. Protecting oneself became second nature after a while, an acquired instinct, provided one survived long enough to pick it up.

Anil was swaying from side to side in the open, looking murderous.

'Move out the way, cunts.' His speech was slurred. He slouched up to them like a sailor on a rolling deck in a parody of threatening machismo.

One of the youngsters raised the muzzle of his weapon and placed it against Anil's chest, resting it there. He did not look angry or insulted; on the contrary, he seemed calm and very much aware that his weapon bestowed command of the situation on him alone. A mere sergeant of police with a Makarov pistol, his expression seemed to say, posed no special problems to someone holding a Kalashnikov with a full clip, a round up the spout and the safety on full automatic.

'Fuck,' said Anil, and in trying to push the barrel away, he tripped over his own feet and almost fell. It should have amused the gunmen, but Luka's boys did not laugh. They were taking themselves far too seriously.

Taher, the only one of the three policemen in uniform, took a more dignified approach. He had his warrant card out and held it up so the gunmen could see it.

They weren't interested.

'Mate of yours, is he?' one of the teenagers asked of Taher, indicating Anil, who was now staggering about, trying unsuccessfully to light a cigarette.

Rosso went up to them then, hands in his pockets. He could see the exchange was getting nowhere. His victory in summoning these people to this place was turning out to be Pyrrhic. The best he could do would be to prevent any unpleasantness. Anil seemed to be taking his role of village idiot too far. At worst, it would end with one of them shooting Anil or Taher or both. Dr Misic wisely hung back in the fog.

'I'm chief of detectives,' said Rosso. 'We're not here to give you problems. But we are investigating a suspected murder. We would like to enter the building.'

'Sorry. Orders. No-one in, no-one out.'

'In that case I would like to see your commander.'

'Sure.' The two fighters exchanged glances and the younger – he could not have been more than seventeen – slouched off.

'He won't be a minute.'

'If you don't mind me asking, why all the security?'

The gunman shrugged.

'Cigarette?' Taher held out his packet.

'Thanks.'

Taher lit it for him.

'You know what this place is called, don't you?'

Rosso didn't answer.

The soldier took a long draw on his cigarette, pulling the fumes into his lungs sharply. Gave Rosso a knowing look.

'It's the Monkey House.' House was pronounced 'arse' so that Rosso was momentarily confused by the accent.

'Why's it called that?'

'God, I thought you coppers was supposed to know everything.'

'Obviously I don't.'

'See any bullet holes, any damage on this particular building, do you?'

'No, can't say I do.'

'See, then. That's why.'

'I'm afraid I don't see.'

The gunman sighed. 'Serbs live here, see. Most of them what's left, anyway. The Cetniks up there never shoot at their brothers. Them that lives here knows they're safe, like. Know what I mean?'

'Is that why you're here?'

The gunman didn't reply. His comrade had returned, running.

'He's coming,' the youth said.

'No hard feelings, then, right?'

'Course not,' Rosso said.

The more senior of the two gunmen looked reassured.

'That's OK. You have a good talk with the boss. He'll sort you out. He isn't a bad sort.'

The commander did not run. He strolled up to the doorway, his rifle reversed over his shoulder. He held it with one hand, clasping the barrel. He was a good fifteen years younger than Rosso. He had very short blond hair and a gold ring in one ear. He was short and stocky and frowned at Rosso. Grenades and a very large knife hung from his belt.

'Superintendent Rosso,' said the detective.

The commander nodded.

'We're investigating a death in one of the flats. I want to take my men in, along with a doctor to conduct an examination.'

Another nod. It was not immediately clear if this was a nod signalling permission to enter, or simply a nod of comprehension.

'May we go in?' Rosso took a step forward.

'No.'

'May I ask why not?'

'Security.'

Rosso picked up on a foreign accent.

'What does that mean? I'm a policeman.'

'You can come back in the morning.'

He was a foreigner, Rosso thought. No doubt about it.

'I need to do this tonight.'

'No. There was an attack here today. It's not safe. It's not safe for you. You are very close to the front line. The Cetniks are only forty metres away. You would be wise to go home and come back tomorrow. It is curfew soon.' The young commander started to move away.

'Are you a member of Luka's force?'

That infuriating nod again.

'Who are you again?' the commander asked.

'Detective Superintendent Rosso.'

'This is a military area. Our jurisdiction.'

There was no sign on the man's face that the name Rosso meant anything. He wasn't a Bosnian. He was a western European, and as everyone knows, young Westerners have lost their history. Fifty years and five hundred years are all the same to them.

'Can I ask you a few questions?'

The commander had turned away. He said something in German to the two sentries which Rosso didn't catch.

'Tomorrow. You hear? Tomorrow,' the fighter said over his shoulder. Rosso could not see him any more in the gloom.

Vasic, poor man, would have to spend the night there, alone and without food. He would curse terribly. He would be convinced

Rosso was deliberately punishing him for his indiscretion, his outburst. Rosso turned back to the car. There was nothing else he could do. Not with Luka's boys in the way.

Seen from the front, the presidency seemed to have survived three years of war relatively unscathed. There were the usual sprays of bullet holes like patches of eczema across the plasterwork, symbolic piles of crumbling sandbags, the odd, football-sized bite into the masonry and piles of roof tiles scattered across the pavement, but there was otherwise little sign from the main street that the centre of the Bosnian government's policy-making was a target.

It was never a pretty place at the best of times and as times go it was not likely to get much worse. The presidency was rectangular, four storeys with the usual neo-classical vanities and big Habsburg sash-windows. The walls were dressed in stone, buttressed like belts of armour on a dreadnought. Its wartime virtue was that it was proving hard to demolish. More lucrative, easily destructible targets were at hand. There was something graceless about the presidency's proportions. It was too large, above all too squat, to please the eye. Unlike many other civic buildings of its kind in the former Yugoslavia that were given a coat of jaunty Mediterranean yellow or warm ochre, the presidency was dressed in a uniform sooty grey like a battleship in winter colours, entirely appropriate for the spirit of the age. Rosso thought that if the Serb predators gazing down on the city chose their victims in terms of architectural aesthetics then it would explain why the presidency survived. The presidency certainly wasn't as tempting as a graceful sixteenth-century mosque or a pretty Romanesque cathedral and the insurgents had already destroyed the capital's magnificent post office.

To Rosso it all boiled down to two players in a murderously unequal game. There was the hapless city itself – passive, inert, a victim oozing its lifeblood onto the broken streets from a thousand wounds – and its relentlessly cruel, almost invisible tormentor who waited up there in the mist, content to kill the city by degrees, bit by bit and day by day. For Rosso, the Serb separatists were intent not simply on killing the living and the present. More than 7,000 ancient texts had gone up in smoke when they destroyed the Gazi Husrev-beg library just up the road one sunny August afternoon (as he drove past now, Rosso saw people, including children, still ripping out what remained of the wooden rafters and window frames for firewood), more than 5,000 more manuscripts had been burnt when the Cetniks systematically levelled the Oriental Institute a few minutes' walk away. The Historical Archives and the National Library followed, reduced to rubble by high explosive and then set on fire with phosphorus; the destruction of a nation's past, the works of scholars, dervish and soldier poets who wrote the old script, the poetry and erotic songs in Arabic metres, ballads and epic love stories enjoyed by Moslem and Christian alike. Truly, Rosso thought, the Serb nationalists could say Bosnia was a cultural desert, that Islam had brought nothing but bigotry and superstition to the Balkans, that Moslems were simply Christians converted under threat of decapitation, a people who had lost their birthright.

The rear of the presidency was the worst hit. There was a screen of oak trees – their branches regrettably bare of leaves – but otherwise this end of the building faced the Serbs across the river in Mrakusa and Sirokaca and further up the white, whale-backed slopes of Mount Trebevic. The windows had been boarded up and the presidency's officials – who had only recently counted themselves fortunate with such a fine, uninterrupted view – had moved deeper into the bureaucratic labyrinth and out of the line of fire.

Rosso left his car out front and walked round the side of the building, keeping close to its stout walls. He showed his police pass at the rear entrance and climbed the broad stairs, almost deserted now that night was approaching, and found his way to Luka's office on the second floor at the far end of a gloomy passage. He asked his way twice of departing secretaries, showing his warrant card, and received terse replies from people anxious to be off the streets before darkness settled across the city. No-one was willing to linger. It was believed evil things went on in the backstreets at night, and not even policemen ventured out on foot after dusk.

The door was unlocked. Rosso knocked and walked in. There was a small outer office for a typist, then Luka's desk and chair, an uncomfortable sofa – from which the stuffing oozed like furry intestine – a wobbly and badly scratched coffee-table of vaguely Ottoman origin and an ancient Bakelite telephone. The furniture seemed to have been dug out of the cellars when they were converting them for use as a shelter, dusted off and put in here, when it was decided that the national interest dictated that Luka should be granted at least the trappings of official power. The rest of the decor was Luka's own and typical of the man-child who commanded respect, terror, hero-worship. There were first and foremost artefacts from his war collection: a massive brass shell casing from a Serb gun emplacement; a jumble of street signs, presumably places where Luka had fought; a tattered regimental flag with the double-headed eagle of old Serbia; a Serb officer's cap splashed with dried blood; an ancient gas mask and finally a deactivated hand-grenade as paperweight, superfluous on a paperless desk. Behind Luka's chair, on the wall, was a faded print of Bonaparte crowning himself emperor.

Rosso would have to find Luka at home. He knew the score. If he turned up at Block Nine in the morning, another commander would shrug and tell him he could not carry out his investigation in an area under military jurisdiction without a piece of paper, signed by Luka and countersigned by a minister. It was the run-around treatment and he would get it in full because he was a cop.

Only Luka could solve the problem.

As he turned to leave, Rosso felt the air move around him. The windows of Luka's office shook, humming faintly as they vibrated to the distant explosions of projectiles from multiple rocket launchers screaming into the city. Specks of dust writhed in the disturbed air, caught in the pale, dying light filtering in from the dirty windows.

The lull was over.

*　　*　　*

The shot came from across the bridge, a good 800 metres or so away, and it knocked the woman down.

Tanja heard the crack of the bullet as it passed her, the tell-tale thump of the sniper's rifle a moment later, that gave her the direction and approximate range of the shot.

The woman threw up her arms, dropping her basket. She went flying like a rag doll, tumbling soundlessly, all arms and legs – black against the snow. She made no sound that Tanja could hear and then she lay very still; just a smear of black on a white sheet. In a few minutes she would have been invisible, the snow was falling so heavily. Tanja could look away and look back and it would be as if she had never been there at all. The pedestrians – now on their knees and clutching one another in some instinctive need – shouted to Tanja not to go, but she ran out nevertheless. One man reached up and tried to grab her jacket. His mouth was open, and as if she had taken a snapshot of him at that moment, she saw his mouth as a large O and full of rotten, stained teeth. She did not hear him shouting at her for the blood roaring in her ears. Tanja did not think – she simply went, running into the road. She did not feel frightened. Tanja thought only of the woman and where she had been hit and whether it was bad and how she would deal with it. The snow slowed her feet, and Tanja was breathless when she reached the woman. She remembered how tiring it had been running through sand as a child when her parents had taken her to the seaside. Her parents . . . her own mother and father were dead. Tanja pushed this mental baggage out of her mind and looked down. She could hear her own heart pumping loudly in her ears as she unzipped the little first-aid kit she carried on her belt. She sensed the sniper watching her, imagined his finger tighten on the trigger.

The woman was elderly. Well, in her fifties anyhow. To a nineteen-year-old that is elderly. The victim lay on her back. Snowflakes fell on her cheeks. There were little droplets of water in her eyelashes. Tanja bent right over, very low, so her face was less than an inch from the woman's. It was like two people hugging, whispering; an intimate gesture between old friends. Tanja's hair brushed the woman's forehead.

She's breathing, Tanja told herself.

Still on her knees, Tanja worked her way round to the top of the woman's head. With great care she put one hand under the woman's jaw, the other on top of the skull and gently tipped the head back to clear the airway. Then, on her knees, she felt the woman's scalp with her fingers, the back of her neck. Tanja tugged off her own gloves with her teeth. She ran her hands over collar-bone, chest, back, hips. Nothing. Tanja spoke aloud: 'If it's your back, mother, there's not much I can do for you.' Sometimes a broken back or neck left a sort of step in the vertebrae, sometimes not. Then she saw the fresh blood, and the leg twisted under her, unnaturally turned.

She bent again, and assuring herself that the woman was still breathing, began to work on the leg, ever so gently lifting and straightening it. 'There,' Tanja said. 'There.' It was a good thing she was unconscious in a way.

That would have hurt.

There was no more shooting. It was so quiet. It was like being alone on a desert island, white sand all around.

The bullet had torn into the leg above the knee, possibly a ricochet from the angle of entry. The sniper had shot too low. A shard of bone protruded from the wound and the gash bled sluggishly. The cold helped.

Tanja cut away the clothing around the wound, coiled one of her dressings round, rather like a doughnut with a hole in the middle, and placed it over the ugly rupture in the tissue so that the protruding bone wasn't under pressure, but settled in the centre of the ring of the bandage. She placed another on top, and tied it on firmly, grunting with the effort of wrapping the ends of the dressing around the woman's thigh.

Tanja checked again for breathing. You're not going to die on me now, dear, are you?

Had she knocked herself unconscious when she fell? Had it

73

been the pain? She could not have lost enough blood to go into shock, surely.

Whatever it was, Tanja needed to get the injured woman to hospital. Tanja gently pulled the woman's two legs together, straightening them as best she could and immobilizing the woman's feet, tying an old bandage into a figure of eight. Then she used the woman's scarf as padding between her legs to help secure them. Finally, she used two old, reused triangular dressings – the kind used to make a sling for a broken arm or collar-bone – folding them flat and narrow to bind the legs together just above and below the wound.

That would have to do. Tanja stood. She was sweating despite the cold.

She grabbed the woman under the armpits, and pulled. It would have been better to have kept the legs raised. Now the wounded limb was being dragged along the ground, leaving a furrow in the snow.

It could not be helped.

'I'm sorry, dear,' Tanja said to the woman. 'I'm sorry.'

Each tug pulled her a few inches out of the road and the sniper's line of fire. Tanja was wondering if the Cetnik was watching the two women, if she was in his sights now. She tugged again, and began to feel an irrational fury at the woman for having got herself shot in the first place. 'Wake up,' Tanja hissed. 'Wake up. Don't expect me to carry you.'

It was when Tanja let the woman down gently and stood back, wondering what she would do with an unconscious woman with a gunshot wound on a deserted street, that she saw the car approach. It put its lights on and off and moved with agonizing slowness. The sky, the world around them, was getting darker by the second. Instinctively Tanja raised her arm, as if hailing a taxi. The driver won't see me, she thought. She left the woman lying there and took a step out onto the street.

It was vaguely familar. It was only when the vehicle drew level

74

that she realized it was her stepfather's car, the little Yugo with its rusty door frames and the grandiose coat of arms on the front. She called Rosso her stepfather because, as she told him often enough, she did not believe in God. If she was mistaken and there was a god, she used to say, and he permitted all this misery, then he wasn't worth the effort.

She bent down.

Rosso leant across the front seat and opened the door.

'I've got an injured woman,' she said.

Rosso left the engine running but put on the handbrake and got out. Tanja told him how to lift her and then they both carried the woman over and got her onto the back seat.

Rosso carefully turned the car around.

'French hospital is closest,' Tanja said.

There seemed to be an unspoken agreement between them that formal greetings and polite inquiries about one another's health and the rest of it could be dispensed with. In that respect, Rosso thought, and in that respect alone, they were like a married couple.

What a family! Rosso's wife was a member of a nation that was, geographically speaking, poised like a bird of prey over Bosnia. As for himself, Rosso originated from a people who could only successfully blunt the Serbian advance towards the Adriatic by possessing Bosnia, or at least by hiving off or dominating part of it. And in the centre, torn between them, was their orphaned god-daughter, Tanja, a member of a Moslem nation the Serbs and Croats both viewed as apostates.

Tanja turned around now, kneeling in the front passenger seat and bending over into the back to attend to the injured woman who seemed to be coming round, for she was moaning very softly. Blood was oozing to the surface of the dressing on her leg and Tanja was trying to place another on top of it, thereby increasing the pressure on the wound and reducing the flow still further. Textbook stuff.

'Not long now,' said Rosso.

The hospital towered above them on three sides. Tanja moved

quickly, pulling open the rear doors and then getting in the back herself to help lift the woman's head and shoulders. A hospital orderly helped her. The woman, who was beginning to cry with the pain, was placed gently on a stretcher of some kind. It had wheels that squeaked terribly, like fingernails scraped along a school blackboard.

'Coming in?' She shut the rear doors.

'I don't think so,' Rosso said. 'Will you be long?'

'I want to get some more dressings. I'll make my own way home.'

'Home? Or Luka's place?'

'Home.'

Rosso put the car into gear.

'Wait,' she said, bending down.

'What is it?'

Tanja had long hair and she put her hand up to tuck it behind one ear, out of her face.

'Father.' She called him that on formal occasions or when she wanted something from him. She seemed to know it always touched him deeply in a way he never understood.

She looked quickly over her shoulder, as if anxious she should not be overheard. There wasn't anybody about.

'Are you in some kind of trouble?'

'No,' he said. 'Why?

He tried to smile as a way of turning it into something lighthearted. He wanted to appear relaxed but a vague anxiety weighed down on him.

Tanja put her hand out, briefly touched his cheek and withdrew it. Then she took her eyes off his face and looked down. She appeared to take a sudden interest in the paintwork on the side of the Yugo.

'Promise me something.'

'What is it?'

'You won't go out tonight,' she said. Then she frowned, as if

76

she was having difficulty choosing the right words. 'You'll stay home. You'll be careful. I know you're a policeman, but you will be careful. Father?'

'I promise. But is there something you should tell me—'

Tanja had straightened up. She turned and ran inside, pushing open the hospital doors without breaking step.

Rosso sat still for a moment or two. Had Luka won her over? Was she lost to them now? He started off again, the car moving slowly into the night. From inside, where it was dark and she knew he would not see her watching, Tanja stood pressed to the window, staring out until the car's tail-lights vanished.

5

'Mendacity is a system that we live in.
Liquor is one way out an' death's the other.'
TENNESSEE WILLIAMS, *CAT ON A HOT TIN ROOF*

ROSSO LET HIMSELF IN. HE WAS TAKING THE KEY OUT OF THE LOCK
when his wife came out of the bedroom. Sabina had on her pyjamas
and Rosso wasn't sure whether she had changed into them (people
generally went to bed early as there was no light and nothing much
else to do) or had been that way all day. The jacket and pants
were flannel, with little pink flowers on them. Sabina gave him
her best smile and kissed him on the cheek. He could smell the
drink on her.

'How are you?'

Rosso knew it was an inane question. He knew how she was.
He wondered where she had secreted the bottles. For the few days
he was away she had no need to hide them. He knew she looked
forward to his brief absences for that reason. Alcoholism was a

disease of the Balkan intelligentsia, and the need made its victims, like his wife, extraordinarily cunning. It made the faithful feckless, turned the truthful into barefaced liars. It fractured personality in a terrible way. Sabina was no exception.

'Would you like to eat? I have something ready.'

She was on her best behaviour; that was always a relief. Yet behind the cheerfulness, experience taught Rosso that a storm was brewing. It made him wary of her.

Sabina was painfully thin and there were dark smudges under her eyes. The pyjamas that had once fitted her so well were now huge, hanging shapelessly from her thin shoulders. In a moment of self-awareness, she touched her hair. It was grey and lifeless and badly in need of a wash. There was no shampoo, no running water either. Her hand fell limply back to her side.

The policeman wanted to hug his wife. While still in the doorway, standing on the mat, he awkwardly put his arms around her, squeezing his eyes shut against the tears springing up behind his eyelids, like the inexorable rise of water in some artesian well, but she slipped easily away from him, objecting that she needed a bath, should have changed. Wasn't he hungry, she asked, flustered. It must have been ages since he last ate and what time did he leave for the airport that morning – she used words and questions like the clouds of metal strips dispersed by aircraft to deceive ground radar, bombarding him with them, showering him with fragments of sentiment.

Food was of no interest to her. It never had been. Now she saw it as a subject she could still talk about, reaching back into some dimly lit recess of memory and dredging up an idealized image of the young wife preparing meals for her ambitious husband. She had always been a good cook, though seldom finding the results appetizing herself and as a consequence, quickly losing interest.

It always began like this. Sabina would put on a brave face whenever he got back. She would promise herself, and him, that things would get better. Sabina would get better: a better wife. She seemed to believe that if she behaved better, she would get better.

It was not made any easier by her painful awareness that violent death intruded into every conversation; it was on everyone's lips. No subject, no matter how trivial, escaped references to death, its occurrence, its manner, its inevitability. It was like the fine sand that blows into people's mouths no matter how tightly they keep them shut in the face of a desert storm. Perversely perhaps, Sabina allowed it into everything she said by her insistence on not mentioning it, or the war, at all, at deliberately excluding it. Again, by not mentioning it, she seemed to believe it could be willed to disappear. Yet this insistence only rendered it omnipresent.

Rosso sat on the bed; the only furniture in the flat was their double bed and a wardrobe and Tanja's narrow army cot out in the corridor. Everything else had been sold or broken up for firewood, but in their case the firewood had been sold, not burnt in their tiny wood stove. Her little collection of jewellery had gone, then the silver-plate tea service, finally the curtains. She had taken his things too. He never said a word of reproach. Cuff-links, a pair of boots, a leather jacket. What was the point of curtains when there was no glass left in the windows? When there was no electric light?

What was the point of cuff-links? These things had no value and it was too great a feat of imagination for Sabina to think that they could again, someday, matter. She would say she could not take her belongings with her. Sarajevans had accustomed themselves to the inevitability of an early and violent end, if not this week, then next month, or even next year. What did any of it matter?

The neighbours had sold everything they had for food, or firewood. But the Rossos were different. Every dinar he gave her went on drink, and everything she had went to the market – for drink. As the dinar sank in value, the amount of alcohol it could buy evaporated and she became increasingly desperate, ruthless in her quest. There had been a time when she had received treatment as an out-patient at the psychiatric wing of Kosovo hospital, on the hill above the cemetery. Now they would turn her away – they had more important things to worry about. What drugs they had were used to sedate the ward of catatonics, schizophrenics and manic-depressives lest they run amok under the artillery bombardments.

Rosso was home half an hour when he found the first bottle, tied around the neck with twine and hung from the bathroom window, the other end fastened to the window catch. It was half full. Rosso hesitated; he hadn't the heart to empty it. Not now, not tonight. Instead he would join the pretence, allowing her some success in deception, if only to extend her good mood.

It was the war, she would say. She called her drink problem her migraines. 'I have a migraine, dear,' and she would shuffle into their room and close the door, furtively lifting a floorboard or reaching into a pile of laundry for her liquor. She would lie on their bed in the dark, sometimes for days.

He did not give her the perfume. She would only find a way to sell it and if that failed, she would probably try and drink it. It would not be the first time.

It was the war.

After this is over, he told himself, she can go back to her family in Banja Luka. Sarajevo will be no place for a Serb under this Moslem government. They had talked about it. The last time she had one of her bouts of hysteria, screaming at him that he didn't love her, never had loved her (that, at least, wasn't true) and that he wanted to be rid of her. She had torn at his clothes, tried to hit him with her fists. A fucking Croatian. Eventually she had fallen back, exhausted, sobbing, begging his forgiveness, which he readily gave.

He felt humiliation. For both of them.

He knew how it was. From being a member of Yugoslavia's *nomenklatura*, one of the Party's beautiful people, she had become a non-person. It had been a long way to fall. Nationalism was no safety net. It repelled her. She saw the writing on the wall before he did: she knew what was going to happen when Slobodan Milosevic, then head of the Serbian Communist Party, stripped Kosovo's ethnic Albanians and Vojvodina's Hungarians of their autonomous status. It was the decision that made inevitable the wars to follow and those to come. Sabina had known, and it came about as she said it would.

It had driven her to the bottle and half round the bend.

People Sabina had known for years nowadays refused to acknowledge her, crossing the road rather than pass by her or greet her. They whispered about her, pointed at her. Their local Serb and an ex-communist and, what was more, married to the son of a notorious Ustasha, a Croatian fascist. Some were openly hostile, cursing her – even spitting at her.

It was the war.

Rosso gave her the cigarettes. She asked about his mother, showing polite but feigned interest. It was the next drink that she was thinking about. It was all she thought about. She hardly ate, even on the rare occasions they had food. She could hardly digest solids anyway. She tried to smile, to be bright, to show interest in his work, and he found himself telling her about the oxygen and the Ilyushin he had taken back to the city. She plucked at her pyjamas, fidgeted, tried to concentrate and failed. Little interested her these days.

She was bothered by something, though.

'Is there someone else?' She looked up at him, her pale face tense, drawn.

'What?'

'You've been to Zagreb three times in as many months. Don't tell me it's your bloody mother.'

'She's seventy-three this year.'

'She's as strong as a horse.'

'There's no need to excite yourself.'

'Excite myself?' Her voice rose sharply.

'It's OK,' Rosso said soothingly. He made placating movements with his hands.

'It's a woman, isn't it?'

'Yes, it's a woman. An Englishwoman. Turned seventy-three this year, with an inordinate love of that disgustingly sugary Viennese chocolate cake – *sachetorte*. My mother. You met her, remember?

I seem to recall you took an immediate dislike to one another.'
Rosso couldn't help but laugh.

'You're trying to change the subject, to humour me.'

'Yes.'

'Don't think I'm jealous.'

'I don't.'

Rosso's tactics were to agree with anything and everything she
said, to avoid confrontation.

'Then tell me why you went.'

Rosso told her then of his efforts to collect supplies for his friend
Misic at the hospital. It was a half-truth, one of many Rosso kept in
reserve to prevent people he cared about from hurting themselves,
to save them unnecessary worry. The truth was too brutal taken
straight. It needed to be diluted, rationed. He continued to talk to
his wife: with the name Rosso he thought he could still open doors
in Zagreb. He said he rather liked the idea of the son of a Nazi
using his father's notoriety to help the victims of aggression half
a century later. It was a way of settling the account, or at least a
small part of it. He told Sabina about the hospital committee of
Serb – and Serbian – staff and their efforts to gain the co-operation
of medical professionals across the 'ethnic' barricades, their efforts
to get medical supplies, power and water flowing again to the city.
The committee had asked him to do what he could in Croatia. He
said he felt obliged to help. That was another half-truth.

When he finished, Sabina spoke softly, insistently.

'You're not cut out for heroism,' she said. 'It's not your style.
The cemetery is full of heroes. You're a policeman. That's your
contribution. I thought you were immune from the glory-seekers,
the idealists, the romantics. I thought we'd both come through
all that, finished with it when we finished with the Party. Was I
wrong?'

'In Zagreb the name Rosso means something.'

'Oh, dear me, yes. I'm sure it does. You trade on your father's
reputation.' She seemed to tremble, but it wasn't the damp air in
the flat.

His father's memory was an awkwardness between them that would never quite go away. Like the pictures his mother still insisted on cherishing, deaf to Rosso's appeals and oblivious to his shame, she lovingly took them out each day in her Zagreb apartment, handling the old album like some sacred text and inviting Rosso to sit beside her, to admire as she did, touching each worn snapshot with fingers that still carried her late husband's engagement and wedding rings. The puppy-faced Zagreb student rowing barefoot, smiling at the camera. The stiff, proud adolescent, rigidly at attention in his black uniform. A gaunt, hardened *Obersturmführer*, already grey and shorn of any illusions about the romance of war, receiving the coveted *Ritterkreuz* at the hands of the Führer himself and photographed for the Party newspaper against Bavarian spruce.

Rosso did not want to hurt the old woman. He had sat obediently on the arm of her chair. Looked, as she bade him. He loved her after all. She would not have understood how he felt about the past and it was too late to try to explain.

Whatever Sabina might say.

What should he tell her now, half a century later? That the men who wore the Death's Head badge had their headquarters in Buchenwald? That their casualty replacements were drawn from among concentration-camp guards? That they never took prisoners? That what was initially a racially 'pure' force became a multinational army one million strong, with a reputation for unrivalled ferocity both on the battlefield and off it? That Bosnians were among the last to defend Berlin? That the Germans and their Ustashe allies shot 400 Serb civilians for every German killed?

Then there were the photographs clipped from the newspapers after it was over. Long after they had last heard from him. She kept those too, yellowed with age. Dozens of them folded into a cardboard shoebox in the bottom of the old war widow's wardrobe; photographs of a sea of men as far as the horizon, stumbling across the Russian steppe into captivity or worse. Mostly worse. The starving faces, feet wrapped in rags, the old bandages seeping blood, the endless snowscapes. She wept when she looked at the pictures, mumbled prayers for a son of the Death's Head Division of the Waffen SS. She still hoped. Still stared at the old pictures of survivors freed from Soviet camps decades later, keenly seeking his face.

Lest we forget, thought Rosso. For we can never forgive. Hatred was the gruel on which the Party force-fed its members, not forgiveness. It was hard to overcome the old doctrine. Hard for both Rosso and Sabina.

My father, God help me.

The old man would have been eighty-four.

Rosso was still talking to Sabina about his day. He told it as a joke against himself: the desolation of headquarters, the paperwork, Anil's predilection for marijuana, Vasic's near-hysterical reaction to the murder, their search of the woman's flat, his reluctant witnessing of Misic's operation, finally the frustration at being barred entry to the New Town apartment block. He told her about his chance encounter with Tanja on a snowy street and their mercy run to hospital with a wounded woman. How Tanja seemed to warn him. All this time, as Rosso became aware how hungry and tired he was, Sabina watched him carefully, as if he were a piece of porcelain dangerously close to the edge of a shelf. He told her nothing of the murder victim's role as a police informer, of the investigation into Luka's affairs.

'Why?'

'Why what?'

'Why get involved?'

'I'm a cop. You said it yourself. It's my contribution.'

'That's not what I mean.'

'What do you mean?'

'Take this committee. It's more than you say it is. It's unofficially the voice of the Serbs in the city. They call themselves Loyal Serbs. Others see them as the fig-leaf of ethnic harmony, hiding growing sectarian hatred. Loyalty is a contrivance, a label, like the term terrorist.'

'I'll take your word for it, but I know nothing of this.'

'There's a lot you don't know. You're a bit of a fool, you know. An innocent.' He looked at her blankly, letting it pass. He had let so much pass, why take offence now? 'The city's Croats want the president to accept partition of Sarajevo,' she continued. 'The president – well, the poor man's being elbowed aside by people like Luka. Luka's the coming man. It's dangerous, don't you realize that? You're out of your depth. There's too much at stake. We both promised each other—'

Rosso interrupted her.

'I'm investigating a murder.'

'Get someone else.'

'There isn't anyone else.'

'It's not just a murder, don't you see?'

'Frankly, no.'

'You say this woman was a Serbian. A dentist. Known to Misic. A member of his committee. She's found murdered on Luka's territory. It stinks, the whole business, and you're pressing your luck too far. Leave it to one of the others. Punch the clock, sign the papers. Don't get involved.'

He noticed Sabina's hands shook. How prescient she is, he thought. She has this unnerving ability to focus on the weak link in any tale. How typical that she should sense that the murder, and the murder victim, are not all that they seem.

'And Tanja,' he said.

She looked away for a moment, as if it was something she did not want to think about.

'She and Luka . . .'

'She's an adult. She's not our child.' Sabina spoke angrily, dismissively. This, she seemed to be saying, is not our cross to bear. We have enough already.

Hearing the sound of a car below in the alley, Rosso leant out of the window and looked down. There were headlights, and their reflection showed a large, light-coloured vehicle. It looked to Rosso like one of the powerful four-wheel-drive cars the senior UN staff used. It was edging slowly alongside the building, its tyres crunching on the fresh snow. When the car stopped, the lights were doused and the driver's door swung open for a moment and then closed again.

'Who is it?' Sabina asked.

'I think it's the UN,' he said.

Sabina got up and after a few moments came and stood next to Rosso. She leant out and looked down, also. She must have taken the opportunity when his back was turned to slip out to the bathroom for a quick one. He could smell it strongly on her breath. He was sure her speech was slightly slurred.

'It's that tart on the third,' Sabina said.

'What tart?' Rosso asked.

'They come to see her all hours of the day and night. She only has foreign clients. Bosnians aren't good enough for her. It's the German marks. She's probably the only person in our block who's going to come out of the war richer than when it started. Well, good luck to her.'

'You sound envious.'

'No. Sickened by it all.'

'How do you know about her?'

'People talk, even to me. Her name's Nadia. Not her real name, I suppose. There are some people who want to throw her out because she's a whore and throw me out because I'm a Serbian.' Sabina laughed a drunken laugh, a sort of reckless cackle that made Rosso's hackles rise.

'They won't throw you out.'

'Ha! They'll let Nadia stay and throw me out. She's got money.'

'Of course they won't.'

'You're bloody naïve for a policeman, you know that? It's not only Serbs they're throwing out of their homes. Croats too. You can't blame them; Croats and Serbs started this mess.'

87

'No, you're wrong. They are putting refugees in the homes that have been left empty by Croats. Not the same thing at all.'

Rosso looked up. The city was so very dark, but flashes from distant and unseen guns lit up the surrounding hills. They looked like cakes covered in sticky icing. There was a dull reddish glow in the sky to the south. Something was burning, a village or factory. Luka's sector, he thought, probably in Stup or Ilidza. There was a low rumble, not unlike thunder.

Rosso turned away from the window, and walked through to the bedroom. It was freezing in there and he was tempted to crawl under the bedclothes.

Instead he found his patrolman's torch. He switched it on and off to check the batteries. Satisfied, he stuck it in his jacket pocket and went out to the hall.

When was the last time he had touched Sabina, wanted her? Rosso honestly could not remember. She would know. Sabina would know the date, the time, the colour and texture of the sheets. She would recall what they had said, how it had been. She was like that. She would tease him with her power of memory.

And now? They would lie together in bed, sometimes, hands touching. It was some comfort, that was all. He could see the veins in her hands and arms, blue beneath the pale skin. She was so vulnerable he wanted to weep for her, for them, and instead grew angry with himself. Why couldn't he relent, give more of himself? Was it his Englishness that cut him off? Sometimes he ached for her, not out of desire, but out of companionship, out of sorrow for another human being's suffering and he had no idea how to get that across, how to express what little he did still feel. It was as if he, Rosso, had a finite reservoir of feeling and most of it had been used up already trying to function as a member of the human race. Perhaps everybody had a tankful of feeling. Only people expended it at varying rates; there were the emotional gas-guzzlers, or the emotionally thrifty who saved it for themselves: cowards or killers.

It would be great to walk away from this. Better still, sleep through it.

He pitied his wife – the last thing she would have wanted – yet the smell of her, the very proximity of her, nauseated him. It was the sickly sweet smell of the drink on her breath, and the old *eau de toilette* she used to try and mask the odours of her unwashed body, the skin scaly and dry: a stench of decay. They all carried that smell, the living and the dead.

Rosso told himself it was only the war. When that was over, everything would get better. Everything.

He sometimes thought of hope as man's worst enemy.

'Where are you going?'

'That vehicle outside.'

'You haven't heard a thing I've been saying to you.'

'Yes I have.'

'Leave it. It doesn't matter. She doesn't matter. You can't clean up the streets on your own.'

'I'm going nonetheless.'

'No. You're not.'

'I am. Now move out of the way.'

He felt a peculiar rage grow inside him and take hold, as if all the frustrations of the day were taking the shape of that one vehicle.

She stood in front of him, barring his way out.

'Move, please.'

'Please don't.'

'Don't make me hurt you. Step aside.'

'Don't, oh, don't.'

'Don't fuss woman.'

He took her arm firmly but gently, and turned her aside.

He opened the door and stepped out.

'For God's sake be careful.'

'You forget I'm a police officer.'

'You forget times have changed. Nobody respects that badge of yours. That popgun you're carrying' – Rosso had taken it out and was checking it was loaded – 'is worse than useless.'

He left her in the doorway, shivering in her pink floral pyjamas, making a slobbering noise, tears making her face wet and not really knowing any more what she was doing or why. She was frantic, craving a drink from the bottle hanging from the bathroom window. Burning for him to go yet begging him not to. The self-loathing and guilt were plain.

Sabina was right about the pistol.

It was no defence.

Branston Flett Jnr, Sarajevo correspondent of the US president's favourite daily newspaper, turned his four-wheel-drive vehicle into an alley-way off the main street. It was a sheltered spot between two apartment blocks, huge cliffs that loomed blackly out of the darkness. There were no street lights. Flett braked gently, switched off the ignition, killed the lights. The car was very conspicuous. This was as good a place as any to hide it. It was a huge, rugged US-built eight-seater, custom-made for the US Secret Service and acquired third-hand and flown in across the Adriatic from Ancona in Italy at his editor's great expense to help ensure Flett's survival. The reporter knew everyone in the city regarded the foreign aid workers, soldiers and journalists as fair game, an international hand-out. If anyone found his car, they would slip underneath, cut the fuel pipe and use a can to catch the liquid gold even while he sat there.

Flett opened his door, whistling to himself tunelessly. The interior lights came on. He turned back to the woman beside him. 'One moment,' he said. He leant towards her and kissed her on the corner of her mouth, tasting her lipstick.

She turned towards him, lifted her face, her eyes half closed, lips parted.

Here, he thought. Now. Let's christen my new car.

Let's fuck.

Flett pulled the door shut again and the interior lights went off. It felt good in the dark. He bent eagerly, his right arm encircling her, pulling her close.

The rumble of guns seemed so very far off, not least because of the triple layers of glass that could withstand a high-velocity bullet fired at close range.

A man could buy women for cigarettes in this town. No doubt many of them did. Flett knew what went on in the back of the UN four-tonners at night in the French base. It was rumoured that husbands even brought along their wives to earn enough to eat. The peacekeepers were making a fortune in marks flogging cigarettes. He had put it all down on his list of feature ideas, subjects to be tackled when it was quiet.

She drew his tongue into her mouth.

The women were so vulnerable, their faces had the pained look of wounded creatures, their eyes hopeless, pleading, desperate. Let's face it, he thought, that's one hell of a turn-on.

Her hand was on his thigh, fingers spread. They moved up.

Flett was already tumescent, painfully so, and when her hand cupped his fullness and knowingly pressed and stroked, he broke free for air. She pulled his head down again.

'Kiss me, Blanston darling,' she said.

'Branston.'

'Yes. Blanston.'

The long fingers and painted nails of both the woman's hands were working on him now, taking by frontal assault their objective: an army belt bought in a Washington army-surplus store and ideal for keeping the wearer in and an impatient young woman out.

After the belt clasp came the fly; no zip but a line of large solid buttons sewn onto thick cotton.

Flett tried to make it easier by moving down in the seat, sucking in his stomach. She was dexterous and quick, pulling him clear of the tangle of shirt, underpants and the rough, stiff trouser material.

'There,' she said, as if to a child. 'Feel good?'

Her left hand caressed the back of his neck, her right held on to his newly released organ, cool and expert, gently coaxing the engorged member. It needed little encouragement.

He felt good all right.

'Honey,' he said. 'Honey, please.'

Neither heard the sound of feet behind them, the distinctive creak of leather boots in dry snow.

She bent forward, her hair brushing Flett's cheek.

'You big man,' she said.

'Sweetie,' he said with an intake of breath. 'Nadia.' Whether in surprise, pleasure or reproof, or all three, neither of them could tell. At least he had her name right this time. He was so useless with the names of the girls he picked up.

Sexual pleasure depended on risk, Flett thought. Fear and risk went hand in hand.

What was pleasure but transgression?

The reporter shut his eyes. The woman's hair smelt of strawberries.

When he opened them again a moment later, he saw, to his considerable alarm, that their passion had a witness. A flashlight danced across the rear window, slid down the side window and came to rest at Flett's left shoulder as whoever held it walked around the vehicle.

Flett tensed, tried to straighten. Unaware, his partner resisted, increasing the pace of what she was doing.

He could see the glass face of the flashlight inches away through the thick, reinforced glass.

'No,' the correspondent said. Then, louder: 'No!'

'Darling,' Nadia said encouragingly.

For a terrible moment Flett thought he was going to be whacked, that this was an assassination, a hit. The thought passed through his mind that he had been set up. He imagined his body slumped against the wheel, brains and bone all over the dashboard and mixed with seminal fluid in his lap.

Flett had to remind himself that he was sitting in an armoured vehicle behind bullet-proof glass. Short of someone firing a rocket-propelled grenade or .50 calibre machine-gun slug at them, this vehicle was impregnable.

Cold drops of sweat from his armpits rolled down his sides. He felt suddenly angry. Let the bastard watch!

The beam of light was diffused by the triple layer of glass, but the person behind it must have been aware of what he had found nonetheless. The light moved across Flett's shoulders, up to his face, then down to his lap.

Flett squirmed, trying to shift away from the window.

He bellowed at Nadia this time. She stopped.

'You no like?' She smiled up at him with the unshakable confidence of someone who knows very well what men like.

The torchlight caught her attention. In an instant she was upright, pulling down Flett's grey cable-stitch sweater to cover his disarray. The torch followed her movements, then pulled away from the window. The light was extinguished.

Flett cupped his hands against the glass, staring into the blackness. He could see nothing. For her part, Nadia found it easier to get the American back into his trousers than it had been to get him out of them, now that the rod of desire had turned to a limp fumble of panic. She tried and failed to suppress a giggle. Men!

Flett thought it was over when there was a loud crack next to his head. Someone was banging hard on the window with something metallic. It was as if whoever had found them with the flashlight had given them a few moments to cover their embarrassment before approaching the car again.

It was a pistol. The butt was being repeatedly struck against the glass.

'Oh shit,' Flett said.

He turned the key in the ignition and the powerful engine rumbled into life. He gripped the steering wheel.

'Don't you want to come up to my place?' She smiled up at him, a conspiratorial smirk.

She was a blonde, with legs up to her armpits and breasts that seemed to point at him in unmistakable invitation. He felt his ache for her begin again, expanding from groin to throat.

To hell with the Bosnians, the United Nations and nosy bastards with torches and guns. Let the fucker eat his heart out. He put the vehicle into gear, pressed the accelerator with his foot. The hotel would be better.

The car responded with a throaty roar. Flett gunned it out of the alley, feeling its power and the back wheels kicking up a cloud of snow behind them. For a moment it lost traction, skidded and then righted itself as he turned the wheel into the skid.

Flett glanced across at the woman. She smiled, and moved up against him, sliding her hand between his legs.

'You no want?' she said silkily.

'Course I do,' he said, his voice thick with need. Why was it, he wondered, that he salivated when he felt lust?

Whoever said Moslem women didn't play around had never been out at night in Sarajevo, obviously. They were no different, he told himself, from women anywhere else. Flett glanced in the mirror. The street, at least what he could see of it, was still and empty, like a white bedsheet stretched out behind them. There was no sign of the madman with the gun.

He turned right, into Marsala Tito and headed for the hotel. Flett would take her to his room. What should he care if they were seen? What harm would it do? A little gossip would do his reputation as a war correspondent no harm at all.

There was no risk, surely.

6

'Every day men sleep with women they do not love
and do not sleep with women they do love.'
DENIS DIDEROT, *JACQUES LE FATALISTE*

ROSSO STARTED AFTER THEM ON IMPULSE.

He was irritated by the arrogance of these foreign voyeurs
and Sabina's attempt to stop him had only spurred him on. The
armoured glass had prevented Rosso from clearly identifying Flett.
It was the Press sign pasted on the flanks of the vehicle with black
masking tape that gave him away. And with the near-certainty it
was Flett, suspicion insinuated its way into Rosso's mind.

It was after curfew. That, too, of course. They could be shot at,
or arrested at one of the many checkpoints flung up by the security
forces after dark – outposts that said more about the territory
controlled by the Army, military police, Rosso's own civil police,
Luka's militia and the presidential security service. All jostling for
turf, for a share of the State's diminishing power. But that wasn't

why Rosso went to his Yugo, twisting the key back and forth in the ignition and stamping on the accelerator until the car coughed reluctantly into life.

He was several minutes behind, but was just in time to see the Jeep pull up at the rear of the hotel. It was too late for Flett to make for the basement garage. It was closed at nine by the guard who ran the place, a hunchback armed with a World War II German submachine-gun who pocketed foreign currency tips not to steal the foreigners' coveted petrol – he did that anyway. Like other latecomers, Flett parked as close as he could to the back door.

Rosso, from across the street, saw the driver jump down into the snow.

Where was the passenger?

Rosso followed, passing a guard slumped at his desk just inside the door, head on his arms, fast asleep. Rosso almost tiptoed through an intervening door into the cavernous interior of the lobby and took cover behind the lifts. Flett had already retrieved his room key from the reception desk and was walking away from it. Rosso could hear Flett's rubber-soled boots squeaking on the parquet flooring.

He was alone.

The atrium was huge. It stretched to the very ceiling, the guests' rooms set around internal balconies marking the eight floors of the place. The hotel had been designed in primary colours, the lines like broad, confident brush strokes for a more brash, confident age. This was where the *nouveaux riches* held their weddings, where Rosso, as a young police lieutenant, had received a merit award and, much later, his twenty-year service badge. That same evening he had danced with Sabina at the annual ball. His wife had worn the red dress he liked, off the shoulder with sprays of chiffon that showed off her narrow waist and legs. She was admired then, envied. How different things were. How proud he was in a proud age, so full of promise. It seemed a century ago, another life. This had been the place to see and be seen. It used to be busy with prices to match, packed with foreign businessmen, tourists and local socialites ostentatiously enjoying an evening out. Now the lobby was freezing and quite dark. Rosso edged closer to the reception desk which had been closed in with a wall of cardboard and cellophane in a pathetic attempt to retain some warmth. He hid behind a notice-board festooned with handwritten notes – begging letters, really – pinned up by people offering their services as drivers, translators, fixers. The lucky ones were paid upwards of $100 a day and people who earned that much suddenly came to realize just how large their extended families really were.

Where was she?

Flett was walking off into the gloom, towards the staircase at the far end of the lobby, past the circular stainless-steel bar with its clusters of blue velvet cocktail seats.

Rosso followed.

To the left he could see the reddish dots of cigarette ends, moving like glow-warms, and the faint outline of the hotel's night people – the journalists who could not sleep, or waited for a telephone call that would never come; the foreign currency tarts waiting for a client; the black marketeers trying to sell or buy drink, cigarettes and petrol; the con men and plausibly insane offering to sell stories or their sisters for hard cash; the money-changers; the president's intelligence service agents watching and listening and no doubt enjoying the odd kickback; in short, the flotsam and jetsam every war produces when the media are in town. As Rosso climbed, their muttering ceased, the glow-worms stopped moving. They were watching him, waiting for him to move on up the staircase.

'It's you!'

'Surprised to see me?'

'You'd better come in, Superintendent.'

'That's a great car you have there.'

'Impressive, huh?'

Rosso stepped into the hotel room, curious to see how the American lived. Flett stood aside, putting his hand up to his eyes, momentarily shutting them as if looking into a bright sun. Rosso

97

recognized the gesture as one of acute embarrassment. He knew he was the last person Flett wanted to see at that moment and he relished the reporter's agitation. It was unkind, but Rosso couldn't help himself.

He must know I was the one who caught him out.

'Where is she?'

'Oh.' Flett paused. 'We had a bit of a row. She wouldn't come to the hotel. Said there were too many cops and secret police around. She wanted me to go to her place. I don't know why, exactly – I didn't feel right. Safe, I mean.'

It wasn't Tanja. Just some girl Flett had picked up.

Rosso felt enormous relief.

'I thought you were UN,' he said.

'What would you have done if I had been?'

'I don't know. Arrested you. Kicked up a fuss.'

'Was I breaking the law?'

'Sure. Creating a disturbance, threat to public order, endangering security, violating the curfew, illegal parking, dangerous driving, driving under the influence.'

Rosso paused, saw the relief on the newspaperman's face.

'Lewd sexual conduct in a public place,' Rosso added. 'Fornication with a minor; and that's only for starters.'

'A minor!'

The look of relief had been replaced by one of alarm.

'Do you know how old she is?'

'Well, to be honest, no. Not exactly.'

Rosso could see Flett was shaken. That was how he wanted him to be. He had probably paid the woman to disappear when the desire to sleep dulled the urge for sex in the few minutes Rosso had been starting the Yugo.

There was nothing romantic about this hotel room. It smelt like the city zoo. Rosso sniffed; he identified the constituents – unwashed feet, cigarette ends, drink, grime, damp and a foul bathroom. Maybe she was the one who had had second thoughts, marks or no marks.

'I'd say a good six months with good behaviour,' Rosso said. By the look on his face, Flett was unsure whether to take Rosso seriously.

The American's room was on the fourth floor, west facing. The fourth was good. Too low and a guest would receive small-arms fire with the room service. Too high and he would risk leaving skid-marks on the bedsheets, courtesy of the Bosnian Serb artillery and armour, dug in a mile away on the other side of town. Flett's window – and it was not a window he spent a lot of time looking out of for obvious reasons – commanded a view of what had been a small formal garden, much neglected and at this time of year knee-deep in snow drifts, carved and smoothed by the wind to form a sparkling, undulating crust. Flett did not stand near the window for any length of time if he could possibly help it. A large bullet hole in the double-glazed pane was a useful reminder of what happened to those foolish enough to offer themselves as targets.

'Drink?'

'Fine.'

'You look exhausted.'

'I am. So do you.'

'Tell you what. I haven't eaten. The restaurant closes in ten minutes. Will you join me?'

'Why not?' It was a principle of survival to eat whenever the opportunity presented itself. Rosso was looking around, at the CD player, the profusion of cables on the floor leading to what appeared to be a computer, keyboard, printer and an enormous stack of paper. There were paperback books by the bedside, batteries, notebook, torch, glasses and a full bottle of Scotch, the bed itself was a jumble of bedclothes, as if someone had just got out of it. A map of Yugoslavia crudely pinned to the wall, covered in clear plastic and festooned with arrows and flags in china pencil; red, green, black and blue. Blue for the peacekeeping formations, green for the Moslem-led government army, black for the Croats, red for the Serb secessionist army – the so-called Cetniks.

Rosso pushed the bathroom door. It swung open to reveal a dark interior, sour with urine.

'Would you have arrested her too?'

Rosso smiled.

The journalists made good wartime guests. They seldom quibbled at the room charge of $80, at the damp and grimy accommodation, at the sheets worn threadbare, the almost inedible food, the fitful lighting, the purely symbolic presence of televisions, the telephones that worked every other day for an hour or two, the lack of water and warmth. They often brought their own generators, satellite telephones as well as sleeping bags, food and drink. The American television crews employed people whose sole task was to drive back and forth through the lines carrying fresh food – eggs, fruit, meat, vegetables, cereal, beer, chocolate – luxuries beyond the pockets and wildest fantasies of the townsfolk. The strangers – the locals called them tourists – had thermal underwear, walkie-talkie radios, stout boots and padded jackets, they cooked over gas fires, they wrote on battery-powered computers and they talked daily to their loved ones at a cost of $20 a minute. They paid through the nose for black-market petrol and drove about in huge vehicles that had been especially 'hardened' against gunfire and airfreighted in. They wore body armour made of ceramic plate that could withstand high-velocity rifle bullets. They were, in short, Rosso decided, a breed apart. If they were privately resented by the citizenry, they were publicly courted. Their reports, their film, their images kept the Bosnian government's cause alive, and in turn they built their reputation on the city's agony. But for all their faults they bled to death just like other people. They did not have to be there.

Rosso knew Flett had influence out of all proportion to his age, experience, or even skill. Americans were disinclined to visit Sarajevo for long, or in great numbers and those who did tended, on the whole, to be television people. They followed in the wake of high body counts. By staying on through the worst of it, by hanging in there as he would have put it, Flett won the newspaper's attention.

The newspaper had the president's attention over breakfast in the White House. That gave Flett clout inside the Beltway. He had a monopoly on Bosnia. Not even the combined resources of the State Department could match Flett for his command of this niche market in print journalism and its impact on US policy or lack of it.

The other side of the coin was that the Bosnian government, and the presidency in particular, had a very high regard for Flett and they were acutely sensitive to anything he might say or write about the government and its war effort. Flett, six going on thirty, was a pro-consular figure. He was a celebrity.

But Rosso knew the newspaperman was after stories that could hurt as well as help. If Flett understood the dangers of his work – of his favourite term 'objective' – he showed little sign of heeding them. To Rosso he was like someone driving at breakneck speed through a succession of red lights. He could hit people and sometimes did. It didn't seem to matter, at least not to Flett. He would pass the damage off as being in the greater public good. That was how things were done in the West, apparently. Morally, Rosso thought, Flett occupied another plane from the rest of humanity, certainly from the citizens hobbling about on Sarajevo's cratered streets.

Flett was generous, but there was a price to his hospitality – even a bottle of beer or the meal the exhausted, unshaven waiter in the stained red jacket was about to bring them – and Rosso did not want to get burnt in anyone's crusade for the truth. Not when the authorities and their foes had penetrated one another's intelligence services, when a note on somebody's file automatically ended up on the same person's file, held by the other side; when a careless word of sympathy towards one side was invariably noted as a word of hostility towards the opposition.

Rosso had to be careful.

They weren't asked what they wanted. There was no menu, but Flett did ask for wine. The first plate contained a cabbage salad with a dollop of reddish sauce in the centre. It turned out to be tomato paste out of a can. The cabbage was soaked in vinegar. The main course was a stew of some kind, with dumplings, followed by caramel custard and coffee. It was lousy food by any standards save those of Bosnia's besieged Moslem towns. In Sarajevo, Tuzla, Maglaj and Gorazde it would be classed as nothing short of a culinary miracle.

The only other people in the dining-room were a group of young French journalists, sitting at the far end of the large room, very noisy and very drunk. Their revelry allowed Rosso and Flett to talk without fear of being overheard.

'New car?'

'Flown in today. From Ancona.'

'Looks pretty good.'

'Sure. It's a Secret Service car – the people who protect the president. Armoured top and bottom. It's even got a James Bond device; pull a red switch and it pours a mixture of gas and oil on the road behind, pull the other and it sets it alight.'

Flett giggled with pleasure, with pride. 'Hee-hee-hee.'

'You planning to try this device out on our streets?'

'Hell no,' Flett chortled again, very pleased and throwing up his hands. 'Maybe a Serb roadblock.'

'What happened to the white one?'

'Told the car-hire folks to pick it up.'

'I'd like to have seen their faces when they did.'

Rosso had first met the reporter after the American arrived in the spring of 1992, just as the war had begun and the terrible truth began to dawn on the city. Flett had been determined to make his name in the conflict. Like so many young people, the American was more afraid of showing fear than anything else. He found in Rosso a man who understood that only too well, that tribal fear of fear itself. The whole idea of not showing fear, of keeping what the English called a stiff upper lip, was born of fear. The military fomented it, worked on it to reduce the individual's range of choices. It was called discipline. It meant doing the opposite of what comes naturally to most people when confronted by danger.

Rosso had been working in his office and shovelling the endless tide of paper when Flett had walked in on him. In fact he had not walked in at all, but dived through the open door during a particularly vicious artillery attack and crawled the rest of the way on his hands and knees. Rosso remembered it well. Eighty-seven Sarajevans died that day and nearly 300 were wounded. At least 3,000 shells had rained upon the city.

Flett had spotted a crumpled magazine – one of the popular US current affairs weeklies – lying on top of a pile of old dossiers and asked if he could read it. Rosso, without looking up, had said of course he could, then wondered at Flett's Southern drawl.

Rosso offered him a chair; the only chair other than the one Rosso was sitting on himself.

'I prefer the floor, thanks,' Flett replied.

Only then had the American introduced himself.

Rosso never again offered Flett a seat. He realized then that Flett had been terrified of being hit, that he had the imagination to dwell on something coming through the blinds at the end of the open-plan office, flying through the intervening space and slicing through Rosso's office, cutting him down off the chair. As well it might have.

That was the bond between celebrity reporter and cop: fear. They both felt it, had both learnt to live with it, control it, adapt it, make use of it. That took a special form of courage. In the months that followed, Flett gradually conquered his feelings by being reckless, by steeling himself to go to the front in the thick of the fighting, by scorning body armour, driving a thin-skinned car when the other media people all had armoured vehicles of one kind or another.

Other journalists, perhaps because they had run out of ideas, soon began to send their editors features about Flett, his superstitious nature; he always wore socks of different colours – red on one foot, green on the other. He wore black shirts, black trousers or jeans and a black jacket and he never went out onto the streets without a tie. It too was black. Sarajevo's own James Dean. Cruisin', Flett called it. Ah'm gonna go cruisin', fellas. That golden tan, the uncombed locks, the white teeth. A Hollywood wet dream on wheels, under fire.

Flett was very brave, everyone agreed. The bravest man around as far as the press corps was concerned.

His secret was safe with Rosso.

Did Flett know that? The reporter sometimes behaved as if he resented the fact that Rosso was the only human being who knew how he truly felt under the braggadocio.

The policeman had the distinct feeling – and it was no more than that – that Flett hated him for it.

Their plates pushed aside, Flett looked steadily at Rosso.

'I owe you an explanation,' the American said.

'What about?'

'Tonight.'

'Not really. Your sex life is your affair. You just happened to be right outside my window.'

'I'm sorry. I didn't know. I have a terrible—' He hesitated, as if seeking the right word. 'Urge, I s'pose you'd call it. Whenever I come back from the front.'

'You're not alone. But you're young, American and you're famous. You can have the pick of the translators and fixers.' He might have added: but my god-daughter turned you down.

'I couldn't bear to have someone waiting for me,' Flett was saying. 'Someone waiting for me to say I love them. I can barely keep myself together—' a shadow seemed to pass over his face. 'It's so much easier—'

'That's all right.'

'Is it?' He was looking agitated. He wanted reassurance. 'There was only one woman—'

Rosso did not want to have to listen to a long, impassioned confession about unrequited love. He was too old for that. Too tired, also. He held up his hand.

'Look. Branston. Venereal disease is sweeping through this city like a forest fire. Aids can't be far behind.'

Flett's face fell.

'So if you must pay for it, do use a condom.'

The journalist nodded. He looked like a child caught stealing or cheating. Guilty. Rosso thought it impossible to tell his age because Americans seemed preternaturally young, their faces instrinsically innocent. Nothing seemed to touch them. No vice, no atrocity seemed to age them. Flett looked a child among the Slavs, Rosso thought. Women would want to mother him, smother him, but he suffered from the Protestant belief in his own innate sinfulness. Having a good time, being spontaneous, wasn't something that came naturally to Flett.

Maybe that was why he turned to 100-mark whores. For men like him, the fun was in doing wrong, satisfaction in uncomplicated coupling, unsullied by the fear of failure.

'You were out there today?'

Flett nodded. He poured the rest of the wine into Rosso's glass. It was good wine, a Croatian dry white, one of the best in a distinctive rectangular bottle of dark green glass. Rosso was feeling tipsy.

'How was it?'

'Want a preview?' Flett took some papers out of his jacket pocket. It was in fact a single piece of paper, a long scroll folded up several times.

'Here. Tomorrow's front page.'

'Do you mind if I read it later?'

Flett shook his head, but his expression said he did. When you were offered a story hot off Flett's printer, before it hit the Beltway, you were supposed to read it immediately and show your appreciation.

There was a surge of noise from the end of the dining-room. Someone had fallen off the table, prompting gales of laughter among the French.

'Your daughter—' Flett had to raise his voice.

'Tanja. She is fine, thank you, but she is not my daughter.'

Rosso thought that it could never occur to Flett that, in the circumstances, to ask about the policeman's god-daughter was downright crass, in bad taste. It would do no good to point it

105

out to him, either. It was just the way Westerners were. A matter of cultural conditioning. They tended to say whatever they were thinking. It made for honesty and cruelty.

'I'm sorry. She's your—'

'God-daughter.'

'I didn't know. She calls you her stepfather.'

'She's doing well.'

'She works as a paramedic.'

'That's right.'

'Do you approve?'

'It doesn't matter whether I do or not. She's an adult.'

'But you must have a view.'

'I do, and I'm not sure it's any of your affair.'

'I'm sorry. I shouldn't have asked. It's just—'

'Just what?'

'Just that people are saying that she is seeing Luka. You know him, I suppose.'

'I see. I know of him.'

'How do you feel about it?'

'About Tanja? I love her as a godparent should. About Luka? That's politics. About their relationship, if there is one? I've told you. I have my own views. They are none of your business.'

There was always a price for Flett's hospitality.

'OK.' Flett looked dissatisfied, unhappy, as if he had failed to obtain whatever it was he wanted.

'Now you tell me something.'

'Shoot.'

'What is the Monkey House?'

The French were now singing 'La Marseillaise', but those who stood up fell down again, collapsing onto one another on the floor. A girl was shrieking, whether from pleasure or terror wasn't entirely clear and probably wasn't to her either. The waiter was shaking his head and rolling his eyes at the mess they were making.

'It's that high-rise development. You know. Ali something. Hell, I can't pronounce it. People say a lot of the city's remaining Serbs live there in one of the tower blocks, so they call it the Monkey House. It's a nickname. Not a nice one. Racist.' Flett fiddled with his coffee cup. 'It's the way things are headed. There was something similar – an apartment block near Tito barracks in Zagreb in '91. It was also called that by the Cro' troops.'

'They are forced to live there?'

'No. It's just that there's rumoured to be an unusually high proportion of Serbs in the place. Also, it's become a centre for local drug addicts. I suppose that's because the Serbs in Sarajevo are the poorest now. The street kids hang around there, waiting for the dealers to show so they can get a fix.'

'Since I came back from Zagreb—' Rosso continued, thinking that it was only that morning. It felt like a week. 'Since I got back, today, I've been hearing rumours.'

'It's rumour city. Such as?'

'Something about the Serbs being allowed through the Kiseljak sector, a build-up of some kind, a concentration in the Sarajevo area—'

Flett was nodding.

'Another Dien Bien Phu, the French troops are calling it.' He smiled. 'A bit over the top, but the geography is not entirely dissimilar.'

'There's talk of changes at the top, in the presidency, shifts in power,' Rosso said.

'There's always talk, of the president being shunted aside. It keeps me busy, but the harder you look at it, the harder it is to make out.'

'And the troop movements?'

'I get hints, straws in the wind. You'll see what I mean when you read what I was writing today, what I saw today. It's not conclusive . . .'

'If you don't know—'

'This government isn't going to signal its punches, Superintendent, certainly not to me.' Flett leant forward. 'Contrary to popular opinion, I don't know everything that goes on. In some ways I'm the last person they'd use to get a message like that across.'

How modest of you, thought Rosso.

'Like what?'

'It's winter,' Flett said. 'It's the time of year when both sides thin out their lines, send the boys home to their wives and mothers for Christmas. When I asked them why the government's regular troops were moving out of the city, they gave me a line on thinning-out as an official explanation.'

'Troops moving out?'

'Yeah. All non-Sarajevans, all regulars, slipping out of the city. That's the word on the street. Some say it's for a winter offensive up north, others that it's a deliberate ploy to draw the Serbs into an all-out assault on the capital, to force the West's hand.'

'But you say it's speculation.'

'Right now it is.'

Flett raised an arm and imperiously clicked his fingers in what seemed to Rosso to be a parody of the ill-mannered foreign tourist. The waiter didn't seem to mind. He smiled and actually bowed at Flett's elbow. Why show foreigners such deference, Rosso wondered. They've done nothing but leave us in the lurch. Flett ordered two double brandies. For the road, as he put it. To Rosso's surprise the waiter brought them within a minute or two, and they were the genuine article. With marks a man could buy anything.

'Off the record ...' Rosso began. Maybe he could supply that very something the reporter was looking for. Feed the beast.

'Yes?'

Rosso swilled his brandy around the balloon glass.

'Or rather, on a background basis, no name, nothing that will point the finger at me.'

'OK.'

'The presence of troops from outside town is widely blamed for a surge in crime. It's caused a hell of a fuss in the presidency. Locally raised units have been very upset, saying their families are at risk when their backs are turned, facing the enemy, from outsiders in our midst.'

'Interesting.'

'It fits in with your theory of a redeployment of regulars,' Rosso said. The brandy hit him hard, making his head spin. He told himself he wouldn't finish it.

'It sure does,' Flett said.

'If you're really interested in the criminal angle, I could perhaps give you some help.'

'Great!' Flett sounded genuinely enthusiastic.

'But there have to be ground rules.'

Rosso knew he was harnessing an unguided missile and he had to do something to try and limit the collateral damage.

'I won't accept conditions, Superintendent.'

The waiter started collecting the candles. They could barely make each other out across the table. The French continued to party on regardless.

'Ground rules, not conditions.' For some reason the darkness made Rosso lower his voice to a stage whisper.

'What are they?' Flett leant forward again to hear him.

'You don't identify me in any way as a source.'

'Agreed.'

'Then we're cookin'. Isn't that what you Americans say?'

'Sure. And we'll forget about that incident earlier, right?'

'No problem.'

'Want a lift?'

'I'm safer in my own car.'

'You can always get a room here.'

'No, it's fine. I—'

By the look on Flett's face, someone was approaching the table from behind Rosso. Whoever it was had pushed open the door from the landing above the lobby and a shaft of faint moonlight illuminated Flett. The American's expression changed from surprised to pleased, from pleased to anxious.

Rosso was watching Flett as the reporter pushed back his chair and stood up. Pleasure and worry were battling for supremacy on his youthful face.

'Branston,' said the woman. She was walking quickly, her heels tapping loudly on the parquet floor.

Rosso knew that soft, feminine voice.

The superintendent turned in his chair, twisting round awkwardly at the same time as a familiar perfume wafted over him. It was the same brand of scent he had brought from Zagreb. She wasn't an under-age, 100-mark whore named Nadia, at least not the woman or woman-child Rosso had anticipated. The superintendent rose unsteadily to his feet, putting a hand out to steady himself.

In his mind's eye he saw the body of the woman, Bukovac.

Every detail.

Rosso felt ill.

The dining-room seemed to undulate, the noise of the French party seemed louder than ever. Rosso sucked air greedily into his lungs. His legs felt rubbery. It must be the wine, the shock of so much food all at once. He was sweating.

It was Tanja, his god-daughter.

When Rosso reached home Sabina was asleep, lying on her back. Her lips were parted. She looked almost girlish, but every now and then she would release a guttural snore that was not at all ladylike. From one angle she looked the very picture of peacefulness. But if Rosso raised himself above his wife and leant over her, gazing down, she seemed to have a fixed snarl on her face and he drew back, shaken by her grimace, her curled upper lip and bared teeth.

It was almost midnight. He managed to slip in under the bedclothes without waking his wife, gently lifting her right arm and moving it to make way for himself, listening to her breathing. He turned onto his side to face the window as was his habit. It was a clear night, and the stars winked down on the maimed and darkened city.

Rosso's last conscious thoughts before he slept recalled his stumbling blindly from the dining-room, pushing past his god-daughter, too confused to respond, to react, even to speak. He felt confused, drunk and he had blundered into the dark, reeling from the hotel, stumbling twice in snowdrifts before he reached his car. He had driven home as if in a trance. At first, as the blood pounded in his head, he felt he had been the victim of a conspiracy that hid from him the fact that Tanja was on the game, turning tricks outside, or perhaps in his very home and using Rosso's status as protection. (At this point an appalling vision had risen before him: of Luka as the pimp, Sabina the accomplice, in receipt of immoral earnings to supply her terrible craving and, further, taking her clients to their bed while Sabina sat in the living-room, drinking the proceeds.) After a while the cold air sobered him, calmed him, and the policeman pushed the evil thoughts aside, telling himself they were outrageous, his own worst fears laid bare and the fruit of fatigue and too much Croatian wine. He went over what he remembered of the conversation with Flett. The journalist had indeed been trying to tell him something, only the detective hadn't let him finish, had interrupted, scornful of the young Westerner's self-centred ramblings and anxious to find out what Flett knew, if anything, of the rumours circulating about the city's fate; impatient also to harness the unwitting Westerner to the cause of bringing Luka to book. That was a mistake. He should have listened.

He had assumed the woman was a prostitute. Sabina had assumed the vehicle below their balcony belonged to the client of a tart named Nadia. Nadia might or might not exist. She could have been dreamt up by Tanja to explain (to Sabina) the comings and goings of Flett, and presumably Luka also, outside their building. At any rate, Rosso had followed Flett on the assumption that the woman was a whore. He hadn't seen her clearly through the armoured glass. After all, she had been busy . . . He didn't want to think about that. Not Tanja. Not that. Rosso wasn't Tanja's lover, or her father. He had no right to feel rage, disgust, possessiveness or anything else. She was old enough to decide these things for herself. Her life was her own. If she had two men in her bed, so be it. She would have to live with the consequences. She was a modern young woman – whatever that meant. She had volunteered to help Rosso gather information about Luka. He hadn't coerced her. God, he had given Flett advice about venereal disease, told him to use a condom. Did Flett know he suspected it had been Tanja? What a fool he must seem in the American's eyes. He felt, well, face it, he felt cuckolded. That was absurd. This isn't your woman, he told himself. She's nineteen. You could be her father, easily. If you were, you might have justification for feeling as you do. Rosso scolded himself. You self-centred fool. What mattered was not the trifle of Tanja's amorous affairs, or how he appeared in the estimation of a perpetually juvenile American newspaperman, but the murdered woman literally rotting away in a bath of water, blood and faeces.

That was where his duty lay.

Rosso woke some time later. A Serb anti-aircraft cannon was firing sporadically into the old quarter, Bistrica, making the rooftops echo and groan with the whipcrack of each double or triple burst. The policeman did not feel particularly apprehensive. He was used to it. He slid noiselessly out of bed, pulling on his outer clothes. He rubbed his face, feeling the stubble against his palm. He could smell his own body, slightly sour; it was perspiration mixed with the remnants of the wine and whatever it was that had been in the stew.

He put on his shoes without socks and oblivious of the cold, stepped out onto the balcony and urinated over the edge into the snow below. No-one would see him. It was cleaner than peeing into a lavatory bowl without water.

Back inside, he ran his tongue over his teeth. They felt furry, in need of a brush. His hair stood on end. He ran his fingers through it, tried to part it. There was no shower, no bath. At best he could stand in the bath and sluice himself down with melted snow. Later, much later; when he couldn't stand his own smell he would resort to such extremes. Right now he wanted to stay warm. He pulled on the rest of his clothes.

From the window came a flash of artillery, that tell-tale flickering of the projectiles impacting, along with the lazy, almost graceful curve of tracer over the city rooftops. Someone's awake, someone's pushing forward, or trying to, Rosso thought. Tracer lulled the inexperienced into thinking it was harmless. After all, it looked so leisurely. Tiny sparks of flame, green or red, spinning out across the sky. Little did the inexperienced realize until it was too late that only one in four of the rounds were illuminated. Between each little firefly were three more. It was vicious, and people died in those Christmassy storms of steel. Who, anyway, was inexperienced? Only those who lay beneath grave markers up on the hill in Lion Cemetery and the journalists and peacekeepers. In this city, even toddlers knew when to take cover.

Sabina was curled up, her back to him. Rosso turned towards his wife and taking care not to startle her, put his right arm around her shoulder and gently pressed himself against her. He listened to her breathing.

Tanja had not come home. He would know if she had.

Just a little rest, then to work.

Rosso closed his eyes.

DAY TWO

7

'All of life is six to five against.'
DAMON RUNYON, *A NICE PRICE*

EVERYTHING LOOKED SO DIFFERENT IN DAYLIGHT. THE SKY WAS clear, a brittle blue, pink at the eastern rim of hills where the sun was breaking through a layer of tall spruce, the crests of the trees powdered white. Huge stalactites sprang from the eaves of houses. The snow, covered in a hard carapace, winked back at Rosso from a million reflected surfaces. The world had frozen. The muddy ruts in the streets that would have swallowed a man's boots to the ankles yesterday were iron-hard ribs that would wreck a car's suspension today. The very air itself seemed brilliant, as if the city had been scrubbed clean.

It took Rosso some time to get the Yugo running and when he did, he found himself alone on the streets. Even the cat-sized rats he was used to seeing scurrying about stayed in their holes. Rosso slowed down before the first checkpoint but put his foot down again when he saw no-one was going to emerge to challenge him. It was too early, and far too cold.

Alipasino Polje was as he had hoped it would be: deserted. If the evening gloom had reminded the detective of how the place looked when it was built, daylight revealed how run-down the place had become. The grassy areas were churned up into a sea of mud, now frozen hard. The lower parts of the apartment blocks were festooned with graffiti, spray-painted in huge, garish shapes. They included caricatures of French and British peacekeepers and the names of foreign football teams. There were also political slogans, messages of hate directed at the residents of the so-called Monkey House, and even a poor imitation of Arabic script, full of misspellings. 'God is Great', said one. 'Death to Cetniks', said another. The upper floors of the blocks closest to the front line had been torn, holed, raked and battered as if by some huge, mad animal and its iron claws. Balconies sagged, masonry gaped and reinforced concrete threatened to fall to the pavement below. Plaster and paint had peeled away like skin, leaving splashes of exposed brickwork.

Rosso climbed the stairs of Block Nine slowly, quietly. He had no wish to draw attention to himself. He would relieve Vasic, send him off in the Yugo to round up the others, find Dr Misic. They would conduct the informal post-mortem right there in the apartment and start questioning neighbours. If Rosso could corral five or six officers for the murder team, they would at least make a serious effort at investigation. Thirty officers would have been the minimum for a murder inquiry before the war.

The broken door stood ajar.

'Vasic?'

He pushed it wider and took a step forward. He had to use his shoulder to squeeze in.

'Inspector?'

He fumbled under his jacket for his gun.

It took only one glance to see that the place had been ransacked. The sofa was upside down, the stuffing pulled from it. The little brass-topped coffee-table had lost its legs. The rug was, for some unaccountable reason, torn or slashed into strips. A picture had been taken down from the wall and smashed, the glass all over the floor. Someone, apparently out of sheer vindictiveness, had broken the frame into several pieces.

'Vasic!'

Rosso did not wait, but walked quickly down the corridor.

The smell was there, but it was overlaid by something else. A strong stench of chemical, of carbolic, some sort of industrial-strength cleaner.

The bath was empty. The woman's body was gone. The bath had been drained and a pinkish fluid – that corrosive bleach or whatever it was – had been poured liberally over the glutinous mess that remained. The fumes seared the tissue inside Rosso's nostrils and instinctively he put his hand to his face and stepped back.

Whoever they were, they didn't have water to sluice the bath down. There wasn't any, and they knew that beforehand, so they brought a can of this stuff with them.

Rosso went into the bedroom, stood there, panting, trembling. Whatever it was, the pink stuff was on his shoes and made sucking noises underfoot. It will ruin the woodblock floor, he thought stupidly. As if it mattered.

The chest of drawers had been demolished. The drawers had been taken out, their contents decanted onto the floor, and then the chest itself had been trashed. Clothes hanging in the wardrobe had been ripped up.

Rosso turned back, his boots crunching on wood splinters.

The bed in the alcove had been tipped over, the mattress sliced open and gutted, the frame broken up, the slats smashed. Most people, Rosso thought, would have taken the wood with them. It was too valuable as firewood to leave behind.

This evil had a purpose. Whoever he was – whoever they were, Rosso corrected himself – they wanted something, were in a hurry to find it.

He stood there, looking at the mess, when he heard something.

Rosso froze. It was a tinkling sound, a metallic clink, like a spoon dropped to the floor. The back of his neck tingled. His heart pushed the blood past his ears like the roar of a tidal wave.

His right hand tightened on the automatic, his thumb finding the safety-catch and pushing it forward to reveal the little red dot that told him it was ready to fire.

Someone else was there with him.

The detective lurched forward, a shambling run.

There were only four or five paces to the kitchen and as he started to move, turning into the corridor, there were three sharp cracks and he saw the rounds in front of his face, striking the wall and showering him with paint and plaster. He hardly registered the sting where the bits and pieces struck him in the cheek and neck.

Rosso threw himself to the floor. Gun in hand, he pulled himself along on his forearms, using his elbows, hips and knees like a snake. His weight and clothing were pulling the debris of the flat along with him. He grunted with the effort.

The gunfire was deafening, raking the place, the rounds coming in through the railings of the balcony, some of them ricocheting off with mournful insect-like sounds, others slapping into the walls, sweeping across the living-room and into the passage, impacting inches above Rosso as he worked his way forward, throwing down paint, dust and plaster.

Crack-bang, crack-bang, crack-crack-crack-baaanggg.

Zzzzzzzzzzziiiiiiiiiiiiiiiiiiiiinggggggggg.

The cracks of the bullets and the bangs of the weapon firing were almost inseparable. Whoever he was, he was close.

There was no going back.

He can see me, fuck it! Rosso reached the kitchen and wriggled in, making the last part a lunge to draw his legs to safety, in and over the carpet of knives and forks, broken plates, sugar, tea-leaves and lentils – he was just about to pull himself up into a sitting position when he looked right into the face of a child.

They were both startled. The girl opened her mouth wide, as if she were going to scream and seemed to shrink back, wriggling into the corner.

It was a dirty face and a very frightened one.

She sat with her back to the cupboard under the sink, her skinny arms around her shins that were drawn up so her chin rested on her knees.

The sight of Rosso, clasping his gun and almost on top of her, only seemed to frighten the girl more. She was making a whimpering sound and seemed to tremble.

'It's OK. It's OK,' Rosso gasped.

He pulled himself up into a similar squatting position, putting the automatic on safe and stuffing it into a pocket.

The shooting stopped.

Rosso looked around. The fittings had been smashed, the little food that the woman had left behind her now scattered around, as if the people who had done this had no concerns when it came to the matter of their next meal.

The girl was looking at him and the shivers still racked her skinny frame. She wore wooden clogs, thick socks that had been patched, an old floral print dress several times too large and a grey pullover, a man's by the look of it, and unravelling in several places. The sleeves were so long they covered her hands almost entirely, swinging loosely and emptily. Her hair was short, dark and filthy.

It occurred to the policeman then that she had probably been in the process of emptying the cupboard of the stale contents when the gunfire erupted. Scavenging.

'What's your name?' Rosso spoke softly, putting his head on one side the way a man does when he wants to calm a frightened or unstable dog.

She continued to look at him, yet it seemed her eyes were glazed over, as if they were focused too short to actually take him in, as if he were just a strange and scary blur.

'Do you live here? In this block?'

She only shivered more violently.

'Were you looking for food? Was that it?'

Rosso wasn't sure if the child had nodded or not.

She must be about eleven, he thought to himself.

'I've got a daughter,' he said. 'She's a god-daughter. Do you know what that is? Well, anyway, she's a little older than you. I'm sure you'd like her. She helps people when they are hurt.' He felt talking might do some good.

'A nurse,' the girl said. She spoke so quietly, so normally, it was as if they were seated at a table, having a perfectly normal conversation, which was what Rosso had striven to achieve, a pretence at normality. No matter that someone had just tried to kill them, or that someone had been murdered in the bathroom, that he was missing a detective inspector and that they were squatting on the floor of a kitchen covered by food some people would kill to get hold of to fill their bellies.

'People call me Rosso,' he said.

Whoever had tried to kill him could still be out there, watching. Worse, moving his position, changing his angle of fire. It was always the same question: to move or not to move.

When she said nothing, he added: 'My god-daughter's name is Tanja. Do you know any Tanjas?'

For his pains he won a quick shake of the head.

He noticed she wasn't shivering any more but the eyes still had a downcast, short-sighted look to them. She had laced her fingers together, hugging her knees close to her chest. The hands were black, the nails short and rimmed with grime. Nonetheless, they were a child's hands; grime may have worked its way into the pores of their skin but they had a kind of innocence, a softness that belied her vagabond appearance.

There was a distant mutter of gunfire, a pattering.

Was he still out there?

'You live here?'

That quick nod, those lowered eyes, just a glint of moist eyeball below the dark eyelashes.

'With your family?'

A pause, and another nod, the chin lifting a little.

Rosso sensed a lie, or half-truth.

Crrraaaaaaaaaaaaaaaaaack.

Three rounds at least, whipping through the broken kitchen window above their heads. Everything seemed to jump about, and there was another cascade of splinters, glass and plaster onto their heads and necks.

The girl whimpered. Rosso moved closer. It was instinct that made him pull the child down, covering her with the upper part of his body, pulling her head under his shoulder. Her cheek was against his chest. She did not resist. On the contrary, she took hold of his jacket with her small fist. Tears squeezed out of the corners of her tightly shut eyes. She shook, uncontrollable tremors rolling up and down her.

'It's OK,' he said. 'It's all right. It's really all right. There now.' He was speaking to himself as much as to the girl. 'They can't hit us here. You're safe. We're both safe.'

He felt her shaking subside, her hand release his clothing. He moved a little, giving her more room, putting a little distance between them.

'All right?'

She raised her face to him. The tears left pale streaks down her unwashed cheeks. He smiled at her.

'We're going to wait a little while. Wait until whoever it is out there gets impatient or tired and goes away and finds something else to shoot at.'

She didn't respond, just sat, jaw clenched, enduring.

The first ten minutes dragged by. Rosso thought hard about their options. If he had been alone, he would have run for it, dashed for the front door. If they stayed put, the gunman – assuming he wasn't a Serb sniper but someone with access to the building – could decide to take a closer look.

'Noor!'

The girl looked up. Her face came to life, her thin body tensing. She looked excited, relieved, then worried for the owner of the voice.

The name reached them from afar, as if from the stairwell.

'Noor?' A man's voice.

'Is Noor your name?' Rosso asked.

'Yes,' she whispered.

They heard feet in the corridor.

'Noor!'

'Pa. It's me, Pa. Be careful!'

'Are you all right?'

Rosso answered this time, introducing himself by name, saying they were pinned down and advising Noor's father not to enter.

'Hey, it's our top cop. It's Mahmud, Superintendent. The guy who occasionally buys things from you at the checkpoint. Is my daughter OK?'

'She's safe, Mahmud. Have you got your rifle?'

'Surely.'

'Can you get to another window and give us covering fire while we make a run for the door? I'll carry your daughter.'

A couple of minutes later and Mahmud emptied the magazine of his rifle. At the third loud crack from Mahmud's weapon, Rosso lifted Noor, holding her to him with one arm, and propelled himself out of the apartment into the corridor, a wild, shambling confused lurch through the kitchen door to the hallway, pulling aside the broken front door.

The girl hugged her father, wrapping her arms around his fat thighs. 'I'm sorry, Pa. Really sorry.'

Mahmud looked embarrassed, conscious of Rosso standing there.

'Child, there's nothing to be sorry for.' Bending down despite his bulk, he hugged and kissed her and told her to dry her eyes. Then, looking at Rosso, Mahmud explained that he sent her on forays to find food or wood. She was resourceful, he said, but always felt bad on the few occasions she returned empty-handed.

'You live here?'

'Come with us,' said Mahmud. 'Noor will make you a really decent cup of coffee, better than Zagreb even. You'll see.'

He held his daughter's hand while with the other he slung his bolt-action hunting rifle over his shoulder. Rosso noticed that since he had last seen it, the weapon had been fitted with a telescopic sight.

'It was you who gave me the note . . .'

'You won't refuse our hospitality, will you, Superintendent?' Stepping closer to Rosso, the burly fighter lowered his voice to a whisper.

'We see things. Hear things too, chief. But we don't speak about them here, understand?' Mahmud jerked his head in the direction of the stairs.

'Come.'

Rosso followed them up.

Mahmud and Noor were all that were left of their family. Noor's mother had died on a perilous night flight from Gorazde over the mountains. They stumbled along goat tracks, harassed by mortar and artillery fire. She collapsed from cold, exhaustion and hunger and died in her husband's arms, right there, in the snow. Noor's brother had earlier succumbed to hepatitis and pneumonia, aged five, during the Serb siege of the town. Before the war, Mahmud said, he had been a nightclub doorman, a bouncer and a member of Yugoslavia's amateur weightlifting team. Looking at him, Rosso could believe it: he was built like a bus.

Father and daughter lived in the loft, under the sloping roof of the apartment block. It was a maze of rough cement floors, pillars, pipes, water tanks and rafters; a separate world that seemed to touch the very sky. Their bed and living space were several wooden planks laid together to form an even surface and their beds a horsehair mattress and a dozen blankets to keep out the cold. Near by lay Noor's prime responsibility, a tiny wood-burning stove on which she now boiled up water for coffee.

Rosso imagined at first that Mahmud must be some sort of caretaker – until the ex-weightlifting champion showed him his work, not a dozen paces from their living area.

It consisted of a trestle-table, placed close to a ladder, the kind that opens out into an inverted V and can stand alone, unsupported. On top of the table was a simple wooden chair with a grubby leather cushion on the seat to make Mahmud's long hours at work less of a strain. Directly opposite the chair – at shoulder height of a seated man, one of the ladder steps had been wrapped in sacking and fastened with twine.

It was a makeshift killing machine, Rosso realized.

A device for execution, a guillotine by gunshot.

Mahmud demonstrated. He laid the rifle on the table. Then he climbed onto it – he was remarkably nimble for such a thickset individual, Rosso thought – and took up the weapon. He sat down on the chair and placed the rifle in front of him on the padded step. Leaning forward, planting his elbows on the step below, he pulled the rifle into his shoulder and sighted through the scope. The aiming area was a small hole where perhaps two or three bricks had been removed from the outside wall. It gave Mahmud a narrow view of Serb positions, but out there anyone searching for a Moslem sniper would see more than a dozen such holes, crevices, windows and other possible firing points. Neither the rifle barrel nor the muzzle flash when he fired would give his position away.

Mahmud put his hand in his pocket. Withdrawing his fist again and opening it, he showed Rosso three empty cartridge cases. He explained that he kept the cartridge cases of the rounds that found their mark, and dropped the 'misses' to the floor. After each day's shoot, Noor and he counted up both scores, and marked the figures down in a big logbook along with any details of the target. Not unlike the sort of gamebooks that farmers kept when foreigners or local Party bosses came to hunt on their land. Every two or three days Mahmud and Noor moved the table, ladder and their little stove to another spot, rotating the firing positions, so to speak, to keep the enemy on his toes and to try and reduce the risk to themselves.

'Noor's a pretty name,' Rosso told the girl when she handed him his coffee.

'It means light,' she said. 'In Arabic.'

She smiled, but appeared to look away from him.

'You can hardly tell, can you?' said Mahmud.

'Tell what?'

'That she's nearly blind.'

Mahmud explained that cataracts had started to grow over his daughter's eyes shortly after her mother's death. The sniper said he though it was nature's way of protecting the child, of not looking at an intrinsically evil world, or perhaps it was a way of escaping the unendurable.

'It's a simple operation,' said Rosso.

'Not so simple in Sarajevo,' replied Mahmud. He went on to say that he did his best to teach Noor the basics of spelling and arithmetic but her eyesight was getting so bad that it was becoming impossible to make further progress. No schools were open anyway in Sarajevo, but he was coming round to the view that the only thing he could do now was get them both out of the city into a refugee camp somewhere in Croatia or Slovenia where she would get medical attention and some education.

'What do you want to do when you grow up?' Rosso asked her.

'I want to be a sniper like Daddy,' she said.

'So you didn't see what happened in that flat?'

Noor shook her head.

'But I heard them,' she said. 'I heard them.' Her face clouded over. She sat on her father's knee and hugged him close when she said that. She turned away from Rosso, buried her face in her father's chest.

'What did you hear?'

'It upsets her to talk about it.'

'I know. But somebody was killed there. A woman.'

'So this is official business, Superintendent?'

Rosso nodded.

'I kept your note,' he said. 'I read it when I got to my office, then came straight here and saw the body.'

'We don't want any trouble. We've enough troubles of our own. I don't want it to get any worse.'

'Sure. I see that.'

'Still, things are bad round here. If you keep us out of it, make sure we're not dragged into the shit—'

'I'll keep you out of it.'

'You won't identify us?'

'Not if you don't want me to.'

'No way.'

'As you wish.'

'You won't call on us to give evidence?'

'You can refuse.'

'Tell him,' Mahmud said to his daughter. He said it in a kindly way. 'Tell him what you heard.'

Noor wiped her eyes with a sleeve of her ragged pullover. She brought the detective a second cup of coffee and he agreed it was better than anything he had had for a long time, even in Zagreb, or Vienna for that matter.

Hesitatingly, Noor began her story.

'I was looking for food, for firewood. People sometimes give me things. There are kind people in the apartments. I know them all, good and bad. There's one lady, Mrs Hadzic, who gives me milk powder and sometimes bread and the coffee you are drinking now. She's rich and very old. She lives on the sixth floor. I went to visit her. I am careful, you know. It's dangerous because the Serbs shoot if they see any movement, even a cat or a child. So I go slowly. I duck under windows. I stop and listen every few steps. Daddy taught me.

'It was the day before yesterday. It was dark and I don't see so well, so I feel my way along the corridors. I can feel the doors, the draughts of air and this door was open. It was three doors before Mrs Hadzic. I didn't know anyone in the flat. I did not know anyone there before. I thought it was empty, you know, left by people who ran away. It was open, just a little, so I stopped. I listened for a while, then I went in. I went into the kitchen. I thought maybe there's some food or something. I heard footsteps, then men's voices. They were angry. They were carrying or dragging something. There was a lot of shouting. I think they were in the flat and then they went into the front room, right next to where I was. I was frightened by the noise so I hid in the cupboard under the sink.

'They were shouting at a woman. She was crying. She was begging them not to do something. Not to hurt her. They were shouting at her because she had something they wanted. She told them she didn't know anything. They beat her. I put my hands over my ears because it was so horrible, but I still heard everything. They were shouting and then hitting her all the time and she was screaming at them to stop. I heard them say they would kill her if she didn't tell them where it was. She begged them not to. She said this wasn't her place, it was her husband's. They accused her of stealing, of taking money. They called her names. They said she worked for the police. They called her a spy and kept hitting her, then they took her out of the room. I thought they would find me.' Noor started to cry, the sobs shaking her. 'I waited there a long time and when it got dark I came home.'

'Did you search the place before you left?'

'No. I was scared.'

'You didn't go into the bathroom?'

Noor glanced at her father. A fraction of a second's pause.

'No.'

Why, Rosso wondered, did that sound like a lie?

'Did you find the woman before you left?'

'No.'

'You didn't make out the men's faces.'

'No.' Noor shook her head.

'You wouldn't recognize their voices.'

'Yes,' Noor said. 'I know one voice.'

'Whose?'

'There was one giving orders, doing most of the shouting. He seemed to be the one who was the most angry.'

'How would you know his voice?'

'I've heard it before.'

She looked at her father again, a worried expression on her face.

'Whose voice is it?'

Mahmud clasped Noor to him, hugging her.

'It's OK,' he told her quietly. 'Answer him.'

'Luka,' Noor said. 'It was Luka's voice.' She started to shake all over once more.

'He was terribly angry,' she said. 'He was screaming at her. Liar, liar, liar. While they hit her.'

Rosso had a rough idea where Luka had his militia headquarters. It was above the old town, on the hillside, one of the wealthier suburbs of modern apartments and chalet-style homes of the new managerial class and professionals of Tito's Yugoslavia. Once in the area, it did not take him more than a few minutes. After driving round the silent, icy streets he caught sight of the gangster's black-uniformed thugs warming themselves at a brazier on a quiet, tree-lined avenue. When he showed them his warrant card through the lowered window of the Yugo, they waved him through without a word and went back to their fire, keeping their weapons slung over their shoulders and holding their gloved hands over the coals. They were roasting chestnuts for breakfast. Rosso thought he would try to buy some later and take them back to Mahmud and Noor.

An array of German cars and Japanese four-wheel-drive vehicles was parked outside a modern, whitewashed villa below the road. Looking at the cars, Rosso thought the war had been good to all the wrong people. It had certainly been no good to little Noor. Rosso was searched this time, his pistol taken and its number recorded by a serious young man with a crew cut and a fancy, cut-away holster in his armpit. Rosso was given a receipt. He could have made a fuss, demanded to keep his side-arm, but what was the point of face-saving? There was some discussion on a mobile telephone before Rosso was finally escorted through a wrought-iron gate down a flight of frost-covered steps to a paved courtyard where a woman beckoned to him. She was very short, with dark curls around a plump, smiling face. She wore the inevitable black overalls, vaguely sinister and on her, at least, vaguely suggestive. She led him up a winding staircase to the converted attic in which Luka slept. Rosso could hear the rattle of typewriters and the murmur of voices behind closed doors as they climbed.

'Superintendent, what a surprise.'

If Luka felt guilt, or shame, he gave no sign of it.

He sounded cheery, pleased to see the police officer.

Luka sat on the edge of his disordered bed, rubbing his face and pulling a tracksuit top over a Manchester United football shirt. The air was stale. It was after eight, but he appeared to have just woken and hauled himself out of the blankets. Rosso knew how these people lived – he had arrested several of Luka's kind in the old days. The city mafiosi traditionally spent all night in cafés, buying and selling bootleg whisky and cigarettes, dealing in guns and ammunition and stolen cars, gambling, drinking, whoring and occasionally brawling over their turf. Now and then one of them would be found dumped in a ditch, shot in the face or the back after a row over a woman, a marked card or a deal gone bad. The newspapers would dismiss it as a gangland killing. Well, here he was: the chief of the mafiosi, the big fish, the man Rosso would give his right arm to put behind bars for a long stretch. Now he was sitting in front of him, half dressed, smiling.

'I'm sorry if I disturbed your sleep.' Rosso's apology was not without irony.

'Not at all, Superintendent. It's not every day that I receive policemen, and certainly not one as senior as yourself. It must be important.'

A livid scar ran across Luka's cheek. The skin was grey and puckered where it had been grafted on by Misic and his hospital colleagues from the inside of his thigh. The lantern jaw was itself disjointed and seemed to move in different directions when the gangster spoke. He was vain enough to try and keep his better

131

side towards whoever he was talking to. Doctor Misic had been a member of the team that had twice operated on Luka and he later told Rosso what had happened, at least those details that did not appear in the police files.

It was the summer before war broke out in Bosnia. Fighting still raged in Croatia. Dubrovnik and Karlovac were taking a vicious beating from the Serbs. The far-sighted in Bosnia said it was only a matter of time before the war rolled across the borders. Assorted patriots, devout Moslems and gangsters – Luka among them – were preparing for war in Bosnia. Unidentified attackers had intercepted Luka's car near the presidency, hurling two grenades at it. One bounced off the bonnet and exploded, smashing the windscreen, killing his wife outright and slicing Luka's face to ribbons. According to Misic, who had seen the wounded gangster on his arrival in hospital, Luka's lips and cheeks appeared to hang from his skull like raw meat. Luka's little girl had been on the back seat, and she took the full brunt of the second blast, killing her instantly.

No-one seemed to be sure if it had been political, or simply a rival gang, or possibly both. Politics and gangsterism were inextricably mixed, even then. When the doctors operated, Luka's men stood in the surgery, guns at the ready, and threatening to shoot if they failed to save their boss's life.

Looking at him now, Rosso wondered what it was that Tanja saw in him. Luka's accent, his manner, were of the streets. His forehead was low, his eyes deep-set. He would always have to walk with the aid of a stick. There was a pile of comic books on the bedside table next to spare clips of ammunition and a CB radio. Luka was dyslexic, semi-literate at best. Not that any of that mattered, as long as he had other qualities. Luka had physical courage in large measure, of that there was no doubt whatsoever. He was ruthless, and had the ability to lead. Men like Luka were all that had stood between Rosso and a Cetnik bullet when the war started.

They weren't alone. Three of Luka's men – armed, their uniforms bulging with extra magazines of ammunition and grenades – sat forward, forearms resting on their knees, alert and watchful. Luka dismissed them with a few words and they left, staring over their shoulders at the visitor. The woman with black curly hair brought a tray of coffee, Luka lit a cigarette and looked Rosso up and down, as if trying to read his intentions in his clothing, his posture. He insisted the policeman sit on the bed next to him.

'What can I do for you, Superintendent?'

He thinks he's got me in his pocket, that we're going to decide my price.

'Do you know of the existence of a group of Sarajevo Serbs, a humanitarian committee of medical people?'

Luka scowled.

'Yes, I've heard of it.'

'Do you know a Doctor Misic?'

'Yes. He was one of the doctors who helped me when I was injured a couple of years back.'

'Is this committee purely humanitarian or does it have some kind of unofficial political function?'

'From what I hear, it's both.'

'What do you hear?'

'What is this, Superintendent? A general knowledge quiz?'

'I am making inquiries and need your help.'

'Am I under suspicion? Should I call my lawyer?'

Luka was making fun of Rosso, a sly grin on his face.

'Do you know a woman called Bukovac?'

'I don't think so.' Luka shrugged in a way Rosso thought was exaggerated.

'She's a dentist and a committee member.'

Luka shrugged again.

'I don't know, really.'

'Do you know the Monkey House?'

'I've heard of it.'

'Do you know it?'

'Maybe. It's in Alipasino Polje.'

'Have you been there?'

'I may have been.'

'Were you there three days ago, in the afternoon?'

'I don't think so, but it's possible.'

'On the sixth floor? In a flat occupied by one Bukovac?'

'What is this? Am I being cited in a divorce case?' Luka grinned at Rosso.

'Were you or weren't you?'

'It's possible. I don't remember.'

'Think.'

'I've thought. I don't recall. The name means nothing to me. Why?'

'Bukovac was a dentist. She was murdered. An inspector of mine keeping an eye on the place has disappeared. The woman's body has vanished as well. You wouldn't know anything about it, would you?'

'No. It sounds like a mess.'

'It's in your sector.'

'I'll ask, OK?'

'Please do.'

'What's so important about this woman?'

'Nothing in particular – other than the fact that she was murdered and I'm investigating it.'

'There are plenty of fresh stiffs every day, Superintendent. The murderers are plain for all to see. I don't know what the fuss is about unless of course you're still trying to fit me up.'

'There's a witness,' said Rosso.

'Yeah?' Luka got up, took his orthopaedic stick, gathered up the ammunition on the table.

'Someone saw you there.'

They wouldn't suspect a blind girl.

'I think I know why you've come to see me.'

'I'm investigating a murder.'

'People are dying every day, and you've bothered about one lousy Serb. Come off it. That's bollocks.'

Luka was obviously about to leave, so Rosso rose, also.

'You think I'm just a gangster, a smuggler. It's people like me,' – Luka's voice rose – 'who kept this city out of Serb hands, Superintendent. Every day they demand more of me. The presidency, I mean. Now they want all my men at the front – even the clerks and drivers. Every one of them.'

Luka had never liked being questioned and it showed. He was tense and his voice had risen. Spittle struck Rosso in the face. He didn't wince or wipe it away.

'OK, copper.' Luka's voice had dropped. He had managed, unusually, to bring himself under control. 'You want answers to so many questions. Come with us now. I'll show you. You'll see for yourself.'

Luka flung open the door and began shouting a stream of orders, punctuated by oaths. Other doors opened and shut. His voice seemed to electrify his staff. Luka began to hobble awkwardly down the stairs. When he wasn't shouting, he was muttering to himself.

Rosso followed.

'Where are we going?'

'To the front, Superintendent. Where else?'

8

'The lion and the calf shall lie down
but the calf won't get much sleep.'
WOODY ALLEN

FLETT'S MORNING DID NOT BEGIN WELL.

Standing in the sandbagged entrance to the post and telegraph building that served as the UN peacekeepers' headquarters in Sarajevo, the journalist looked out across the car park and part of the city dominated by a low-lying line of hills to the north-west. He stamped up and down, rubbing each arm in turn, impatiently waiting for his escort in the form of an Australian captain and a squad of surly Ukrainians, soldiers who seemed to regard their duties as a heaven-sent opportunity to trade everything they had for hard currency.

Flett knew from the UN briefings that there had been skirmishing in the south-west suburb of Stup, where the Bosnian government army was trying to pinch off a Serb-held finger of territory at

Ilidza. The Serbs reacted by putting the squeeze on Luka's men. The Australian was going to give Flett a bird's-eye view of the affair from the hills to the north-west, notably a promontory directly looking down on Stup itself. Flett was looking forward to it; it would give him the big picture, the broad view for his next piece. It was perfect for a foreign reporter; he would see the action yet remain out of harm's way. Both the Australian and the Ukrainian squad were late. Flett glanced at the fat Rolex on his wrist. It was 9.33. He would remember the time because that was when he heard the ugly sound of a tank shell whirr past him and crash out of sight beyond the parapet around the car park. It was a very noisy impact, a blast of tremendous resonance, as if, Flett imagined, the shell had a mind of its own and was announcing to the city its own satisfaction at the destructiveness it brought. Flett did not at once know it was a tank shell. All he knew was that it was very close, it had a flat trajectory, it made an ominous, busy, spinning sound and the detonation was not unlike a head-on crash between two cars at speed.

Three more followed within a minute.

Flett huddled down behind the wall of sandbags that protected the doorway. He squatted down in a foetal position, holding himself, folding his arms across his body as if afraid bits of him might fall off, or as if he was very cold. He had always hated artillery, and that is what he thought it was. He had never been that close to live tank fire before.

It could have taken my head off.

There was a pause, and it was long enough for the horror to retreat from the front of his brain. Instead he saw a French sentry on the other side of the glass doors. The Frenchman was eyeing him with some curiosity and Flett stood up. The soldier had his rifle slung over his shoulder and his thumbs were tucked nonchalantly into the shoulder flaps of his body armour. To show he was not afraid and to escape the Frenchman's droll stare, Flett stepped out into the open.

Flett knew it was not a very sensible thing to do. He sensed it through the fog of fear, the way people with bad eyesight can sense something bearing down on them through a blurr of short-sightedness. It was too late now. Flett wasn't going to show the French, of all people, that he was afraid.

He saw the fifth tank shell in flight: something fuzzy with a hard, black centre passed from right to left. It struck the top of the iron fire-escape that ran down the side of the building, all three floors, about 30 metres away.

It did not explode. There was a crunch and then the shell started to fall. It tumbled down the steps of the fire-escape. As it hit each step it made an ear-splitting metallic crash, as if a vast gong was being struck with an iron ball. It quite literally bounced down, turning end over end so slowly it seemed almost languid.

Clang, clang-clang.

With each bounce, Flett expected it to explode.

He flung himself to the ground, all his celebrated insouciance gone.

It seemed to take ages.

Clang. Clang.

Flett felt something sharp in his side. I'm hit. This is it. All is terribly clear, normal, but I'm hit someplace.

The Australian stood over him. The captain had given him a not-so-gentle nudge in the ribs with an army boot that had long forgotten what boot polish was.

'Solid shot,' said the Australian in a conversational tone of voice. 'Anti-tank round. By the way, I'm Captain Heart.'

Flett did not mention the kick, although he harboured the suspicion that all Australians relished the chance to kick a newspaperman – especially an American one – lying on the ground and terrified witless.

'Got your brown trousers and bicycle clips, have you?' Captain Heart asked. 'From where I'm standing, it looks like you may need 'em.'

Luka climbed awkwardly into the front of the Mercedes, placing

138

his orthopaedic stick between the bucket seats. He insisted the superintendent sit next to him. Another of Luka's female acolytes came up and passed a brown-paper package through Luka's window. Shutting the window again, Luka opened the package to reveal what appeared to be a large sandwich which he proceeded to tear in half. He held up one half and waved it at Rosso. The policeman shook his head.

'Eat,' commanded Luka, waving the sandwich so violently that Rosso was afraid he might spill the contents all over his legs and the car's leather seats.

Rosso took his share. Luka's mouth was already full, his jaw moving in several places at once. It was prosciutto and basil, olive oil, sun-dried tomato paste and Italian bread.

Rosso had to question Luka, but had no wish to visit the front. He couldn't refuse, not now. It would mean considerable loss of face. It seemed hard to believe he was sitting next to a killer, a smuggler, and sharing his breakfast.

Evil is so commonplace.

Various people came and went to Luka's window, which whooshed up and down at the touch of a button. Luka spoke to them with his mouth full, the disjointed jaws jumping and pulsing this way and that as the food was slowly ground down and ingested. It was like watching some sort of giant lizard consume its prey. Orders were given, questions asked, individuals thanked, praised, teased and, on one occasion, threatened. The chewing continued.

Finally Luka flung the ball of paper out into the street. He turned and looked at Rosso as he started the car.

'It's not the dead woman that brought you.'

'What do you mean?'

'I know why you're here. It's Tanja. You disapprove. She told me. So you thought you'd take a look. See what kind of a savage you've been trying to get behind bars all these years.'

The irony of the situation suddenly struck Rosso and the detective couldn't stop himself: he threw his head back and laughed.

Luka wanted his approval. Even gangsters are traditionalists.

Instead of threatening to kill me, Rosso said to himself, he wants my blessing.

'It's true: I don't approve of your friendship. It's true you were under investigation before the war. It's true the department has been unable to pin anything on you and it's certainly not for lack of trying. But you're wrong about why I came to see you. It's Bukovac I want to know about.'

'About a Serb,' Luka sneered.

'About a murder.'

'Who the fuck cares, Superintendent? Your precious taxpayer? He's got other things to worry about.'

Hadn't Vasic said the same thing, more or less?

'Bukovac was a taxpayer.'

Luka turned the big car out onto the street, one eye on the rear-view mirror, the little finger of his left hand probing his teeth for bits of ham wedged between his gums. Unlike Rosso's Yugo, the Merc had chains on all four tyres.

The Serbs were close. The trees up there were usually just a mass of nothing, a blur of growth, a brooding presence. Now every single treetop seemed to stand out, every branch counted, each dollop of snow slipping off and sliding down could be weighed, watched. They had telescopic sights on their machine-guns. Surely they would see the sleek banker's car and recognize it as Luka's. Rosso felt the twinge of fear like toothache, a nuisance and a familiar one, yet not so bad that he couldn't push it out of his mind.

Toothache.

That was it. He had forgotten all about it. He remembered Bukovac clearly now. She had stood in his office, in front of his desk, telling him she was a dentist. How she would do his teeth, for free. She wouldn't stop talking. She had waved her hands about frantically. Rosso had summoned Anil, introduced them and asked Anil to take care of it. He mumbled his excuses to the woman and left them to it. Later the same afternoon he had glimpsed her again, sitting on a bench near Anil's desk, smoking a cigarette and still talking, this time to no-one in particular. He had taken Anil aside, told him to make the best of a bad job. She was clearly a mess and would make a lousy witness. She couldn't stop talking. The siege did that to people. It couldn't be helped. But she's what we're looking for, Rosso had said. She can bait the trap for us. Give her plenty of rope, Rosso had told Anil.

Whatever it takes. I'll authorize it.

That must have been three months ago.

Rosso tried to concentrate on the road ahead. It was littered with debris – hub-caps, piles of spent cartridges, lampposts bent like hairpins (how the hell do they get like that, he wondered), tramlines twisted into Salvador Dali whiskers from the heat of blazing trolleys, pieces of discarded clothing, roof tiles and lumps of masonry gouged from buildings stuck up out of the ice. It was horribly open, bereft of cover. In those places where there was no ice and where the snow for some reason had retreated, mortar bombs that had fallen vertically and detonated with contact fuses left distinctive star-shaped craters, quite small, delicate and with a surrounding frieze of tooth marks where the flying, red-hot splinters had splayed outwards in a cloud, the lowest ones clawing at the surface of the street. The patterns the bombs made looked puny, almost harmless, belying the truth. The hard surface considerably extended the killing zone of each impact, sending those hailstorms, those sprays of razor-sharp hot splinters, out further.

Luka looked composed, even relaxed. He was quite brazen, like Flett, in his defiance of the odds. Luka was pushing the car hard down the centre of Sniper's Alley, and the car seemed to purr, lapping it up, leaping forward whenever Luka touched the accelerator, as if it liked speed.

Not yet. Wait.

The big car quivered. Luka was accelerating, taking them past the collapsed newspaper building – it had been so savagely shelled that its tall and futuristic towers reminded Rosso of photographs of the smashed superstructure of battleships tipped over and half sunk in Pearl Harbour.

10.40. The dreaded flyover was ahead. The policeman told

himself the Serbs wouldn't start until they had their mid-morning *rakiya*, plum brandy, to fortify themselves against the cold and the killing. With luck, Rosso thought, they'd be wherever it was they were going and back by eleven, before well-oiled Cetniks sauntered back from the bar to tug the lanyards on their guns.

He wondered if Luka had simply watched Bukovac die, or had lent a helping hand. Even taken the lead.

Two ambulances bore down on them, weaving unsteadily from side to side on the ice, two old Citroën estates, 100 metres apart, their suspension long gone, their windows painted white with red crosses, the white bodywork grey with old mud. Luka did not even spare them a glance; he was concentrating on a battered four-tonner some way ahead, its tailboard up and canvas flap lashed securely. It was an ancient Russian Zil, painted sky blue, rattling along.

As Luka overtook the truck, the driver waved. Luka seemed to nod in return. They soon left the Zil far behind.

Our Father, who art in heaven . . .

It was the only prayer Rosso could remember, learnt as a child from his mother. It made him feel better, just as extract of lettuce had been prescribed for a sore throat and always made him feel better. Then he did not know what lettuce was, or what extract meant. They were magical words. Even now he did not know what the words of the Lord's Prayer meant exactly, but it was an incantation, a mark of good, a stand taken of some kind, an appeal of last resort, no more nor less than the superstition of a blue stone worn around the neck or above a door lintel to ward off the evil eye.

A movement to the left caught Rosso's attention.

In the courtyard of a large building – some sort of government establishment – dozens of government soldiers milled about. Many of them held loaves of bread.

'Who are they?'

Luka didn't bother to turn.

'Eighth and Seventeenth brigades.'

'What are they doing?'

142

'Collecting rations before leaving.'

'Leaving? Leaving for where?'

Luka glanced at the policeman but said nothing.

There were more of them, scores tramping away from the city. They did not turn to stare as Luka sped past. They were split into groups or squads, well spaced out in single file. They were veterans; older men, weapons across their shoulders, swathed in belted ammunition, bedrolls slung from their shoulders or belts, rocket-propelled grenades stacked in haversacks high on their backs. Despite the weight they marched with that confident, rolling lope of men who know they have far to go and who also know they are fit enough to do whatever is asked of them.

They were not men in retreat. They were too calm, too assured for that.

Now and then the Merc passed a horse-drawn cart, piled high with mattresses, blankets, cooking pots and mortar base plates.

'It's an army on the move,' said Rosso.

'Something like that.'

'Tell me why you killed her.'

Luka did not reply.

At 10.37 Flett was invited to clamber into the Ukrainian armoured vehicle through a hatch in the side that seemed to him to have been designed for midgets. It was preposterously small and the journalist was tall and broad. He had to suffer the indignity of being tugged at one end and pushed at the other by a squad of spotty-faced Ukrainians barely old enough to shave and who thought the whole process hugely funny.

All the while, Captain Heart sat on top of the BTR-60, smoking his pipe and tapping with one dirty boot on the machine-gun mount to show his impatience while he contemplated the struggle going on below him.

Captain Heart had neither smiled nor offered his hand; he made Flett feel he was on trial, not yet qualified for membership of what the captain would regard as the human race. Heart simply looked

Flett up and down with an expression bordering on contempt and diffidently indicated where the civilian should climb into the long, sausage-like armoured personnel carrier with its boat-shaped prow and enormous rubber wheels. That was it; Flett was a civilian – anathema to a professional soldier.

Flett was thankful there were no television cameras on hand to record the humiliating start to the patrol, and once he had collected himself and his equipment – tape recorder, laptop computer, autofocus camera – and squatted awkwardly on a tiny flip-up leather seat (the leather was badly torn and what little padding there had been was breaking off in tufts and distributing itself all over the interior) he looked about him. One Ukrainian, who could not have been more than eighteen, manned the 12.7mm DhSK machine-gun, sitting in a sort of ring – a seat like one of those exercise machines in a gymnasium, except the contraption wasn't shiny at all but chipped and covered with grease and dust – the teenager traversing the weapon by turning a handle and squinting into the viewfinder. The big heavy bullets were strung together in a metal belt that looped down into the troop carrier around the gunner like a steel curtain. Another Ukrainian tugged an ancient pair of earphones over his head and twiddled the nobs of a chipped radio set that had lost almost all its green paint. It looked like a World War II artefact, something a war museum might display.

Heart pulled his scarf around his face and swept an arm forward melodramatically as if he were commanding a squadron of cavalry. The BTR-60 coughed obediently into motion, shaking violently as the gears rasped and the whole apparatus lurched forward in a cloud of blue exhaust fumes. Heart, who had his helmet on now, had stuck his pipe back in his mouth through the folds of the scarf, both feet dangling down from the remaining open hatch. A Ukrainian corporal offered Flett a cigarette – half of it formed from a cardboard tube. Bits of black tobacco fell from it. Flett shook his head.

There were gun ports along the sides of the armoured vehicle, but they were absurdly small for anyone trying to get more than a glimpse of the roadside. Flett knew they were there so the infantry could help defend themselves without dismounting, but their field of fire would be extremely limited. Better, he supposed, to have something to do rather than wait to be attacked. Even if they were shot at, Flett knew he would neither see nor hear it, which was comforting in a way. Either the small-arms fire would not be heard above the rattle and whine of the engine and the hot racket of its own machine-gun firing, or there would be a direct hit by something bigger and he wouldn't be any the wiser.

Black smoke rose in front of the Mercedes. It was thick, boiling up with a violence that suggested a huge bonfire of car tyres.

'We're going in,' said Luka. He meant Stup industrial estate, a huddle of warehouses and factories, all quite new, neatly fenced off and surrounded by walkways and loading bays covered in blue-grey gravel.

'We'll take this fast,' he said.

He did. As they came out of the defile, Rosso plainly heard the crack of the bullets. A burst of three. Another of four. Several single rounds, evenly spaced, as if the firer was trying to pace the Mercedes, swinging with the target like a hunter taking a bead on a flighting duck.

Smack. Smack. Smack.

All high and incoming from the left. The Merc plunged downhill, shot under a bridge and emerged the other end, tyres screaming.

Rosso was no longer afraid. The adrenalin had the effect of accelerating his senses, giving them new clarity, making them more vivid and creating the impression that everything around him – including the car – was moving in slow motion.

Luka turned into what looked like a factory gate. There was no-one about, just a pile of sandbags, decorated with a Bosnian flag. It seemed deserted. Whoever had manned it was either flat on his face, eating dirt, or was dead.

The wheels spun on the gravel as Luka gunned the huge car

forward, then turned to the right so it spun through the loose stones. He braked sharply.

Rosso had his door open, but pulled it shut again for the heat. It hit him like a wave of air, ruffling his hair, his clothes. It was like a giant hair-dryer. It felt as if it had given him an instant tan and he put a hand to his face to see if his eyebrows were still there.

The source was a sheet of flame not a dozen paces away, vertical, twisting, sucking at the air around it, trying to leap ever higher to reach the oxygen it craved.

Luka was getting out on his side. Rosso went after him, crawling across the seat, sliding his legs awkwardly under the steering-wheel and thinking it was unwise to leave the car so close to the burning warehouse. But the crackling in his ears wasn't fire, it was gunfire, and he kept his peace.

Luka was hobbling, Rosso tried not to run on ahead of him, to stay with him. He wasn't sure why, but he did it just the same. He saw there were firemen, kneeling in a line to their right, between them and the inferno. They were directing their hoses into the tumult of ash, sparks, smoke, twisted metal and whatever had been in the warehouse in the first place. The firemen worked in pairs, one gripping the nozzle of the hose, the other trying to control the whiplash of the bulging canvas tube that kept twisting and writhing with the pressure of water. The flames leapt 20 feet up into the blue sky, apparently unaffected by the fire brigade's efforts.

It occurred to Rosso that Luka's disposal of Bukovac had been no more than a pre-emptive act, engineered to expunge evidence, erase a potentially hostile witness.

Was he next? It would be a simple matter for Luka to arrange an accident in the middle of a battlefield, a crossfire. The inferno would take care of his remains.

Rosso found himself on his knees next to the wheel of a large red fire-truck, his legs awash in a puddle of water. He badly wanted to stay alive. It took him only a moment to realize why everyone was crouched down. Bullets were coming at him – it seemed so

unlike any golf course he had known and intensely personal –
from two sides, whistling and cracking overhead, punching holes
in the hoop-shaped corrugated iron of the other warehouses still
unaffected by fire, zinging off the ground, off the truck, spinning
crazily past him with a moan. Rosso's legs felt weak and his balls
ached as if they were shrinking, trying to draw themselves up into
his scrotum.

If only they could.

9

'If once a man indulges himself in murder, very soon
he comes to think little of robbing; and from robbing
he comes next to drinking and sabbath-breaking,
and from that to incivility and procrastination.'
THOMAS DE QUINCEY

TWO WAREHOUSES WERE SO FAR UNSCATHED BY FIRE, BUT THE
swarms of sparks, fanned by a freshening breeze, did not augur
well for Luka's hoard of plundered luxuries. The heat generated
by the blaze was tremendous. Unless the wind changed it would
only be a matter of minutes before the two remaining structures
went up in flames. Luka knew it. Despite the ever-louder sound of
battle Luka and several of his men gathered at the first structure,
hacking off the padlock with an axe and tugging at a sliding door,
urgently pulling and pushing it open. It seemed to Rosso they
had driven into a skirmish over access roads to Sarajevo. Tracer
rounds or phosphorus could have set the place ablaze; there was

no particular reason to think it was deliberate. When the firing slackened, Rosso ran over to Luka's people, ran doubled up, his legs paddling crazily. They all moved to the second warehouse and crouched like people caught in a rainburst, sheltering against the thin corrugated iron walls of the godown as if that would somehow protect them from the haphazard squalls of gunfire. Luka and his men laboured furiously, anxious to save as many of the crates and packing cases that lined the 60-metre-long interior as they could.

It was like standing in a circus tent, and walking through one of the structures gave Rosso a false sense of security. They resembled Nissen huts, only much bigger and painted a crisp grey, hoops of corrugated iron perhaps 20 feet high at the apex. Like 44-gallon drums sliced down the middle and laid on the flat side. Inside, the sense of urgency lessened, both in terms of the fire-fight raging outside and the burning warehouses. The strange, soft light and the sound-absorbing nature of the contents seemed to insulate them from the danger. Rosso had the urge to find a comfortable shelf and curl up and go to sleep, but Luka hobbled up and down, shouting orders, cursing, muttering under his breath. Here lay the city's stolen wealth, or part of it, stacked neatly; a canyon dividing cliffs of crates and boxes on either side, right up to the roof. A small fork-lift truck appeared and it made the loading and removal of whisky, cigarettes and stolen UN rations much easier. Luka and his crew went outside again, loading the ancient Zil with as much contraband as it could carry. Rosso helped. He was not unaware of the incongruous nature of what he was doing. He could hardly have done otherwise; to stand back, or rather seek cover and watch from the relative safety of dead ground or the fire-truck, would only provoke hostility. There were five of them, all armed. He wondered if Luka saw the irony of the situation or, indeed, whether that was part of the reason for inviting Rosso to join him in the first place; if not to dispose of this meddlesome detective, then to implicate him in some way in their affairs, to humiliate him, to teach him the political facts of life. One fact of life was that a single container of cigarettes could buy a twenty-minute respite from Serb artillery fire, a truce to exchange prisoners or recover the dead.

This was the source of Luka's power, or part of it.

There wasn't room on the truck for more than a fraction of the goods. Several trips would have to be made if they were to save the contents of the two godowns. Rosso did not rate the truck driver's chances very highly. Or that of the man on the fork-lift. He had to sit high up, exposed more than the rest of them to the shooting, as he shuttled back and forth between the tailboard of the truck and the warehouse. During one run the fork-lift driver passed Rosso and he looked up. They caught one another's eye. It was the foreign gunman Rosso had talked to briefly outside the Monkey House, but if the young man with the crew cut and ring in one ear recognized the policeman he gave no sign of having done so.

One of the firemen tramped over to where Luka and Rosso were standing. He took his time, looking at the ground ahead of his boots, frowning as if in thought, the chin-strap of his big fireman's hat just under his lower lip. The rattle of automatic fire, the crashes of mortar bombs and rocket-propelled grenades seemed to have no effect on him.

'We're pulling out,' he shouted into Luka's ear above the roar of the flames, the shooting, the cries of the firemen.

Luka rounded on him, ready to display his famous temper.

'We'll run out of water in ten minutes. No point in staying,' the fireman declared. He was elderly, probably brought back from retirement. He had a weather-beaten face, his mouth looked all sucked in, as if he had taken his false teeth out for fear he might swallow them if he were hit.

'What about this?' Luka gestured to his two godowns.

The fireman shrugged.

'We can lend a hand getting the stuff out. If the firing gets too hot, we'll have to leave you to it.'

Without waiting for a reply, the fireman tramped back to his men, awkward in his high boots. There was something about the way he walked that said he did not care for Luka and certainly wasn't going to risk his men's lives saving Scotch and cigarettes.

The truck began to move, turning horribly slowly.

Luka staggered in his lopsided way back into the godown and grabbed several cigarette cartons. The foreign gunman did the same, wrenching open a packing case at random and snatching up as much as he could clutch onto. Someone pushed a bottle at Rosso. He took it clumsily, then another.

'C'mon,' Luka shouted in Rosso's ear. 'Let's move.'

The mortar bomb burst a good 150 metres off, near the gate where they'd come in. It struck the gravel driveway, hard ground save for the thin covering of stone chips. There was a white flash of light. Rosso felt the detonation through the soles of his feet, all the way up his shins. The sound followed – a heavy metal thuddddd. Then the slap of air from the blast, a slowly rising curl of smoke, opening up and out, leisurely, plenty of time to kill. Heavy and dark. Opening up a bit like a flower, a big, ugly blossom. The roof above their heads rattled, the walls pinged with the sound of whatever it was the mortar bomb had tossed in their direction. A small, twisted piece of wire struck Rosso's boot. He looked down and saw it lying there, red hot still, hissing in the damp dirt underfoot. The second mortar bomb fell 50 metres the other way. A giant foot kicking up earth and stones and throwing it around. Out of sight but well within killing range. Calibre – 60mm? 81?

We're bracketed, Rosso thought. He was bent over like everyone else, from the waist, head craned forward. As if walking into a storm. Stupid, really. I could get whacked from behind. Up the arse. Both legs. Try as he might, though, Rosso found he could not stand straight.

Next one will be dead centre. Right here. He counted, the way people count the seconds between the lightning flash and the first peal of thunder to know how far off the storm is.

One-and-two-and-three-and-four-and . . .

When-I-get-to-eleven-it'll-happen.

The stunning mortar detonations prompted a revival of small-arms fire, the rounds winging and whupping past them, too high mostly to do any harm. Amazing how much weight of explosive and hot iron was needed to kill one human being. Tons of it.

Rosso never did get to eleven.

They ran to the car, clutching the loot. Rosso, hugging two litre bottles of twelve-year-old Scotch, broke the distance into three legs: a sprint out of the doorway to the fire-truck, around it, and then the longest dash to the car. It was like baseball. First base, second base, home run. He circled the car, skidding and sliding in the mushy ice, feeling it crunchy and soft under his feet, seeing the mud splash, feeling drops of it on his face, opening the car doors, pulling them wide, sucking air into his lungs through his open mouth, then throwing himself in, chest heaving. Finding himself drenched in sweat and still holding the Scotch.

Luka pulled himself into the driving seat, hauling his bad leg in after him with both hands. Rosso helped him with his stick. The German was behind them on the back seat.

Great. A gun in my back.

Luka started the car.

'This is Landser,' he said. 'Landser – meet Detective Superintendent Rosso.'

'Tell me,' said Rosso, turning to look at the German, 'do you know of a woman called Bukovac?'

Landser didn't respond.

Luka glanced at Rosso.

'We do a little business now,' he said.

Rosso thought of the woman and what was left of her in the bath. This is what you died for: Luka's empire. And these are your killers.

Something large and jagged shot across the car bonnet. It made a fluttering sound.

Instinctively Rosso crossed himself.

It was a tremendous view.

152

After another struggle involving raucous Ukrainian merriment, Flett managed to extricate himself from the armoured personnel carrier, now parked on a grassy slope outside a pretty, alpine cottage on the very crown of the hill. His first thought was what a marvellous ski slope the hill would have made before the war. The cottage seemed balanced on the very crest, looking down on the city, its rooftops glinting prettily in the morning sun.

No wonder the 1984 Winter Olympics had been staged in Sarajevo. It was the perfect setting. The city was laid out in a bowl, like a quilt tossed carelessly across a deep hammock. It was a natural amphitheatre. A fine killing ground.

The knoll was covered by green grass. Only in shady, sheltered spots had the snow and ice held, white rinds clinging to the lee of stones and logs. There were vines here and fig trees. Flett was struck by the vivid winter colours, the beauty of it all, his eyes unaccustomed to being able to roam freely. He felt he had been freed from the grim streets of Sarajevo.

They went inside. The whitewashed walls of the living-room of the chalet-style home were still decorated with a crucifix and a picture of a saint, his hand raised in blessing and a halo around his brow. It had been the home of a Bosnian Croat family, long gone – 'cleansed', Heart said, meaning murdered or driven off to a refugee camp. This place had been held by Serbs, by Moslems, by Serbs again and by Croat militia. Now it was a UN observers' post – boots, ration boxes, maps, crates of beer and radio equipment were piled in corners and stacked up the stairs that led to the first-floor balcony.

Heart led Flett up there. An attack was developing directly below them, on the south-western outskirts of the city, little spurts of smoke and dust rising from mortar and artillery impacts in Stup. It was flat terrain, broken by factories, warehouses, the odd patch of wasteland, apple orchards, canals and narrow roads.

Captain Heart diffidently pointed out to Flett the difference between the mortar and artillery detonations: the mortar bombs fell vertically, the oily smoke rising evenly like squat mushrooms;

their killing grounds were circular. The artillery bursts were thrown forward, slanting, the smoke and shell fragments rolling forward like someone with a brush sweeping a dusty floor. They killed in a path that was narrow at the base, broad at the top.

Thank God I'm up here and not down there.

A spent bullet whizzed past the two men. Heart flapped his hand at it as if shooing off a bothersome hornet. Flett couldn't tell if the captain deliberately cultivated mesmerizingly slow gestures, or whether he had simply been exposed to danger too often, too long, to care.

'Shit, look at that, will you? Luka's people are putting in another attack.' Heart pointed off to the right. All Flett could see were the tiny points of light, the flicker of small-arms fire, and the drifting haze of artillery shellbursts. Everything moved slowly in the sunlight, like watching English cricket: so peaceful, so far off, so harmless, both sounds and action somehow muffled. He saw no pattern, no front line, could not tell friend and foe apart. It made no sense to him.

'It's pretty bloody futile,' said the captain.

'What do you mean?'

'I mean,' Captain Heart said. 'I mean' – the heavy emphasis on the world 'mean' suggested he thought he was either talking to someone of extremely low intelligence or else to someone too contemptible to be worth wasting his wisdom on – 'that the Bosnians have the men, but they don't have the fire-power. The Serbs have the fire-power but not the men. It's futile because' – here the emphasis fell on the word 'because' – 'the Bosnians will always lose when they pit flesh and bone against fire-power. Added to which – as you can see for yourself – they don't know how to put in a decent assault. They don't know about fire-and-movement. Their tactics are lousy.'

Captain Heart chain-smoked, lighting a fresh cigarette from the stub between his lips. His fingers were stained yellow.

Flett's gaze turned away from the flickering automatic fire, the ant-like figures darting about, the clouds of smoke and dust, the dull red flashes of shellbursts, to where flames licked and leapt from a warehouse of some kind, black smoke coiling into the blue sky to join the thousand other streams of smoke and dust from the battlefield in a layer of grey smoke, a haze beginning to spread out across the city.

It was like playing toy soldiers.

He saw the car then, sleek and grey, moving rapidly out of the industrial estate, sliding away from the city.

Luka's Mercedes. Mad bastard. Flett felt that if he lobbed a stone down there he could almost hit the car, warn him off. Don't do it. You're heading into the thick of it.

'Fuck,' Captain Heart said after drawing hard on the cigarette. 'Luka's boys have lost several dozen in the last day or two, and for what? Nothing's changed hands, not a bloody inch. They take a few metres in the morning, lose 'em again in the afternoon. Fuck.'

A burst of machine-gun fire that sent bullets snapping past them only feet away, had no discernible impact on Heart. Flett flinched. He couldn't help it.

'Fancy a beer, mate?' Heart asked.

The lessening of the immediate danger, albeit temporary, brought a profound feeling of calm. Rosso felt resigned to whatever lay ahead. What had Luka meant by a 'little business'? Rosso leant back in his seat, gazing up at the sky, at the hills, the houses with their buckled roofs and blackened, windowless walls. They harboured snipers, but that thought did not disturb him. He felt like someone who had just completed strenuous exercise, that peculiar sense of numb bodily well-being induced by endorphins as the exertion dies away.

If only I could die whole, he thought. Quickly, without time to shriek in pain or make a fool of myself, squirming like an animal, squashed and torn in my own blood on the ground.

Not like Bukovac. Not beaten, strangled, drowned in blood and shit.

What if he were brought into hospital on one of those bloodied canvas stretchers and looked up to see Misic, gloved and masked and scalpel in hand, looking down at him, ready to make the first cut?

We are the sum of our parts and our parts are not our own. My legs are my father's, my square-ended toes are my mother's, my thin hands those of my maternal grandmother, my rather bulbous nose that of my grandfather. None is my own. I have inherited other people's bits and pieces, skeins of thought, of marrow, tissue and the rest. I should not worry about losing them to Misic's knife. They live through me as I live. These die, and I being the sum of them, die too, of some mechanical weakness, some flawed gene.

There are bits of me, twists of cells, that fill me with dread: lest I become my father. He is in me, certainly. Not a day goes by without recognizing him in me. What made him what he was could make me, also, if I let it.

Death is not so bad. There are worse things in living.

Luka stopped the car, pulling it over onto the verge and dragging Rosso out of his reverie. Luka kept the engine idling, the gangster's eyes fixed on the rear-view mirror. Rosso saw they must have left the main road at some point, but lost in his own thoughts he had missed the turning. They did not have long to wait. A minute or so passed, no more, and the truck containing the bulk of the cigarettes and whisky rumbled past, slowed and lurched to a halt some 50 metres further on. They seemed to have halted on the edge of a country hamlet, one of those villages which, with time, would become part of the city as its population grew. On the right were three oaks, splintered by shellfire. A lone house immediately ahead, standing on a corner and partly screened by fruit trees, had no roof. It was a mere shell of a place. The gate in the surrounding fence and privet hedge leant drunkenly on its broken hinges.

Landser opened his door and got out. He paused to light a cigarette, the pungent smoke wafting into the car. Luka sat upright, gripping the steering-wheel, waiting.

It was too quiet, too still. Neither sight nor sound of farm animals, no chickens pecking at the dirt, no washing out to dry, not even a cat sunning itself.

156

A Croatian flag, torn and muddy, fluttered sullenly on a telephone wire across the road. It was no ordinary telephone line for it was not attached to any telephone pole that Rosso could see. It was a land-line, an army telephone line looped across the road to link some headquarters with the front. Gusts of wind shook the wire, buffeted the car, rippled the surface of rainwater where wheels of passing vehicles had broken the ice on the puddles in the broken road. The sky began to darken, light skirmishes of cloud racing in to blot out the sun.

The fighting was a continuous sound, a rattling, a drumming. The odd thump or crash, sounding hollow like echoes. A fighter appeared from behind the dilapidated hedge in front of the house, taking a good look at the truck and Mercedes, then vanished. A few moments later he reappeared with two others. They looked like farmers, carelessly dressed in a mixture of ill-fitting civilian and military coats and trousers. When they reached the truck they were close enough for Rosso to make out their HV badges – the Bosnian Croat militia with its white and red Croatian chequer-board shield. One of them carried some sort of machine-pistol or submachine-gun with a long silencer, like a tube, on the end of it. Another cradled a sawn-off shotgun in his arms, holding it fondly, proudly, as a parent holds a baby, in the crook of his arm.

They were weapons for close-in work. For cleansing. For murder. For vengeance. For starting feuds, extending them, creating them. For fulfilling the mythology of Balkan hatred.

The truck driver and two of Luka's men who had been in the back of the truck pulled back the tarpaulin and lowered the tailgate. The Croats climbed up. They appeared to check the truck's cargo. They took their time, and Luka's men lit up cigarettes, smiled, exchanged banter with the Croats.

They know one another, Rosso thought. This is a regular event.

Sure enough, someone produced a bottle.

Old pals. They passed it around, tipping it up, swallowing and wiping the neck of the bottle on a sleeve before passing it to the next man.

Luka did not turn when he spoke.

'Now you see how it is, Policeman. We buy our ammunition, our weapons, from Croats. From Serbs, too.'

'With UN food.'

'Sometimes we buy food. Sometimes we buy ammunition. Which would you do, Policeman? Food or ammunition?'

'Both.'

'And if there isn't enough for both? What then? Guns or butter?'

Luka had both hands on the steering-wheel, gently tapping his fingers. His eyes were still on the Croats and the truck.

'You don't answer. You can't answer. You're a man of principle, Policeman. A man of law. You uphold the law. You ensure order is preserved. Your kind makes sure my kind stays on the outside so the bosses can fill their pockets. Right?'

'I wouldn't put it like that.'

'No. You wouldn't.'

Luka raised his right hand from the wheel, turned it palm upwards, stretching out his arm so the hand was close to Rosso's face, the hand forming a cup.

'Now the fancy folk who pay your wages eat out of my hand. I feed them. I arm them. I give them bullets. The presidency needs me. They want my men. Every day they ask for more of my fighters. Every day more die. For all your laws and smart government and bosses, they turn to me. Me!'

Luka checked himself.

'Tell me, Policeman. If I steal, cheat and kill to save this city, am I hero or villain? If I rob people to pay for artillery shells, am I a criminal? If I steal from the UN to keep the city going, am I a thief? Would you watch your precious Tanja starve, or would you steal so she could eat? You have seen us today, there, right in front of you. We are selling stolen goods for ammunition. Look for yourself. Now tell me, am I not good enough for your Tanja?'

'She's not my Tanja.'

'Oh no?' Luka looked ferocious, his mood transformed again.

158

He jabbed at Rosso's side with his elbow but the superintendent moved too quickly.

'Don't tell me the old pecker doesn't get a thrill when you see her, eh? C'mon.'

Rosso stared straight ahead.

'She's from Bjijeljina, right?'

Rosso said nothing.

'Your old man was in the Waffen SS, wasn't he?'

Rosso felt the colour rise in his face.

'Seventh Mountain Division?'

Rosso gave no sign that he was right.

'The seventh was quartered there in '43. Am I correct?'

'What if it was?' Rosso was thinking that Luka was right – the Seventh was there in 1943. Most soon deserted to the partisans.

His father hadn't.

'Forgive me. I don't have your education.' Luka's tone was sarcastic. 'Just a little theory, mind. That you're eaten up by guilt. Someone like yourself could be so useful. But you're too bloody busy trying to bury the past. You spend all the time carrying your own fucking cross to Calvary. You know something? No-one gives a shit. Because the rest of us are too busy trying to save our skins while you're navel-gazing. Tell me, Copper, what do you believe in? God?' He spat the word out as if it were an obscenity. 'Or the Party?'

'Tell me why you murdered the dentist.'

Rosso looked away from Luka, at the men at the tailgate of the truck. They were loading it now with boxes of ammunition, long wooden boxes with rope handles, two men to a box.

'What do you believe in?' Luka asked.

'I believe in having a job and a home to go to. Without fear of my neighbour. Without my neighbour fearing me.'

It was not very well put, Rosso thought. He did not know the right words. He meant to say without tyranny, with the freedom to be allowed to make a mess of one's own life without having to take someone's permission.

159

'Where's Vasic?' Rosso demanded.

'I don't know a Vasic.'

'Detective Inspector Vasic. The officer I left at the flat where the woman was murdered.'

'Have you checked his home?'

'No.'

'He's probably at home with the wife. He most likely got fed up with being left in some dark, freezing flat on the front line with a stiff to keep him company and went home.'

'What did you do with the body?'

Luka did not answer.

'Bury her at night? Dump her under the bridge?'

Landser was walking back towards the car.

'He was there,' said Rosso, jabbing a finger towards the approaching gunman. 'Your man was there. He turned us away the first time. Did he do your dirty work? Did he kill her?'

Luka said nothing.

'What did you do with her?'

Luka's only response was a shake of the head.

Landser leant against the Mercedes, still smoking, his sub-machine-gun on the roof, its muzzle pointed in the direction of the truck, and beyond it, the ruined house.

'This is the difficult bit,' said Luka. 'This is the time they'll make their move if they're tempted.'

Rosso realized the German was providing the insurance, ready to use his Heckler & Koch at any sign of trouble.

'The Croats of Hercegovina may be many things,' Luka went on, 'but they are not stupid. They see the soldiers pulling out. They listen to the radio, to the Americans and Europeans arguing. They know NATO and the UN don't agree. They know nearly all my men are at the front. What do they do? They put up their prices. And what do they do when we can't pay? They shoot us and grab the lot, get what they can before Johnnie Serb moves in.' Luka chuckled at the thought, as if it gave him pleasure to contemplate it.

'I would do the same myself,' he said quietly. He touched the key in the ignition, as if making sure he could get out of there in a hurry if things began to go awry.

The loading was almost finished.

Landser got back into the car and passed Luka a slip of paper. Luka showed Rosso. There it was, the day's transaction, in black and white on a scrap torn from what looked like a child's exercise book with ruled lines.

The war material was listed in a neat column: 17,000 rounds of 7.62mm ball cartridge ammunition, 11,000 rounds of belted 7.62mm tracer, 1,300 9mm parabellum ammunition, 360 20mm anti-aircraft rounds, 34 rocket-propelled grenades, 17 60mm mortar bombs, 43 fragmentation grenades, 13 Chinese anti-tank mines, 35 kg of industrial explosive, 220 metres of gunpowder cotton and 22 electric detonators and caps.

'See?' Luka held out the piece of paper.

'Where now?' asked Rosso.

Luka turned in his seat and winked at Landser.

'If you don't have some other pressing engagement, Superintendent, we're going to make a few deliveries. If you don't mind, that is.' Luka's words mocked him.

'Do I have a choice?'

'Isn't he catching on fast, our policeman? Eh?'

'He sure is, boss.' Landser grinned mirthlessly, his pale eyes on the road ahead.

'I think you'll enjoy it,' said Luka.

10

'One murder made a villain,
Millions a hero.'
BEILBY PORTEOUS, *DEATH*

TRENCHES AND FOXHOLES RAN ALONG A LINE OF APPLE TREES,
zigzagging across the far side of the orchard. The trees themselves
were mostly bare, the branches grey, the trunks slick and black,
their roots emerging from ground that was soft, wet and uneven,
the grass beaten flat by rain and snow, slippery to touch. Rosso
heard sporadic firing; the double crack of a single Kalashnikov,
the vicious thump of a rocket-propelled grenade, the fast ripple of
a light machine-gun in quick, short bursts like the sound of tearing
cloth, only louder, more abrupt. Brrrp. Brrp. Brrrp. Landser,
speaking to no-one in particular, said the action was taking place
some 400 metres away, off to the right, ahead of them. At two
o'clock, he said. Low buildings could be seen through the trees that
way; a patch of blue sky, something red flapping on a laundry line.

Blood red, Serb red to Moslem green, Croat black. White runnels of snow, black stumps. Torn trees, churned soil, boots sucking in the mud. The drip, drip of snowmelt. Splashes of weak, watery sunshine. So this is the battlefield, Rosso thought. This is what it is like, for us and them.

Rosso realized the pattering and snapping of twigs overhead were the sounds of bullets; incoming, yet too high to do any harm. He looked about him, eyes scanning for cover. The ground was uninviting. It was too wet to hug with any enthusiasm and too flat to do much good if he did; the worst of both worlds. I don't mind getting wet if I'm still alive afterwards. It was bocage country; short murderous rushes, infantry charging in terror against other infantry lying in wait, waiting in terror. Hedgerows only yards apart. You could hear a man breathing behind the one just ahead, lying in his scrape, friend or foe, wondering too, index finger curling around the trigger, waiting for you to cough or sneeze before rising up on his knees in the mud to squeeze off a few into you, quickly, before you do the same to him. Grown-up children playing hide-and-seek. Bang-bang, you're dead. Only someone never does get up again. You work your way around the flank to find there is no flank, only more of the same. A taker of lives, this country. Each tussock costly to seize, too easy to lose. No front, no rear.

Just murder.

The policeman thought of little Noor, of the greyish cataracts forming over the girl's eyes, of her patched clothes, her unwashed hair tied back with an old ribbon. Of Mahmud; burly, brave, bald Mahmud. Of Vasic, winning his battle against anorexia but not winning over life itself. Of Sabina, teetering dangerously on her feet, her face a mask of misapplied make-up, giggling, tipsy. Tanja, bold, defiant, a young face old before its time with knowledge of death. Misic, patrician in his surgical gown. The dentist, Bukovac, or what was left. Had they buried her? Burnt her remains? Left her in a minefield?

What had brought him here seemed suddenly so remote.

Luka had turned the Mercedes off the narrow road into a

163

driveway of what appeared to be a smallholding. To one side of the dirt driveway was a wooden fence; a low hedge on the other. The grass that in summer would have been waist-high on the verge, full of wild flowers, butterflies and grasshoppers, was matted in a slush of snow and mud. There was little natural protection save for a whitewashed cottage, quite modern, with stucco walls and crazy paving outside the front door and in the field beyond the fence a partially built outhouse of some sort, three walls of breeze-blocks, unplastered and roofed in corrugated iron and built on a platform of bricks and cement.

Luka extricated himself from the driver's seat, dismissing with a string of obscenities the German's offer of help, hobbling fast, head and shoulders bobbing up and down, as he dragged his bad leg over to the outhouse and using his stick to push the ground away violently, as if beating it away from him. How he hated his own disability. Once there, Luka leant against the raised cement foundation, propped up his stick against it and rolled a cigarette. He wrapped his scarf tighter around his neck. After the car it seemed colder than it really was. The truck pulled up and everyone save Luka and the superintendent began off-loading ammunition, stacking some of the long wooden boxes in the outhouse. It was mostly small-arms ammunition, with a dozen rocket-propelled grenades. Luka said 'enough' at one point, the men piled back into the truck and it reversed hurriedly out into the road and moved on for the next delivery, the driver's face sweating behind the dirty windscreen, working the gears furiously to get away.

This was the so-called front – so called, as Luka explained, because what Luka's men held was a narrow finger of real estate with the foe on two sides and within no more than a few hundred metres of the only approach road to Sarajevo. It wasn't really a front. All the other roads were firmly in Serb hands and this route was held, at different points, by Croat and Moslem forces or a combination of both. It wasn't ideal, it wasn't open or free, but it was a lifeline of sorts and the Serbs were anxious to change all that, tighten the noose around the city, another notch, another turn in the garrotte.

As Luka talked, a woman appeared, seemingly out of nowhere. She was clearly a farmer's wife, or perhaps the farmer herself, wearing an apron with a garish pattern of sunflowers and carrying what looked like a large basket of fruit. She simply walked across the field from the house, apparently oblivious to the bangs, thumps and cracks up ahead among the trees in her orchards. She wanted to shake Luka's hand. She must have seen the car and recognized the crooked figure that hurried from it. Middle-aged, thick set, rubber boots on her feet and an old sheepskin coat over her shoulders, smiling, she looked the very picture of rural vitality. She talked quickly in a country accent, slurred around the edges, vowels as chipped as her crockery, as she thrust the basket at Luka, smiled and bobbed in what appeared to be almost a curtsy of respect. She thanked him for saving her family from the enemy. It was an honour to receive him. Would he eat with her family? At least a coffee? She had one son in the Army. Up north, she said. A daughter worked in a city hospital as a nurse. She had six children in all. Her face was round, her eyes bright, hair parted in the centre, braided and pinned up. Luka was courteous: could they escort her back to her home? She smiled, shook her head, touched his hand, shyly, and walked back alone. Rosso held his breath. Please God, don't let her be hit.

She climbed the steps to her front door, vanished inside.

'Mary Mother of God,' Rosso muttered, and turning, saw Landser's gaze upon him, reflective. The German was smoking calmly, his flat blue eyes expressionless.

They fell upon the fruit then, Luka doing the cutting, Rosso with them despite himself.

'This,' said Luka, his mouth full of apple and pointing the blade of the clasp-knife at Rosso's face for emphasis. 'This is my world. Not yours. Here – here you follow my rules.'

Rosso said nothing. Luka rules OK will be his epitaph.

'Here your badge and gun count for fuck all. Nothing. They

won't protect you from being shot. The Serbs don't care. My men don't give a shit, either. Why should they? What are you to them? Just the face of an authority that's long discredited. Fucking pond-life. Where was your precious president when the war started? Talking peace. Trust us, the Government said.' Luka stuffed more apple into his mouth, the jaw rose and fell, rippling under the skin.

There was cheese in the bottom of the basket and bread.

Rosso salivated. He couldn't help it.

Luka cut the loaf into three equal pieces. Then he divided the cheese.

'Take,' he commanded.

Rosso ate quickly. All three did, wolfing it down, cheeks bulging, jaws champing, no words; the habit of men who never know when they'll be interrupted or get another chance to eat.

When they had finished, Luka wagged the knife at Rosso again, but his tone was friendly enough.

'It's all very simple, Policeman. Ask yourself this: what, above all else, will bring the West to the aid of Bosnia?'

'Nothing,' said Rosso. 'There's no oil here, no gold, no uranium. Nothing to gain or lose.'

'I hope you're wrong, Copper. There's only one thing the headline writers, the scribblers, the television people care about: Sarajevo. That's why they're here, see? They don't care about Gorazde because they don't know where it is, how to get there if they could, and they can't. They can't even pronounce it properly. Same with a hundred other towns. They can't get the pictures, see.' He closed the knife, snapping the blade into the wooden shaft and slipping it into a pocket. 'But everyone has heard of Sarajevo. Everyone knows about the archduke and the shot that started World War I, the Winter Olympics in 1984. Right in their sitting-rooms they've seen pictures of the kids dead in the streets. Right? Am I right?'

Rosso nodded.

'It's our trump card, Sarajevo is. So the Government in its infinite

166

wisdom has decided to use Sarajevo as bait. By taking the regulars out of the city, by moving 'em north for some bullshit offensive, they hope to lure the Serbs into making a grab for the city. They're inviting the Serbs to party with us, right, eh, Landser?'

The German did not react. He stared into the middle distance, the cigarette stub burning almost down to his lips.

'It's like a bird dragging its wing along the ground, pretending to be injured and enticing a predator away from the nest,' Luka said. 'Understand, Policeman? We're all that's left. I am the bait. So's he.' He gestured at Landser. 'And so, my friend, are you.' Luka grinned. 'Good, huh?'

'Why are you telling me?'

Luka shrugged.

'I want you to know, to appreciate, how things are, Police-man. I want you to stop playing games. Forget the woman. Forget your war against crime. Forget your bullshit job. Hear me?'

'I hear you.'

'Great. Terrific, Policeman. All we're waiting for now is the big freeze, for the ground to harden. That's when the Cetniks will make a move. When the ground is hard enough for the motherfuckers' tanks.'

'Right,' said Landser.

'You can come work for me,' Luka said. He grabbed Rosso's arm, held it for a moment, shook it, fingers digging into him. 'We could use someone with your talents. All my men are at the front. We could sure use you. Couldn't we Landser, eh?'

'Sure, boss,' Landser said. He didn't sound very convinced. As for Rosso, he said nothing.

They went forward, cautiously, moving in short runs, stumbling really, from tree to hedge, hedge to fence, fence to the first foxhole. It was empty, and so was the next, and the narrow, waist-deep trench after that. The hastily dug depressions and earthworks formed an irregular line, like a trail of blood, through the trees. The firing petered out, only to resume again. In the silences there was the steady drip of water from the trees. Where was everyone? These pitiful, watery holes in the ground bore all the signs of soldiers' sordid front-line existence – spent cartridge cases, a discarded glove, cigarette ends, a torn boot, a small kettle and the smell of faeces from men who shit where they crouch rather than risk being shot for decency's sake. Decency, like everything else, was subordinated to staying alive.

Luka told him: These were our positions.

The inescapable conclusion was that his men had advanced. Advanced! Rosso felt a rush of elation. So it was possible to seize ground from the enemy, to make headway. He had never believed the victories broadcast by Sarajevo radio. Now he was afraid of being left behind in the trees, he hurried to keep up but found himself bumping into Landser.

'What is it?'

'See the house?' Landser whispered. He nodded in its direction, pointing with his chin. Landser cocked his weapon carefully, moving the slide back with the palm of one hand and Rosso was close enough to see a shiny, new round slip easily into the breech. The house stood off to the right, near the road. It was where the superintendent had seen the washing line and the red shirt or sheet or whatever it was hanging on it earlier, only that was around the other side, hidden by the white walls which themselves were still obscured by the trunks and branches of the apple trees. The dwelling was about 200 paces away, Rosso thought. They must be neighbours of the woman with the basket of fruit they'd just eaten.

'There,' said Landser in a low voice. 'Sniper in the roof and upper floor.' Someone like Mahmud, thought Rosso. Some bitter soul with a bitter tale to tell. Someone who kept the score, notching up his kills. Someone with family, with children. Try as he might, Rosso couldn't hate. That was all done with long ago, the hating. Landser turned his head and grinned at Rosso. The policeman was relieved to see he was not the only one whose face was shiny with sweat from their rural ramble.

Rosso nearly tripped over the first body. It was lying against the exposed roots of one of the trees. Then he saw another and another, all in drab uniforms soaked by the snowmelt, the mud. There seemed to be very little blood. It had either drained away into the soil or had been slowed by the cold. The corpses did not look very human. They seemed to be more part of the ground, part of nature, the natural order of things, like the fungi that grew in the forests, which Rosso told himself, in one way or another, they were. The policeman counted seven: seven lumps, bulges, outcrops.

'Cetniks,' muttered the German.

Landser wasn't pale, tense or distraught. On the contrary, he was cheerful. His expression was that of a youth enjoying himself. He might be well within range of the sniper and standing among the corpses of several men, but he gave no sign of it. He was in his late teens, maybe early twenties. For the young, mortality is an abstract idea. Landser was in the middle of an adventure, a child-man who thinks death happens to other people. It is all a game of risk and the others do the dying and the losing. People who get killed have made mistakes and therefore have only themselves to blame. I don't make mistakes so it follows I won't die. Faulty reasoning, but that's how someone like Landser sees it, Rosso thought. Until it happens to him. Then he will look surprised, disbelieving as life ebbs away. This can't be happening, he'll say. It's only a game.

One man had been hit in the back of the head. His face was unmarked, but strangely colourless, almost translucent, like candle wax, in death. The eyes, which were still slightly open, had rolled up into his head so they appeared milky and blank. They seemed to glitter, almost as if the eyelashes were still flickering. Rosso watched, holding his breath, as if at any moment the colour might flow back into the lips and the eyes might open, the mouth smile. Only a game, boys. It was a foolish thought. The policeman saw then that the Serb's brain had fallen out because the rear of the skull had been sheared clean off, and it lay almost intact on the

169

ground, skin and hair still attached. Rosso thought of a coconut, cracked open on a stone. Either the Serb hadn't worn his helmet when he was hit or it had provided no protection worth having. A kitten was feeding on the grey and pink matter, pawing at it and licking it, its tiny tongue lapping at sticky mucus. The animal looked up as the three men drew nearer. It skittered away, almost playfully. It probably lived at the house, had been given scraps by these men when they held the line of trenches. Rosso felt the urge to stamp on the animal, to snuff it out, then he felt remorse. Like everything else alive in Sarajevo, it too was hungry.

The bodies had swollen a little despite the cold. They seemed to lie in groups, as if the dead had crowded together for company. In point of fact, men who are alive tend to bunch up under fire, a natural reaction, but often a fatal one. It takes the kind of training no army in Bosnia provided to keep men well spaced out, especially in retreat. Later, if the temperatures rose further, they would swell hugely, the pressure of the bloated flesh stretching the uniforms tight and bursting the pockets outwards, so that banknotes, handkerchiefs and lovers' letters would tumble out, an additional obscenity to the decomposition of what had once been human beings, fathers, sons, brothers, lovers.

Already these remains had begun to merge with the dirt of which they were a part, the body fluids flowing into the sodden soil and melted snow. Dust to dust, mud to mud.

We are nothing but pus on legs, the policeman thought. Alive we are of little account, dead we are putrefaction. No other creature is so destructive in life or smells so bad dead.

Luka grew more cautious, his eyes searching the ground ahead. He was looking for anti-personnel mines, the small, plastic ones that will take a man's foot off in what Misic would call chronic amputation, just ripping it away, wrenching it off, snapping bones and leaving nerves, blood-vessels and tissue dangling. The superintendent became increasingly conscious of the sound their feet made, creaking in patches of snow, cracking panes of ice that formed over puddles, sucking in oily mud. The shooting came and went like squalls of rain and through it Rosso heard the drone of a Hercules cargo plane leaving Sarajevo, the pilot pulling the aircraft up steeply in an effort to gain height – and safety – as quickly as possible, relieved to be out of it. Home to steak, eggs and beer, a hot bath, clean sheets, safety, plenty of admirers to soak up the boasts of another voyeur of a foreign war.

Rosso let the gangster and his German sidekick lead; sensibly, because they knew better than he what they were doing and selfishly, because he was frightened. He was always frightened. It was a perpetual state for soldiers in combat but Sarajevo civilians had to learn to live with their fright, not in the brief, spasmodic bursts of fighting, but all the time, constantly. There were no non-combatants, and no rear areas. The Serbs, who had the ability to strike at long range, would respond to Bosnian army attacks by hitting civilian targets. Every yard taken in this apple orchard would be paid for by a salvo of shells or mortar bombs behind them, in a market-place, a street, a huddle of houses or apartment blocks. Wives, sisters, daughters paid in blood for whatever their fathers, brothers and husbands achieved at the front. That was the Serb equation: resist us, and we will slaughter your families, raze your homes, starve you. Like pain, fear was usually manageable but there were times – and this was one of them – when Rosso's terror, his desire to live, his awareness of danger became so acute it took conscious effort to keep the devils in his brain and his gut in check. He wanted to yawn, to pee. He felt sick. He wanted to throw up and take a shit at the same time, as if his whole body was saying it wanted to evacuate all non-essential baggage. Keep going, he told himself. Nothing lasts for ever. Rosso put his feet carefully in the tracks left in the mud by the German. He had seen too many feet and legs taken off by mines not to be careful.

Captain Heart was explaining to Flett where the Serbs were: 600 metres to the rear, their lines on the reverse side of the hill. That very morning they had come through Serb positions in their Ukrainian armoured troop carrier, though Flett had been unable to see anything very much from where he sat in the metal toothpaste tube on wheels. As for government forces, the Australian said, they were dug in 400 metres to their front, just over the crest where they stood and on the forward slope of the steep hill. They had tried to claw their way up, but heavy Serb fire always pressed them back. The Serbs had come down to push them off altogether, but the Moslems had held on, repulsing thrusts by the Serbs. So the little Croat house with its fig trees and balcony where the two foreigners now stood, cans of beer in their hands, lay squarely between the two sides in no man's land. Only the ragged blue flag flying from the tiled roof had preserved the cottage, saved it from being reduced to rubble by the two sides. It was certainly in view of fighters on both. That was why, Flett thought to himself, these bullets kept snapping and moaning past them. They're trying to hit us for the sport of it. Throughout the consumption of the second and now third beers the rounds flying around them seemed to increase in number.

It was while he was listening to the captain, keeping a wary eye on the grassy slopes beyond the house and putting his third beer to his mouth – the cold metal against his lips, sucking out the froth and generally enjoying the skirmish unfolding below the hill – that the world seemed to disintegrate. It not only fell apart, but opened up at Flett's very feet. The balcony on which the reporter stood appeared to buckle. He dropped the beer, or rather released it from his grasp, but it chose to stay where it was. How peculiar, he thought. Actually, the beer can was keeping him company; they were both flying through the air. Flett seemed to be horizontal, his feet where his head had been. There was nothing to hold onto. There was thin air where the railing had been.

He seemed to fall for ever. He saw the blue sky, felt on his face a not unwelcome flash of sunlight, but what struck him most forcefully of all was the sight of a cloud of tiles detaching itself from the roof in slow motion, tossed up like so many leaves and starting to cascade down upon him. He felt they were falling

172

together. Beer emerged from the can in a long spurt, a stream that seemed to go on and on. He did not feel afraid. Not at all. Flett felt detached. An embarrassed smile appeared on his face, an apologetic look replacing one of surprise. It occurred to him that this must be an earthquake of the most violent sort. Something so extreme it was right off the scale on which such natural disturbances were measured.

There was a roaring in his ears. The air seemed to quiver with it, to hum; a continuous rushing sound like a river, but one in which there was a series of individual rumbles, linked together, a sound so terrible that he instinctively put his hands to his ears. It seemed to shake the whole world. It reverberated through his teeth. His head pounded with it. He opened his mouth, gasping for air.

For God's sake stop.

He was still floating, falling.

Roof tiles were bursting like clays at a clay-pigeon shoot. Popping. He felt the splinters, the shards hitting his clothes, tugging at the cloth.

Flett felt himself collide with other objects. He was horizontal, moving in grotesque slow motion, or so it seemed, slipping into a pile of military equipment which in turn appeared airborne and was bursting over him like a wave; boots and bottles, clips and cartridges, gas masks and greatcoats.

When it finally did end, Flett's ears still rang and buzzed. He was on his back. Some items came to rest on top of him: tinned steak-and-kidney pie, biscuits and chocolate, strips of dark green canvas festooned with buckles and pouches, T-shirts and big bars of grey soap. His head was in a pool of the beer he had been drinking – what, only a second or two before?

It seemed an age.

11

'Truth will come to light;
murder cannot be hid long.'
WILLIAM SHAKESPEARE, *THE MERCHANT OF VENICE*

HE HEARD HIS NAME. FLETT ROSE GROGGILY TO HIS FEET. HE PUT
his hand to the warm wetness, then looked at his fingers, put them
to his face and sniffed. It was beer, not blood. It had gone down
his neck, down his front. He stretched out the other hand, fingers
making contact with the cool whitewashed wall, and steadied
himself before lifting one foot and placing it carefully in front
of the other, pleased and surprised to find the ground was firm.

Outside, in front of the house, Captain Heart was calling him,
all the while staring up at the roof, or what was left of it, like
some worried householder after a storm.

'Not more than a couple of feet to spare,' Heart said.

It took a moment for Flett's mind to clear, to realize what Heart
was talking about. He squinted at the roof. The rafters were for the

most part intact, but the tiles that had covered them had vanished, had been peeled away. They lay around them now, a carpet of terracotta fragments. Heart explained that the Serbs had fired salvo after salvo from an entire battery of massive Orkan multiple rocket launchers set up close by; down the hill behind the house in fact, deploying them while the two foreigners had been admiring the view and opening their first beers, watching the toy soldiers bleed in the valley below.

The Ukrainians now started up the BTR-60 and it coughed out a steady stream of blue exhaust fumes into the still afternoon air. The shadows were lengthening fast as the sun sank. Sarajevo itself was already entirely in shadow. Flett was wearing thermal underwear, thick skiing socks, two shirts, a pullover, body armour and jacket as well as gloves but he could feel the chill seeping in under his clothes.

'Time to go,' said Heart, lighting another cigarette. If he had been dazed or shaken by the barrage, he gave no sign of it.

Flett meekly followed. The Ukrainians grinned at him, anticipating another entertaining guest performance. Instead, Flett put a boot on one of the fat tyres and heaved himself up, despite the pounding in his head, and he sat on the roof of the vehicle behind Heart. Once up there he realized too late that it would be difficult to get comfortable – there were so many hatches, sharp edges and protuberances – and it would be very cold as they rolled downhill. But Flett had resolved to choose wet and cold in preference to the humiliation of being thrust into this contraption. He reminded himself that he was there to report and that meant using his eyes, not shutting himself away in the dubious sanctuary of this Russian tin can. He pulled up the hood on his jacket, tightened the cords around the waist. With a noisy clash of gears, the BTR-60 slowly reversed and turned.

They had travelled no more than 100 metres when Heart signalled to him and Flett saw the weapons that had caused him so much distress. The rocket launchers, like sets of organ-pipes mounted on the back of a dozen trucks, had been shrouded in canvas by their crews. The weapons stood in an open field and all pointed uphill, at the crest where the cottage stood, the trucks parked in line like a set-piece scene from a Soviet propaganda film. There was no movement – the crews were presumably in the tree line, or in the cabins of the trucks, preparing to bed down for the night. Flett turned up his collar, buried the lower half of his face inside his jacket. His cheeks were already numb.

Rosso saw everyone freeze when the barrage began.

For a brief moment they were caught like an image on a film negative; the light from the explosions etching limbs and faces against a black background. It began with artillery, guns booming away to the south-east, the passage of the shells like ducks flighting overhead, the arc of the projectiles sounding to the policeman like the whackawhackawhacka of wing-beats, then the successive crashes as the shells impacted on the city, on walls, roofs, cobblestones. The guns were followed by the hysterical rumble and rip of rockets, one after the other, dozens of them, each like a giant clearing his throat, a deep and resonant roar. The flickering of the weapons firing and the spectacular flashes of the impacts were continuous, merged into one another, like the light from an old newsreel, or maybe the strobe lights of a discothèque. A Croat fighter was illuminated crossing himself, a Moslem caught in the jerky action of cupping his hands in front of his chest, lifting them to his face as if washing his sins away, murmuring the Prophet's name under his breath. Peace be upon Him. Luka was standing close to Rosso. 'It's the Old Town on the receiving end,' said Luka. The price to pay for those few metres of mud and apple tree that morning. Blood money.

The soldiers sat quietly in their holes and bunkers, waiting, hugging the hurt of it and thinking: hit us, for Chrissake. We're the soldiers – do your worst with us, kill us, maim us if you can. But let our families be. For the soldiers, the city might well be a thousand miles distant for all the good it did them; it would be far better if it was out of sight, out of earshot, out of mind. Instead they could hear and see its agony and that made front-line duty infinitely worse. The impulse to leave their post, to race home, to reassure themselves their people were still alive must have been almost irresistible. As the Serbs hoped it would be.

Mortars began their work. The Serb crews were well trained; they walked the mortar bombs forward, then back, playing with the defenders' nerves, seeking them out, probing for the foxholes, the bunkers. The explosions moved away, came back. A man might curse his own senses, be forgiven for tearing his own ears off not to have to hear that sound of death playing with him and his comrades. There is no hiding from a mortar, not if it is big enough. Rosso could feel the tension rise around him, the glimpses of men in the dark told him by their expressions how they felt; their eyes looked inward, biting down on the abiding fury of living things caged and goaded by their sadistic keepers beyond endurance. He felt it too and was afraid of it; a rage so deep, so intense, distilled and matured for so long in filth, hunger, sleeplessness, pain, loss; like a fine single malt, the end product was nothing like its constituent parts. It gave off the searing pleasure of hatred. All in there had drunk deeply and often of that cup. It was the stuff of which mass murder is made, he told himself. It is infectious, and often fatal to those touched by it.

Luka jostled him. It seemed an odd time to leave. If Luka had declared they would remain there that night, uncomfortable though it undoubtedly would have been, Rosso would have accepted it. All day his had been a passive role, as passenger and spectator, captive audience for Luka's primitive *Weltanschauung*, such as it was, an uncomplaining member of his entourage, powerless, and now leaving the comparative safety of a bunker for an outer world of twilight mist, huge concussive blasts, brilliant bursts of light like a summer electric storm. One moment they were in the dark, in the warmth generated by many unwashed bodies packed together, the next they were half crawling, half running for the car. It felt bitterly cold. The crashes were almost continuous, deafening.

This was what, the second day back? Rosso wasn't sure. Time meant something else here. Time was something that lay between the sound of the impact of a shell and the firing of it, between the lighting of one cigarette and the next, from one meal to the next. Time was what happened until the escape of sleep, then until the ordeal of waking.

By his wrist-watch it was barely two in the afternoon. There was a red glow above the Mercedes, the fires raging through the homes reflected on the underside of low-lying cloud. It lit up their faces in the car: Luka's scarred cheek and twisted jaw, his dark, glittering eyes intent on the road ahead, the chubby young German, leaning forward between the smart bucket seats that still smelt of new leather, weapon in hand, gold ear-ring winking in the reflected light of a city's slow dying.

An hour later, Flett was back in his mouldy hotel room and struggling with a political take-out the foreign editor wanted for the strap at the bottom of the front page.

The man wanted 3,000 words and it was not that often that Flett, famous as he was, was offered the front, albeit below the fold. It had to be good, he told himself. The newsroom back in DC was full of people with fins strapped to their backs, waiting for someone like Flett to slip up. There was no shortage of wannabe heroes.

It wasn't going to be easy, but the Scotch helped.

Serbs were fighting Moslems and Croats. Croats fought Serbs and Moslems. Moslems fought Serbs and Croats and one another.

Then there were regular Croatian troops fighting alongside Bosnia's Croats against the Moslem-dominated Bosnian army with which they were formally allied against the Serbs.

Flett, perched on the stool in front of the dressing-table in his hotel room, stared at the green screen of his laptop. There was a mirror above the table bolted into the wall and it had a crack in it, starring the glass. He tried not to look up at the reflection of himself that was fractured, split – in short, very much the way he felt.

The reporter felt an urgent need for company.

There were Croats, Moslems and Serbs who were loyal to no-one but themselves. An entire class of war profiteers had sprung up, in whose interest it was to prolong not abate the savagery. What did it all mean? Perhaps things would be clearer if he went out, had a drink, something to eat. Then he might be able to explain this Balkan mess to his Kansas City milkman of an uncle in a way that would make him want to read it.

Female company in particular.

Paradox one: The humanitarian relief effort stopped many people from starving, but it kept the war going.

Paradox two: The Serbs harassed the UN peacekeepers, yet it was they and not the Moslems who wanted the world body to keep its soldiers in Bosnia.

Paradox three: The Moslems had signed a plan for partition of Bosnia which they had, in any case, no intention of accepting.

Flett rubbed his temples. It was a contradiction too far. He took a sip from the half-bottle next to the computer. It wasn't even a real war. A real war was industry fully mobilized to project US power abroad and whack some poor jerk with a different alphabet, differently shaped ears or whatever, at minimum cost to the taxpayer. It was about commodity prices, markets and votes. That was the kind of war that made sense.

What were international politics other than piracy played by rules drawn up by the pirates themselves?

Flett took another slug, swilling it around his mouth like mouthwash before swallowing it, feeling it go all the way down.

This was medieval. Here, the enemies knew one another. Intimately – it was so bloody personal. Edged weapons were preferred. It was house-to-house, street against street, village against village. Old drinking pals slit one another's throats, raped one another's wives and daughters. All in the name of history, of religion. Victor took all. Vanquished stumbled away into the sunset to nurse his sense of vengeance until it was his turn.

The Serbs had waited 600 years.

Flett started to tap away at his keyboard.

The Serbs, widely regarded as aggressors, saw themselves as

victims. The Moslems, widely seen as aggression's victims, saw themselves as the eventual victors.

The lights went off.

The detonations reminded the journalist of someone throwing bottles onto a sidewalk – the way they burst, popped and fragmented. Only these impacts, right outside the hotel, were huge flowers of flame. Flett's ears seemed to fizz with the pressure waves. The table vibrated with the explosions.

The newspaperman sprawled onto the floor, the lazy backflip of a terrified lush. He crawled across the carpet to the bed. Still on the floor, he giggled to himself and pulled his body armour out from under the bed and put it on, sliding it over his head and using the big velcro flaps to tighten the ceramic plates around him. Then the helmet. From the bottom of the armour he pulled out a tongue-shaped flap the journalists called the quick-draw-groin-protector.

Balls and brains. The most important bits.

There was masses of time to file. What he needed was a chance to relax.

Outside, the city was crackling, glowing from a hundred fires.

He emptied the bottle, still sitting on the floor.

With luck, the Ragusa bar would let him in; and there was always Bubbles, the city's sole nightclub, for later.

There was much to be said for a war of any kind, especially somebody else's. For one thing you didn't have to think about the utility bills or the rent. And the drinks were on expenses.

He felt better already.

Rosso drew back what was left of the blinds down his side of the office; he had no need to bother about the windows opposite, for most had been shot away. It was like floating in a cloud of fireworks up here, or flying a spaceship through a field of fiery meteoroids – red tracer streamed past horizontally along his side of the building, so close he felt he could lean out and touch it. Green tracer flickered past too, going in the opposite direction on the other side. He found a half-bottle of bourbon in the bottom drawer of his ugly metal desk, sat back in the swivel chair, put his muddy boots up on the desktop – screw the paperwork – and leant back, watching the nightly display, seeing the interior come alive, flickering red and green with the flare of the individual bullets, the impacts of artillery turning the room a slow, dull red that died away slowly again, giving way to darkness. He drank steadily, pacing himself. The whisky hit the policeman quickly. He liked the way it loosened him up, took the aches and pains away, feeling the pleasant fog of oblivion creep up and cradle his mind. He was practised at maintaining the equilibrium he sought, somewhere between sober and drunk; not too much, but not too little or too late to let reality eat its way back like acid.

He was floating; numb, fearless, free.

It was during a particularly spectacular exchange of gunfire across the rooftops that Rosso became aware of a figure sitting next to him, so close he would have heard whoever it was breathing were it not for the dull thumps, cracks and crashes in the darkness beyond the windows. For the first moment he simply dismissed the outline he thought he glimpsed in the pulses of alternating light and dark. No, no. You're drunk. He almost laughed out loud. Took another swig. There it was again. His back went cold, his scalp tingled. His hand dropped to the gun that was no longer in his waistband.

'May I?'

That was all she said. Just 'May I' in a conversational tone; light, gentle, a question put in such a way that it was clear it needed no reply, no assent. She did take the bottle, too, took it gently from his hand, did not bother to wipe the neck, tilted it up, put it down again. She was like that; so quiet, so gentle, so feminine, few knew the chain-mail stubbornness behind it.

Rosso was astonished. He uttered not a sound, couldn't decide whether to rise or sit.

'We have to talk,' she said after a moment or two. It was said with a firmness, as if to say 'I know you've been avoiding me, but now you must face up to things.' Rosso hated that tone of voice. It was patronizing.

He took the bottle. It was nearly finished and he wanted to preserve his pleasantly detached and clouded state of mind for as long as possible. The last thing Rosso wanted to do was to have to think clearly.

Can't I get moderately pissed in private?

The flashes of reflected light from the guns showed her more clearly now. Tanja must have been sitting there waiting for him for God knows how long, and while he mumbled to himself and drank she had sat there listening, watching. He saw she was seated upright, her narrow waist and the delicate V of her back very straight, her swan's neck clear of her long hair which she had carefully plaited and put up. She had on some sort of loose, patterned pullover under a sleeveless jacket as well as ski pants, the kind with a strap under the instep. Her face was turned to him, pale in the shots of light, hands on the desk before her, resting on her beret, the fingers touching it idly, her eyes on him; grave, watchful.

'I would like that,' he heard himself say. 'We don't talk enough.' The sound of his own voice came as a surprise. There was a thickness to it, an impediment of some kind, as if his throat was constricted in some way, like someone with a bad cold. Rosso didn't have a cold, though. He took another swig, replaced the screw top and put the bottle in his lap. He was sure she hadn't drunk the whisky because she liked it or needed it; at best it was to stop him drinking too much of it, or because he stank of it and she thought she wouldn't mind the smell of the drink on his breath so much if she had some herself. It was just like Tanja to do something like that.

'We should talk, yes,' he said, and nodded. Christ, I'm more pissed than I thought I was. The thought took him momentarily back into the apple orchard, and it made him feel dizzy. He brought the chair forward, and sat up straight.

'Are you all right?'

'Yes, of course. I mean no, of course not.'

'Poor Daddy,' she said softly.

'I'm fine. Really. Just tired.'

Bloody hell. If she goes on like this I'll be sobbing my heart out. Get a hold on yourself. Snap out of it.

'Sure?'

'Sure.' Gruff now, a manly voice, irritated. 'How about you?'

'Oh, I'm fine.' Still that soft, calm voice, a voice to cling to, lie down in, surrender to.

A large yellow fire-ball seemed to float past soundlessly. For a moment it lit up the entire floor, a strange brilliant light. Odd, Rosso, thought, there's no explosion. Must be a parachute flare. The darkness, as it seeped back, seemed blacker than ever. He couldn't see her at all now.

'I've been meaning to talk to you,' Tanja said. 'It's just—'

Rosso realized then, in that instant, that he had got it all wrong. Got her all wrong. She was more anxious than he was. She was afraid. Afraid of what she was about to say. Afraid even of him, perhaps.

Their hands were on the desk, the tips of his fingers and the tips of hers barely an inch apart.

He put his hands on hers.

She did not flinch or pull away.

They sat there for what seemed like minutes, not moving, not speaking. It seemed to him they were scarcely breathing.

'I tried,' she began, and faltered, not knowing how to continue. Her hands turned, held his.

'You tried what?'

'The other day. No, it was yesterday. You took me and that, that – woman – to the hospital. You gave us a lift. That's what I meant to say.'

'The woman – did she live?'

Tanja shrugged. It was not a shrug of indifference, but a shrug that said one does what one can, but not everyone always makes it.

'Yes. At least I think so. She wasn't badly hurt.'

'You tried to warn me, is that it?'

'Yes.'

The ramrod-straight poise went, her shoulders sagged. She leant forward and taking her hands from under his, planted her elbows in the mess of papers on his desk and buried her face in her hands, remaining like that for a few moments before straightening again. Rosso could only guess at the expression on her face.

'May I have another drink?'

'Of course.' Rosso produced the bottle.

'Do you mind?'

'No, of course not. Go ahead.' He did mind, though. He watched her finish it. To his regret the policeman felt clear-headed. Quite sober in fact.

'Better?'

'Yes. Thank you.'

He watched the lights dance across her face. He had been wrong about the Scotch too. She drank it because she liked it.

'You went out with Luka today,' Tanja said.

'I wouldn't put it quite like that.'

'You know what I mean.'

'I tried to question him. He showed me his secret cache of stolen goods. I actually helped him load them onto a truck, believe it or not. I'm not sure I can. We then visited the front. He impressed me with his leadership qualities, which was the whole purpose of the exercise, I suppose. I got the de luxe lecture tour. *Son et lumière.* He even offered me a job.'

'Did you take it?'

'What do you think?'

'It would be the best thing you could do. For you. For Sabina. For us. But I know you didn't.'

'What are you trying to tell me?'

'I'm not sure where to begin.'

'The beginning. Try the beginning.'

She did. She started by recalling Rosso's finding her in the corridor of a hotel turned over to refugees. She squatted in a passage, begged what she could, fought off the unwanted attentions of a variety of males, some of them refugees, even policemen, UN soldiers and boys half her age. Rosso took her home, Sabina fed her, they both put her to bed. That was a beginning of sorts. There were still the nightmares, the 'it' that came at her, a blackness at great speed, a vortex that threatened to devour her. She could never find the words to describe this 'it'. She woke screaming, in tears, unable to explain or describe. She always knew it would come the day before. Looking at her hands, she said, something would happen to them. Holding them up to her face in daylight they would swell, grow smaller, swell again and she knew the Terror, the 'it', would visit her again that very night, however much she tried to stay awake.

They hugged her, fed her with whatever they had and it was little enough. They clothed her as best they could. It was, at any rate, sufficient to bring her out of her tunnel of grief and self-loathing (loathing at being alive when her own family were dead) into the light of day. She could see what was happening to Sabina, to the city. She tried to join the Army, but was turned down. She tried the hospitals. It was Luka who pointed her in the direction of the paramedics. It was Luka who took her out, collecting her himself by car, appearing on the doorstep with a bunch of flowers and a stupid grin on his face, his bodyguards smirking in the foyer and the neighbours suddenly looking at Sabina and Rosso with a new respect. He took her bowling and to the last remaining cinema until that too was shut. She went to his late-night haunts, the smugglers' cafés, hung around while he drank, played cards. He liked to show her off to his cronies. He would tell them she had class, whatever that was. His 'bit of class'. She kept her eyes and ears open and she passed on whatever she found out to Rosso.

Sabina and Rosso argued about the relationship, often and loudly.

'Why?' he asked her now.

'Why? After all this time, what a question!'

'You loved him. Still do, presumably.'

'Oh, you are a fool.' She said it gently, kindly.

'You don't?'

'Do you know nothing about women after all this time?'

'Don't answer a question with another.'

'No, I don't love him.'

'He's pretty keen on you.'

'I know. He wants to marry me. I thought he might ask your permission today.'

'So if you didn't love him – correction: don't love him – why do you still go out with him? I hope it's not because you think I need you to keep an eye on him.'

'People say women are made for love, but how many marriages, how many relationships are based on love? Very few. Most women will make do with a lot less. A man who doesn't beat his woman, who's kind, who provides a home, who is amusing, gentle, a man a woman can be proud of, someone to look up to, someone who puts food on the table. There are a thousand reasons. Love is only one.'

'It's a very good reason.'

'Of course. The best. It can also be the worst.'

'You're very cynical.'

Tanja shrugged. 'No. Realistic. You men are such romantics, little boys grown up but keeping a child's illusions. Still climbing trees and playing with toys, only the games are lethal and the toys are other people's lives.'

'You haven't answered my question.'

'Are you interrogating me, Superintendent?'

Rosso shook his head. He felt as if they were both afloat, cast into a stormy sea aboard some strange, hallucinatory craft, without crew or captain. The lights that swept ceiling, walls and one another gave them the sense of movement, of rolling from side to side, or pitching from one crest of a wave to another.

'If you don't love him—'

She interrupted. 'I needed protection. Women generally do. I did. Luka was attractive because of that power he had to protect. I used it, sheltered behind it. Now I think it's you who needs the

186

protection. If it wasn't for his feelings for me he would have moved against you. I'm protecting you. He knows all about your investigation and has done for weeks.'

'What does he know?'

'He knows the interior ministry – you and your department, in other words – are after him.'

'And besides that?'

'He thinks the troop movements are genuine.'

'Do you?'

She didn't answer.

Rosso bowed his head, looked down at his hands. Vasic had made sure Luka knew about the investigation. What happened to Bukovac was Luka's mistake. Maybe a fatal one where Vasic was concerned, too. Rosso waited for a roll of gunfire to recede, just like a crash of thunder and lightning and every bit as bright and electric blue.

'Aren't you going to ask me if I slept with him?'

He looked at her, her face in darkness again.

'Isn't that what this is all about?'

'You're saying I'm sexually jealous.'

'Aren't you?'

He didn't answer. Her voice was light, mellifluous. It was impossible to take offence. It was impossible to feel anything other than an urge to wrap his arms around her. His desire was so strong it was actually searing, a burning pain, a bright sword-point of desire, so sharp that he almost groaned out loud.

'And Branston Flett?'

'Branston?' Her voice rose in surprise.

'Yes, Branston. Weren't you with him the other night? In that blasted car of his. Outside our building. Last night.' He was getting angry at himself.

'I've been out with him. But not last night.'

'For protection?'

'There's no need to be sarcastic.'

'Sleep with him too, did you, for protection?'

187

'That was unworthy of you.'

'Of me?' He was surprised at how relieved he felt that it had not been her.

'Don't you know, haven't you realized, all this time, these – what – two years that we've lived under the same roof that it's you I have loved? That if it hadn't been for Sabina—'

'Stop this for Chrissake!'

'I won't stop, not now. You wanted to know. Well, this is the truth you asked for. Oh, you fool. You loved me, too. I could tell you did. I called you "Father" and "Daddy" because I knew that if I didn't . . .'

Rosso had put his hands over his ears and it was not to block out the sound of the great percussive hammer blows outside. He was used to that. He had his game of golf to think about.

'. . . only now Sabina has gone, there's no need.'

'What did you say?' He sat up abruptly.

'I said Sabina has gone. She went today. It was what I came to tell you and then we got into this. I didn't mean to. I planned to tell you straight away. I'm terribly sorry. I—'

Rosso stood over her, fists clenched, rigid, grinding his teeth, not knowing whether he wanted to strike the woman sitting before him or run from the room out into the night.

'Tell me,' he hissed. 'Tell me. Quickly.'

Tanja said the *Mouhabarat* – the secret police – represented by an officer and two armed men – had appeared at their flat on the morning after Rosso had left for New Town. They probably waited for him to leave before they made their move. Tanja was not there – she had spent the night at the military hospital. It could well have been Luka's work, she added. He could have put them up to it. Maybe they were on Luka's payroll. Plenty of that sort were. Sabina opened the door only when the officials had identified themselves. They told her the flat was confiscated by government order. Whose, which minister, she didn't know. It had been in her name. A Serb name. With two bedrooms, the officer told her, they'd get two Moslem families in there. She would have to go.

Sabina tried at first to brazen it out, mentioning that her husband was a deputy police commissioner (at this point the secret policeman had merely sneered at her), then she tried appealing to his humanity. She told him that they already had a Moslem refugee staying with them. They had nowhere to go. All to no avail. The official notice taking over the property was nailed to the door for everyone to see and the security people left, saying the Rossos had twenty-four hours to vacate the property or face arrest for obstructing the war effort.

Rosso sat down, heavily, with a stunned look.

Sabina had wasted no time, Tanja went on. She scribbled a note, sealed it in an envelope and addressed it to Rosso, leaving it on their bed. Then she had dressed up in her best remaining winter dress (there were only two), packed a small overnight bag, and had walked the two miles in the snow to Luka's headquarters where she had waited patiently for Luka to see her. He lent her 350 marks: the price of a black-market seat on a Red Cross bus, one of several comprising a refugee convoy delayed several times and finally due to leave the city that very day.

Tanja paused. She looked at her wrist-watch. By now, she said, Sabina should be safe in Serb-held territory. Maybe Brcko or even Banja Luka.

Rosso stood, pushing his chair back.

'I was at Luka's this morning. I would know if my wife was there, or had been there. He would have said something. He never mentioned it all day.'

Tanja looked up at him. Reached up, touched his arm.

It was that gesture, a gesture that said everything – it spelt pity, it spelt love, it spoke truth. Of course, Luka had known. He had probably just handed her the money, or kept her waiting in another office so husband and wife would not see one another. How like him. Maybe that was why Luka had invited the policeman to join him at the front – to keep him out of the way, to give Sabina time to join the convoy. He knew Rosso still had the influence to get the order overturned, rescinded.

'Why?' he asked. 'Tell me, Tanja. Why?'

Tanja turned her head away. She was crying. They both were.

'Because I wouldn't marry him. Because he thinks you're stopping me from marrying him, so he wants to weaken you, get you to give in, submit. Everyone else does, you see, so why shouldn't you? He won't have you murdered because if something happened to you he knows I wouldn't have him; anyway it could backfire. Your own men are loyal; your killing would start a civil war in the city. That's what he asked me: what makes Rosso so bloody different? Luka has every woman he wants, but he doesn't have me. He has every policeman – well, practically every policeman – in his pocket. But he wants you. If he gets you, he gets me. That's how he sees it.'

'So he drives my wife out of town.'

'That way he thinks you'll weaken.'

She sniffed and wiped her nose on her sleeve like a child.

'Maybe he's right.'

'No, he's wrong. Not you. Never you.' She spoke with bitterness, anger.

'And you? Will you weaken?'

'Not while we have each other,' Tanja said. 'Not now. And we do have each other, don't we?'

Rosso stared at her. He felt unable to speak.

A strange sensation of being lifted up towards the ceiling overtook him. He seemed to be looking down at Tanja as if she were at the bottom of a mine shaft. How was it, he wondered, that Tanja knew about Luka giving Sabina the money? The question hit him like a bucket of icy water and he felt he was back on terra firma again.

'You hate me now, don't you?' she said in a low voice. Her face seemed to break, deconstruct, as emotion gripped her. Her body seemed to go rigid. Perhaps she had seen the unspoken suspicion in his eyes, in the set of his mouth.

'It's all my fault. You think I put him up to it; that it was I who wanted Sabina out of the way. It's not true, but I can't blame you for hating me.'

She let out a howl, so loud and so animal-like that Rosso drew

190

back with surprise as much as anything else. It was an utterly wild sound, and quite unlike the Tanja he knew.

'It is my fault,' she repeated. 'How could I think it would be otherwise? To have you, to lose you in the same instant. It is my fault. It is. Oh, God forgive me, it is.'

12

'Most women are not so young as they are painted.'
MAX BEERBOHM, *A DEFENCE OF COSMETICS*

ROSSO COULD NOT REMEMBER WHEN HE HAD LAST WANTED A woman, when he had felt the insistent urge; not for anyone in particular, just plain horniness directed at womanhood at large. In the past, in peacetime, the arousal and its spawning of sexual fantasy had come at him often, hourly, twice-hourly, sometimes every few minutes or even continuously for hours on end, day or night. It never occurred to him to wonder at it. He assumed everyone – or at least every male – was similar. Since that awkward period of transition from boy to manhood, every interval, each idle, empty moment was plugged with thoughts of the before, the after and the coupling itself, with a thousand imaginary partners, or perhaps a thousand versions of the same woman in every conceivable location, in swimming pool, phone booth, corridor, on staircase, bannister, balcony, in bath, bedroom, on rooftop, wooden floor, rug, table, chair, in a car. In the pubescent beginning the shape, the line and fold of clothing was every bit as important as what filled it, if not more so. The women, to start with, were of the healthy, outdoor kind, generously built with happy, healthy complexions, good teeth, narrow waists. They were usually blonde. Then they were only glimpsed at in the man-child's mind, always in shadow, partial people, two-dimensional at best, robotic, usually pliant, sometimes dominant and invariably without personality. With the onset of manhood that began to change. They became young, old, married, single or divorced, pale or swarthy, fat, thin, short, tall, refined, coarse, flat-chested, well-endowed, naked, partly clothed, with and without underwear. A gesture, a look, a scent, a delicate wrist or elegant throat could provide ignition. As a young man Rosso had devoted considerable energy and time to the realization of some of these imagined encounters. What success he had, in turn fed the fantasy as it was bound to do. He discovered that wanting to please helped. As only young men can, he felt extreme jealousy at the sight of women he did not know and could not have. That there were young women he would never know – know in the carnal sense – vexed him until he reached the relative stability and self-assurance of his late twenties. It had always seemed odd to Rosso that the Roman Catholic Church regarded women as passive, inert, and male lust as the danger to be suppressed, curtailed; whereas the Qur'an, for all the repression and ignorant cruelty perpetrated by a minority in its name, approved of female sexuality, encouraged fulfilment but sought to restrict the woman's behaviour and appetite as if she, not the male, threatened good order. The two seemed to be mirror images of one another.

How different things were now, at least for him.

Both the thought and the instinct had evaporated with Rosso's arrival on the doorstep of middle age and the advent of war; with the constant hunger and fear, the passion for sleep, for escape; with being unwashed, finally filthy with wearing the same sweat-stained clothing day after day, the low self-worth; with the exhausting effort needed merely to endure and to accept there was no alternative to

193

endurance. No wonder, with death at every turn, so many took their own lives out of a sense of guilt at having survived for so long.

It had got to the point when the mere act of sex, shorn of any pretence at love, affection, gentleness, giving and all those other civilized qualities, would have been just one chore too many, and would have required too much effort. Even the stirring power of imagination seemed to have died in the face of terror. Until this evening he thought he had reached the stage where he would no longer have known where to begin. Only extreme danger seemed briefly to stir the juices, the urge to procreate. Yet the chemical, or whatever it is that makes push-button men the way they are, surged through his limbs this night, bursting in his brain, synapses firing, heating his skin. A current of energy tightly beamed on the dark figure next to him in his office, fuelled by the sound of her clothes rustling, the sudden illumination of her mouth, chin, her long fingers, the roundness of a thigh. The flashes of light through the broken venetian blinds stamped bars of colour across her face, imprinting stripes of light on the swell of her breast: his captive desire behind prison bars, his zebra-woman sinuous in the light of a hundred burning homes. Rosso's reason flailed hopelessly against the giddy images of his taking her then and there. The whisky had played its role in breaching the last bastion of self-inflicted inhibition. It was a victory of sorts, but one he still resisted.

The ache stayed with him as he drove home, even as he climbed the stairs; it was still there when he opened the door, stepped inside, made his way through the dark (he knew it so well he hardly needed light). It made him angry, resentful even, though he wasn't sure against what. His own nature? Tanja? It was so bad he could hardly walk straight.

My God-daughter.

What did that matter?

God was a cruel joke, the ultimate lie.

The desire drained away absolutely and as abruptly as it had come the very instant his eyes fell on the envelope. As a reminder of his marriage vows it was innocuous enough – a small white rectangle of cheap, recycled paper lying on the bed where it had been flung; his name on it. He tore it open messily, fingers fumbling at the flap.

The object of his temporary madness had followed him in. Tanja stood inside the doorway, silent, arms folded defensively across her chest while he bent and picked up the envelope, then stood aside as he made his way out of the bedroom again. Neither spoke. He felt her eyes on him. He stepped onto the balcony. There was just enough light from the fires, reflected down off the patchy cloud, to make out the note, written hurriedly, the letters pitching sharply forward to the right. He held the letter up close to his face.

Dearest. Forgive me. There was no time to dwell on it. I fear we may repent at our leisure but I want you to know, and believe, that whatever has happened in the past and whatever may happen in future, I love you dearly. We loved one another from the start despite everything, everyone. Despite my family and yours. With time it grew stronger. It was strong. At least it was until I let you down. I am so sorry, so ashamed. I was weak. What I am doing is best for us both. I will be safe. You will have less to worry about. I was a burden. Don't deny it. I was. I was killing off what you felt for me. I think you even hated me a little. Don't protest – it is the truth. I knew this would happen eventually. It was bound to. Maybe they will be seen as having done us a big favour. All you have to do now is survive as best you can. I will not judge you. Just live through this. Do not hate. Do not seek revenge. The debt to Luka is my own. You owe him nothing. When we meet again I WILL be better. I love you. This will pass. Remember, also, that Tanja cannot help herself. Do not blame her. If you must blame anyone, blame me. Your loving Sabina, always.

Rosso read through it a second time, stuffed it into his coat pocket. You're playing the blasted heroine, the saint. He felt an irrational anger rise up like bile at the letter and the hand that wrote it and felt immediately ashamed with himself for it. Damn. This is not worthy of you. Of her. He took the crumpled note out and read it a third time as if it would reveal something new, something different, and then put it back again. He would have liked to have stood out there for a while, collecting himself. He needed time to take it in, think it through, absorb what she had done, how she had done it, what it must have been like for her – but it was too cold. He quivered with the chill, he had no resistance left, no spare fat left from his Zagreb trip. By now Sabina would be at Metkovic, or even further. Safe, at any rate. Rosso went back inside where he knew Tanja would be waiting. He found her sitting on his side of the bed, he noticed, with that quietude, that stillness of the watchful. She had regained that self-possessed, cat-like assurance that he found so alluring, so enigmatic, as if nothing had happened. He sat down next to her, not touching, yet careful to seem neither distant nor too familiar. It was a game of some kind, he realized, a ritual perhaps or a contest and one without any rules that he could recognize. He sensed that whatever it was, and wherever it led, she was – for reasons he did not fully understand – by far the stronger player. He did not want to hurt her feelings by avoiding physical contact, and he did not want to touch her for fear of reigniting his own desire. He felt sure she knew that and, like a chess player, was already several moves ahead.

What had Sabina meant when she said Tanja could not help herself? That she should not be blamed? For what? In some ways the letter's banal sentiment showed considerable guile; by blaming herself, by playing the role of repentent sinner, by heaping fault on herself, Sabina had ensured that Rosso would regard himself as being in her debt. She had successfully inserted a strong element of doubt about Tanja into his mind. Of guilt, also. It would fester there.

Was it deliberate? Of course.

Why did he always try to do the right thing even when he had lost sight of it?

The problem sorted itself out, or to put it more accurately, was quickly submerged by other news. Tanja had a good deal more to tell him. Sabina's sudden departure was the worst news Tanja had delivered on Rosso's return from the front, but it was by no means all. Misic and two other members of the committee of Loyal Serbs – all that remained, in fact – had been arrested by the military that very morning, probably at the time the security men were making their way to the Rossos' flat. The doctor's whereabouts were not known, she said. (Rosso showed no surprise at this, but thought to himself that they would move the doctor about at night, keeping him at different barracks.) The arrest warrants had apparently been signed by the defence minister himself, she went on. Tanja said she had found out about the arrests at the hospital, hearing it from distraught nurses in the obstetrics department where she usually managed to scrounge dressings and other medical paraphernalia. Finally, Tanja said that Luka had confided the previous evening – and this was the issue which had prompted her veiled warning to Rosso when he had dropped her and the sniper victim off at the hospital – that what was left of the police department was to be disbanded with effect from midnight the next day – little more than twenty-four hours away. He looked at his watch. Remaining officers were to be drafted into the armed forces or the military police. Those too old for either would join civil defence teams, no more than glorified burial parties, collecting the dead in handcarts and barrows, scraping intestine off walls with shovels. The presidential war council had told Luka the city was desperately short of troops; they had sent their best regulars to reinforce the 5th and 3rd Corps and wanted him to provide every able-bodied fighter he could find.

In effect, it was martial law.

Had Luka agreed?

Tanja said he had.

Rosso lay back, closed his eyes and marvelled at the way in which Luka was walking into the trap set for him, designed to match Luka's sense of his own importance.

While Tanja was still talking, he covered himself with the bedclothes against the cold night air.

*   *   *

197

Flett stopped for a couple of drinks *en route* to the garage and two at the lobby bar were quickly followed by two more, for the road, as his colleagues put it. It was a very tipsy reporter who was finally cheered on his way and who staggered down the spiral staircase into the subterranean garage, and it was with some difficulty – he dented the door of one car belonging to Italian journalists and knocked a wing mirror off one of the BBC's Land Rovers – that Flett managed to manoeuvre his beloved armoured vehicle up the circular ramp and onto the street beyond. His colleagues thought him mad to go out and had told him so. That only made him more determined to pursue his quest, to add lustre to the living legend.

What he found was not particularly promising. The shelling had all but ceased, but the city's buildings loomed above him, dark and menacing. They were split, like the walls of some great canyon, by snowy alleys. He hardly recognized the place. The only sign of life, or rather death, was the odd burst of tracer, the illuminated rounds curving lazily through the black night sky, the glow from a burning house. There were no street signs that he could see, and if there had been, there were no lights to allow Flett to make any sense of them. He dare not use the headlamps. For a while he searched for the Ragusa bar and after forty minutes of pointless circling around the city centre, gave up. Now and again he rode the huge vehicle up onto a pavement, the rear end skidding wildly on the icy surface. The snow was so deep and the streets so icy the befuddled newspaperman could not tell where tarmac ended and kerb began. It was only an instinctive sense of the whereabouts of Sarajevo's *demi-monde* and an act of supreme will that broke through his state of inebriation that allowed Flett, like some errant homing pigeon, to find the nightclub. As it came into view, Flett told himself he was safe. He was, after all, a US citizen. He had clout inside the Beltway. He had friends in the Bosnian presidency.

No-one was going to mess with him.

There was no neon, no sign in fact of any kind that Flett could see;

just a doorway, scores of young people gathered outside on muddy cobblestones, drawn like moths from their chilly, ill-lit homes to the one beacon that promised an hour or two of forgetfulness, of escape.

Bubbles was a vast underground complex, a series of basements linked by corridors and lined with mirrors. It was packed with twenty-somethings, dozens deep around the bar, though few had the money for as much as a fruit juice. The smoke was so thick it would make a chain-smoker's eyes water. At the entrance, girls who looked no more than twelve or fourteen waited, their backs to the grimy, yellow-tiled walls, chatting desultorily with one another, eyes constantly watching newcomers, weighing their wallets, assessing their desirability and puffing on cigarettes they could ill afford; round young faces pasted with make-up in a crude effort to look older, waiting to be chatted up for the price of a Coke and considerably more for a pack of cigarettes or bar of chocolate. They were children without childhood. These pitiful creatures' targets were the youths in uniform, the combat-suited thuggerati with money to throw around, young men with baby faces below crew cuts, with guns on their belts who would not know the front if they tripped over it and whose parents would go to extraordinary lengths to avoid their heirs being sent there.

Flett appreciated it for what it was: a meat market. It was sordid, pecuniary and it appealed to him. He had tasted the contaminated delights of other stew pots of a not-dissimilar nature: Bangkok's Patpong, Manila's Ermita, London's West End clubs. As for Sarajevo, the moral order, family life and the rest of it, was being torn apart, turned on its head, by the siege. The process of corruption and disintegration was tangible. It fascinated Flett. He told himself a new order was rising from the primordial soup. He was there to record it.

He carried out a reconnaissance, diving into the crowds and using his shoulders to forge a path through the heaving, steaming mass of humanity. The dance floor was as crowded as the rest of it, with the usual crust of young men around the sides staring fixedly at the women performing self-consciously together in the centre under the flashing strobe lights. He fought an orderly withdrawal to the bar and took up residence there, carving out a few inches of Formica. He could watch the sea of faces behind the two barmen. It took him no more than the price of three local beers and half an hour before he found Nadia, or she found him. She was with a female friend of hers, a sharp, predatory old-young face under a mass of black unruly curls and an ugly scarlet gash for a mouth. Flett knew enough Serbo-Croat to realize after a few minutes that he was the subject of their heated discussion. They seemed to be arguing over possession. He liked that. It excited him. Nadia claimed prior property rights over the American. Her friend gave up, vanishing into the heaving mass of faces and bodies with a toss of her head. The music was deafening. Flett had ordered and paid for three vodkas and Coke and Nadia smiled and shrugged and took her friend's drink as well as her own, throwing them both back one after the other, like water.

'You come,' Nadia screamed into Flett's ear.

She was stripped for action, wearing a dark body stocking of some kind; bare-backed, low in front and ending in very short hot pants that seemed to have been moulded to her buttocks. Below them she had on black stockings and big black-and-white shoes on her feet, the heavy clumpy sort with high heels that were fashionable among Western teenagers.

Her hair smelt of strawberries as it had that night in the car.

'Where?' Flett asked. He had to put his mouth to her ear and at the same time he slid his right arm around her.

'My place. You stay with me, no?'

They pushed their way out of the club. Nadia led, occasionally casting Flett backward glances, as if to ensure that he had not fallen behind or slipped away. Not that there was anywhere for Flett to slip away to. The crowd had increased substantially since he had arrived and if it wasn't for the slim figure ahead, ruthlessly pummelling and kicking her way through, he would have been trapped in the sweaty press of humanity. It didn't do to think what a single 160mm mortar round would do to them all. To him.

Once outside in the cold, fresh air, she pulled a fake fur coat around her shoulders.

'We walk, yes,' Nadia told him, tugging and holding him upright at the same time.

'What about curfew?'

'Fuck curfew. No problem. Flat very close. You come.'

Flett was not entirely sure if his companion was a professional or simply an amateur enthusiast. In some ways, a professional was safer. He began to worry, in a confused and inconclusive manner, about safe sex. He had no condoms on him. They were back in his hotel room, stashed away in his suitcase for fear someone else – the cleaning woman, perhaps – would find them. That made him think of Rosso, and the lecture the policeman had delivered the previous evening, before he had leapt to his feet, pale and shaken, and rushed from the hotel dining-room as if the very devil were after him.

Flett skidded on the ice, laughing like an idiot. A cat snarled at them out of the darkness. Nadia held him tighter.

'You be good,' she commanded him. He wasn't sure what that meant. He had no intention of being good. His desire for this strange woman was becoming more urgent by the minute.

They held one another up, his drunken state matched by the difficulties Nadia had in keeping a purchase on a particularly icy stretch of road with her high heels. Flett laughed louder, she swore in Serbo-Croat. They clung to one another, arms flailing to keep their balance, Flett hooting insanely, Nadia cursing. For all he knew or cared she was swearing at him. It was like a three-legged race down a precipitous mountain.

They were rushing into the darkness one moment and the next they seemed to have been immobilized.

It was a flash of light so powerful it seemed to stun both of them. Flett raised his free arm to shield his eyes.

He told himself it was some sort of searchlight. Then he thought it was the headlight of a passing car, but it was like gazing into the sun. It seemed to sear his eyeballs. He flinched from it, yet the white beam seemed to transfix them both like insects impaled on a collector's pin.

He heard a shout; are they shouting at me? he wondered, incredulous. Then he was being pushed, none too gently, against a wall. Feet tramped about in front of him, came near, receded. More boots crunched towards them in the snow.

'Let me go, bastard,' the girl was yelling. 'Motherfuckers, fascists.'

'I'm an American,' Flett said in his most authoritative voice. '*Nominari*! Press!'

He had straightened up, stood erect to increase his sense of authority. He felt clear-headed all of a sudden, sober even. He searched his pockets for the UN press accreditation he always carried, only he couldn't remember which pocket he had slipped it into when he left the hotel.

They weren't interested. The hand that had been searching diligently for proof of identity was grabbed, twisted and forced behind him so that he was spun round to face the way he had come. It all happened so fast. The arm was then pulled up as high as it would go, into the middle of his back, so that he was forced onto his toes to avoid the pain. Someone grabbed his thick crop of hair and with it rammed his nose against what must have been a brick wall. It was rough and hard, and Flett felt his nose make a sort of soft crunching noise when it connected. His attention was on another sound, now, the very distinctive metallic click and slide of a Kalashnikov being cocked. Blood trickled into his mouth. It tasted warm, salty, familiar.

'Pricks!' screamed Nadia.

'Whoremasters!'

'Fuckwits!'

Flett distinctly heard a slap, a sharp smacking sound, followed by a scuffling. Nadia was quiet for a moment, then he heard her murmur: 'Cunts!'

202

Flett's hands had been pushed above his head and rested on the rough surface of the bricks. Now he felt his wrist-watch being slipped off his raised left hand. It was a $3,000 Rolex, watertight down to 100 metres with an oyster strap. Not that he had ever been down 10 metres, let alone 100.

He made no effort to resist.

God-damn.

Whoever they were, they were frisking him, turning out his pockets and dropping whatever they found and whatever did not interest them into the mush at his feet. Keep the greenbacks, boys. Take the plastic too – fat lot it'll do you in Sarajevo. Just let me have my press card and my nice leather wallet. He felt hands move down his thighs, his legs. And if they take my boots, he thought, then I know I'm done for: it's a sign that you're not going to make it out alive, though they could always shoot him and then take the boots. He debated this point as they searched him. If you shoot a man while he's got his boots on, chances are his blood will be all over them. They'll be more difficult to get off, too. On balance, he thought, I'd take a man's boots off and THEN shoot him.

At least his underwear was clean that morning. Hell, he wouldn't want some preppy State Department jerk lugging his remains back to the Zagreb consulate in dirty shorts, or for his ma and pa to receive their son's corpse wearing them . . .

Flett had never been religious. Yet he tried to pray now. 'Oh God,' he mumbled, unsure and awkward with the words. 'Get me out of this and I'll never go to that club again. Never pick up girls, never get drunk and never, ever cover this piss-awful war again.

'I promise, Lord.'

Flett could not sleep for the cold. He fidgeted, dozed off, woke abruptly, rubbed his arms and legs, dozed and woke again. He had the cell to himself – a concession to his status as a foreign journalist, perhaps. He tried to prop himself up in the corner on the only furniture: a three-legged stool. So much for his influence inside the Beltway. He had no blanket or mattress, they had taken away his belt and his bootlaces. He stared and stared but could see nothing.

After a while he could discern a window of sorts, but no bigger than the mouth of a drainpipe and set into the very thick wall behind double sets of bars, high up, close to the ceiling. A pale, watery moonlight oozed from it; simply enough to show the prisoner it was there. He could not even see his own hands. The blackness was as suffocating as a blanket held over a man's head. He felt his way around the cell, using his hands, measuring it with his feet, shuffling along the walls like an old man. It was 5 feet from the back wall to the iron door, 4 feet across. Tiny, no more than a cupboard, the air still and cold. A bucket in one corner (he found it by almost falling over it), the stool opposite. The bucket stank, the flagstone floor was wet. The walls were like ice and the cold seemed to seep from them into whichever shoulder Flett leant on. He wondered if there were rats.

No-one knows I'm here. No-one.

His ears strained for sound. Was he imagining it? The odd, irregular sound of water, a faint drip or gurgle. The blood on his face had hardened into a crust that he picked at for lack of anything better to do. His nose felt swollen, sensitive.

The deadline for his front-page piece must have come and gone. They'd curse him, but would they bother to call him?

Flett had no notion of time. He could have been there minutes or hours. To stop himself freezing, he hopped up and down, then set about trying to discover any gaps in the walls, any holes. He pressed his ear against the slabs of cold stone or whatever they were that ran from the floor to the unseen ceiling, listening. Occasionally he thought he heard a drip, drip; it was too faint, too irregular to be sure. Mostly, a nothing blared back at him. Was it possible that silence could deafen? He tried singing, quietly at first, embarrassed. He reasoned if he couldn't hear his neighbours, they would not be able to hear him. He began with 'The Star Spangled Banner'. 'All That Meat And No Potatoes'. 'The Sheikh of Araby'. 'Rock of Ages'. 'What Shall We Do with the Drunken Sailor'. 'Onward

204

Christian Soldiers'. 'I Can't Get No Satisfaction'. Fed up with the sound of his own, flat voice in his ears, he tried to run on the spot but his head was too painful, his stomach too queasy after all the drink. He felt his way with his fingers along the walls, probing, testing, listening. It was remarkable how danger could sober a man up.

Nothing.

I'm going to die here.

He was woken by the sound of the key in the lock, scraping the iron, then finding its way in and turning, roughly, as if whoever was opening it was impatient, hurried. The door swung open onto the corridor.

Flett got to his feet too quickly and felt his head spin.

Strangely, he felt little elation at release. His head pulsated as if it had been pounded with a jackhammer, his mouth tasted like the inside of a boxer's glove and his legs had gone numb with cold. As he reached the door he tried to stretch his arms above his head to get the blood circulating and immediately felt he would throw up if he didn't stay still. The guard waited for him, staring at the foreigner. Flett blanched at the noise of feet on the tiled floor. Wordlessly, another guard, unshaven and puffing on a cigarette, handed over his belt, his shoelaces, his press card, even his credit cards and cash. But no watch. Flett signed some sort of release form, and with a cacophony of locks being turned, bars lifted and pulled, they let the hungover reporter out into the grey morning light, their laughter following him as he held onto the wall of the jail to stop himself from slipping.

Nadia was already there, waiting on the pavement, tapping a stiletto-heeled foot in an impatient tattoo on the ice. He did not recognize her at first. He had never seen her before in anything resembling daylight. Sixteen going on sixty, he thought. Her make-up seemed like a cruel mask that had slipped, her mascara blurred, her lipstick smudged. She still wore her black panther suit, or whatever it was, only the tights were torn, showing circles of pale thigh. Her brown eyes examined him carefully, as a butcher might measure a calf for the knife.

Apparently they had kept her overnight, too.

Flett tried to smile. 'Hello,' his mind said, but no intelligible sound emerged from his dry and foul-tasting mouth. God, he felt like death dug up. Dying might, after all, be a blessed relief.

'We go, yes.' It was more command than question.

'Go?' He felt stupid.

'My place. Now. Yes, Blanston?'

She closed in on him, taking his arm in both hands as if he might make a run for it. All he wanted to do was lie down.

'No,' he said. 'Sleep.' Flett thought that if he spoke again his brain would flop out of his skull, ooze out of his ears. He tottered like someone walking on broken toes.

I must be careful.

'No problem. Sleep.' She smiled encouragingly. Apparently she thought he was apologizing for not being able to perform.

'No. I have to work. Write.' He made a tapping motion with his fingers. 'I go to my hotel, OK.'

'My place,' she insisted.

Even his eyeballs hurt.

'No. Not now.' He tapped his wrist where his watch had been. Even that sent pains shooting through his skull.

Nadia let go of his arm and stood still. For a moment he thought she had given up, that he could go.

'I really have to go,' he said, trying to smile. Only it wasn't a smile. More like a crooked smirk. 'I am sorry,' he added lamely. 'Maybe another time, hey?'

She spat, then. At his feet. Hawked the spittle up from the back of her throat – an accumulation of booze, cigarette smoke and God knows what else had lodged there overnight – and spurted it forcefully out of her mouth, the stream of phlegm striking the pavement in front of his toes. Some of it went on his toecaps. Flett's stomach heaved in revolt.

'Fucking homosexual!'

206

Flett glanced about him, embarrassed and immobilized by amazement. Not that there was anybody about to see or hear them, but Flett was terrified of being spotted by a colleague, standing outside the prison with this fiend of a woman. He wanted to get away, expunge it all from his memory.

Flett plunged his hands into his pockets and pulled out the crumpled banknotes that they had returned to him. 'Look— ' he began, with a shrug of his shoulders. He would at least know whether she took money.

'See— '

She certainly looked and saw. As he thrust a fistful of the marks towards her, waving them at her to take them, she stepped in quickly, very close, leant back from the waist, put her shoulder into it. He felt the slap like an electric shock against his face, snapping his head back and turning his cheek scarlet. It was just like a burn. Half his face was stunned by the blow. He put his fingers up to it, testing. His knees felt they would give way. He wanted to throw up, the sea of acidic ooze lapped at the back of his throat. The buildings on either side of the street seemed to lean crazily one way, then lurch back the other. It was like being seasick.

Nadia was off, head held high, high heels tap-tapping along the wet pavement. Several 10-mark notes fluttered into a puddle. He wanted to pick them up but couldn't bend that far without the pavement rushing up to meet him.

Flett's nose started bleeding again. He could taste the blood at the back of his mouth. He told himself he should have known that amateur enthusiasts have their pride.

DAY THREE

13

'And they shall fight every one against his brother.'
ISAIAH 19:2

ROSSO OPENED HIS EYES. THE FLINTY GREY PRE-DAWN LIGHT MADE them smart, but he had no wish to slip back into sleep again. Quite the contrary: he felt clear-headed, alert. A deep, seemingly dreamless sleep had somehow purged his troubles, calmed him. It was the feeling of someone who takes a pain-killing pill for toothache; the ache is gone, is only dimly remembered. If there had been firing during the night, it had not been sufficiently noisy or close to wake him. The urgent need he felt for Tanja, the sad prick of conscience over Sabina, his suspicions that he was in some way being made to look a fool – these tumultuous feelings seemed to belong to someone else. Rosso rolled onto his back. I know what I must do. He stretched out his arm, pushing his hand through the bedclothes, feeling them grow cold as his fingers moved away from his own body. There was no-one on the other side. Rosso was the sole occupant. Tanja must have left for the hospital. He had the delicious sense the naturally solitary have of being alone. He straightened his legs, increasing his territory. He felt insanely happy, whole. I don't have to justify my own feelings to myself.

Rosso felt brave enough to attempt a strip wash.

Two-litre plastic Coke bottles, cut into tubes and fitted together, linked the gutter that ran along the edge of the roof over the balcony with a large ribbed drum. He took a yellow plastic bucket from the kitchen, set it down beneath the tap on the side of the canister. He wore a woollen check dressing-gown over his musty clothes, and shoes without socks, the shoes themselves cracked and worn from constant use in the snow and wet. Water dribbled reluctantly from the tap. The canister was full – there must have been 30 litres of snowmelt in there – but much of it was frozen hard. He would have to wait.

When finally Rosso shuffled inside with three-quarters of a bucketful the sun was coming up, lightening the sky in the east, turning it the colour of gun-metal blue.

The last clean underwear and socks: he pressed them to his face, smelling the soap, the wood smoke, before setting them down on the floor next to a towel. Would he live long enough to need another change of clothing? He put the bucket close to the bath, panting with effort. On the rim of the bath itself he placed a bar of soap and a large plastic cup. He stripped quickly, stepping into the bath and squatting down. The enamel was icy to the touch. He tried to ignore the cold eating into the soles of his bare feet. He squatted, careful to keep his testicles clear of the white enamel. Around him were the accessories of domestic life, of an era of peace, of inconsequential and material routine: the hand towels, the three toothbrushes in the yellow toothbrush mug, the soap dish with its picture of rabbits, the bottles of shampoo and conditioner from Austria, smaller bottles of mysterious feminine lotions and fragrances, the woolly, sky-blue bath mat, the lavatory brush primly upright in its plastic holder.

This is how Bukovac died. In a bath like this one, surrounded by the trivia of a normal life.

With a grunt he lifted the bucket over the side and put it directly in front of him. Scooping up the water in a cup, he poured it quickly over his back, gasping, furiously dipping and pouring again and again, then his arms, his chest, his groin, his neck. Rosso stood, wet his hands, picked up the soap and rubbed himself down with it, working it into a lather, paying particular attention to his neck, abdomen, armpits, his feet. He worked frantically, gasping with the impact of the cold water. Finally he wet his hair, rubbed in soap. He had used up half the water. The rest was for sluicing away the suds. His head ached with the chill as he splashed, soaped and poured. He stepped out carefully, snatched up the towel and rubbed himself down briskly, seeing his own skin redden with the combination of cold and abrasive drying, the goose bumps standing out on his chest and thighs, spreading like the flush of measles. Below him, in the bottom of the bath, a grey rivulet of dirt made its way towards the plug hole. He had spent his last night in the place that had been his home for more years than he wanted to remember and all he could think of was the torn body of a heroin addict.

It was like old times; well, almost.

The wrecked furniture had been pushed to the far end of the detectives' room, the rest of the desks and chairs organized into neat ranks facing Rosso's corner. But it was the hubbub of voices, the sight of people milling about, the drifting haze of cigarette smoke, the litter of styrofoam cups that had held the brandy, sljivovica, rather than coffee by the sweetish odour that hung in the room, the bursts of laughter, the flourishing of writing pads, the cheerful curses, the holstered guns – the general clatter of a working incident room – that reminded Rosso of better times. And just like those better days, the noise dropped appreciably as he sauntered in among them, walked to the front, turned and put his rear against the edge of the leading desk. He waited while they turned towards him, broke away from their little huddles, set aside the gossip, picked up their belongings, hid the bottles, drifted over, nudged one another, borrowed pens, dug notebooks out of pockets. Here's the boss – watch out! Looking at him now, seeing his wet hair carefully combed, the attempt at a shave, the dab of tissue paper where he had cut himself with the blunt blade; noticing the clean shirt. He waited, a patient, even serene, expression on his face, looking over their heads and seeing only what he wanted to see, until the silence was absolute.

'Who wants to answer the phones?' General laughter. Coping with the flood of calls in any big investigation was the most unpopular job on any team.

'It's a serious question. Because there aren't any lines, or very few, it means more legwork and that means a lot more paper. Zlata? Vladimir?' Rosso looked up. The pair sat together over on the right. They had already been briefed, knew what to expect. The garrulous Zlata and the fastidious Vlad were well matched. She was a lateral thinker, he was methodical.

'You'll maintain the incident book, help your colleagues with their notes and reports.' They nodded in tandem, dutifully. Rosso wondered if they realized how overwhelmed they would be in a few hours. If so, they gave no sign of it.

The superintendent got to his feet, hands in his trouser pockets, and strolled the few steps to the back wall, to the big white board below the blank clock faces. He moved slowly, relishing the sense of tension building, aware that they watched him closely, took their lead from him. Rosso picked up a felt-tip pen and with quick strokes, as if wielding knife, he wrote the murder victim's name across the board in blood-red capital letters: Zeljka Bukovac.

'You're going to like this,' he said. He paused for effect, looked around at the half-circle of faces. What he lacked in people, in cars, in telephones and in time, he knew he would have to make up for in hard work and hard work would depend on how they would follow him. Looking at them now, he realized he had at best eight hours before they started to wilt through sheer exhaustion. Four hours of hard work in this city was equivalent to three or four days in peacetime.

This would be the equivalent of a week with little food and no sleep. He would lead them now, drive them later, cajole, threaten and bully until they turned their backs on him.

However anybody thought about it, what he was proposing, what he was putting them through, was near-hopeless.

'The murder victim,' he said.

He wrote the name Dusan underneath.

'The victim's ex-husband.'

He spoke confidently, with a flourish, like a magician announcing one new trick after another.

Rosso faced the circle of police again. 'Bukovac – Serbian, a dentist, found dead, presumed drowned in a bath at a Novo Grad flat.' Here he heard a suppressed laugh, a muttered curse, an excited exchange of whispers. 'Time of death: up to forty-eight hours previous to the discovery of her remains.'

Rosso put the pen down. Now it was time for the truth.

'We have no autopsy report. We don't even have a body.' The room was utterly still. Their eyes were all on his face, waiting to see if he would falter, if he would show fear.

'Dusan's whereabouts unknown.' People stirred and fidgeted. He could see them thinking it was a lead, an obvious line of inquiry, something to get their teeth into. Would they know, had they guessed, that the officer who had taken the call had bolted, deserted his post?

'The dead woman was a member of a committee of people who were called, or perhaps called themselves, Loyal Serbs. Three other members of that committee are believed' – he put the stress on 'believed' – 'to have been detained by the military. We don't know where they are.' Someone – Rosso could not see who it was – sniggered at this.

'The flat is in a block called, regrettably, the Monkey House. I'm sure some of you at least know where it is and why it is called that. I should also point out that it's under the jurisdiction of the so-called special forces and you won't get much change out of them.'

215

Out of the corner of his eye he saw Salco and Taher exchange glances.

'Bukovac was a snitch. She was also a user.' Rosso paused, letting the information sink in, watching some officers scribble furiously in their notebooks.

'There was a struggle. I personally suspect the victim died from strangulation, but it may well be academic. There was some bruising, a lot of blood. Whoever did it appears to have returned to the scene to look for something, something they failed to find. The place has been ransacked, the woman's remains removed.'

'They?' Rosso could not identify the voice.

'Yes. They. More than one.'

'Witnesses?'

It was the hoarse voice of Murad, a young and newly appointed detective constable.

'One.'

'Will he or she – the witness – be able to identify the killers?' Murad was very ambitious, having spent years studying pathology and reading sociological treatises on the criminal mind with the aid of a State scholarship. A graduate, no less. He had not bargained on a war blighting his upward mobility.

'I believe so.'

'This flat. Did she live there?' Murad again.

'No, I don't believe so.'

'A fuck-pad.' A voice from the back Rosso didn't recognize.

'A safe house,' said Anil, raising his eyebrows at Rosso. As if to say, well, what can you expect?

'Not very safe, then, was it.' People were turning, craning their necks to look at the cynic, whoever he was.

Rosso pulled himself up, away from the desk he had been leaning against.

'We don't have a lot of time.' He walked up to them now, turned and walked along the rank of desks, letting them see him close up, letting them feel his self-confidence.

'How long?' The voice was Anil's. He thrust his right hand with its missing four fingers up in the air like a schoolboy asking a question in class.

'Midnight.'

'What then?' It was Boris this time.

Rosso looked at Anil's partner with a half-smile, said nothing, locking Boris's gaze with his eyes until the lame sergeant looked away again. Rosso walked back, took up his old position, standing with legs apart, hands on hips.

'Any more questions before we start?'

They were silent, impatient to begin.

'A couple of administrative matters. We have three cars, and all three have full tanks. There is very little in reserve, so don't waste it. Samir – where are you? Ah, I see you now – you're in charge of the transport.'

Samir suffered from a perforated ulcer and constant diarrhoea. The detective inspector should not really be working at all, but he had the quiet authority and common sense to keep them from fighting one another for the wheels.

They were starting to gather up their belongings.

'Oh, I almost forgot – the good news.' Rosso had to raise his voice over the hubbub to make himself heard.

'We will be fed, courtesy of the kitchen staff at the Holiday Inn.' A ragged cheer went up. 'It won't be much. Stew for lunch, stew for supper, stew for breakfast . . .'

'Rats or rabbits, boss?' shouted Anil.

'What's the difference? They're the same size nowadays.'

Talking to them, performing his appointed role, was like being on stage. It was an act. Perhaps the last, the most important of Rosso's career. There was no prompt this time, no lighting, no props. The pitch of his voice, what he did with his hands, how he moved – it all sent a constant flow of messages back to the tableau of men and women lounging in a half-circle around him. They were the most cynical of critics; they would know a false move, a gesture of self-doubt, a voice cracked by excessive self-control, a fake effort at over-familiarity, a falling back on a formality that no longer held any meaning. They were students of human nature, schooled on the unforgiving streets of the city. He had to relax them, take the edge out of their laughter, bring them together, draw them into becoming players themselves. Make them feel wanted, make them feel needed, coax them into playing on a team again.

We can make a difference. We are in the right.

All the while he was talking he did his arithmetic, counting, breaking the numbers up, splitting them, reorganizing them, staring out and placing faces only dimly remembered with case histories, seeking out the doers from the thinkers, the dawdlers from the activists, the corporate spirits from the unreconstructed individualists, the sceptical from the idealistic, the footsloggers from the intellectuals; matching their faces turned to him with his memory of their performance ratings and the dusty case files on his office floor.

Nineteen officers, sixteen hours, three cars.

Six had failed to show. Seven, if he included Vasic.

It was a huge bluff and he had to sell it.

It worked out this way: Zlata and Vladimir keeping the incident book, minding the paperchase of investigation; the two biggest uniformed patrolmen, Davor and Munir, the wannabe detectives, at the door with Kalashnikovs, carrying spare clips, grenade launchers; looking mean, looking the part. The gentle, pale Samir in charge of transport; the irrepressible Anil and Boris, Taher and Salco, Zoran and Vejlko would form three teams for the graveyard checks, the search for the woman's remains.

Seven left.

Fatima and Ratimir would visit the clinic.

Ante and Nenad the records office, if it was still there.

Drina and Andrei – both Serb, both detective constables – would tackle Serbs who might know something. They would slip into the Monkey House unnoticed and unarmed, without drawing attention to themselves, without letting on they were police.

He, Rosso, would visit Mahmud and little Noor.

They would regroup for lunch, then he would divide them up again, redistribute them and personally lead the arrest. He had planned it carefully and he would not tell them about it until he had to. He had confided in no-one, could trust no-one.

'Chief?'

Rosso looked up from his papers.

'Me and Boris,' said Anil, giving a nervous shrug of his thin shoulders and shuffling, shifting his weight from one foot to the other. Was it possible he was feeling bad about the dope and drink party the previous morning? When Rosso stared up at him, looked into his face, Anil seemed to wince. For his part, Anil's partner Boris didn't try and squeeze into the office but gazed through the glass partition instead.

'Me and Boris,' Anil said again, clearing his throat. 'We went to Vasic's place as you asked.'

'Yes?'

'There was no-one there, chief.'

'And?'

'We checked with the neighbours.' Anil cast a glance over his shoulder at Boris, as if seeking his help. Boris did not make any attempt to move closer. He stayed where he was.

'Go on.'

'They said he and his wife left yesterday morning, quite early. They came out of the house together – well, it's a maisonnette or something like that, you know, on two floors – and got into a car and were driven away. The neighbours couldn't remember exactly when, but they saw them leave, carrying bags and a suitcase. Sometime between six and seven.'

'Did they say where they were going?'

'No chief.'

'What else?'

Anil shrugged, looked away.

'Come along, tell me.'

'They seemed to believe – the neighbours, that is – that the departure had something to do with Luka.'

'I see. How many neighbours?'

'Two. Two separate addresses.'

'Statements?'

'Yeah.'

'What did the neighbours say about Luka?' That quick, over-the-shoulder glance at Boris.

'That he helped them get out of the city.' Anil shrugged.

'Anything more precise? What about the car?'

'Nothing on the registration. We did have a look round.'

'You broke in.'

'We found an open window.'

'Sure you did. And?'

'They don't seem to have taken much, but they were in a hurry. Clothes scattered about, a suitcase full of stuff left behind near the front door, food on the table. That kind of thing: people in a big rush.'

'Did the neighbours say anything about Luka's relationship with Vasic?'

Anil shook his head.

'Sure?'

'Well there was the usual crap about the cops being in Luka's pocket. You know, them never wanting for food, us neither. You know the sort of stuff.'

'I'm not sure I do. Anyway, thank you. Mention this trip of yours to anyone?'

'No, chief. You said not to.'

'Keep it that way. Make sure your partner keeps his big mouth shut too. I don't want the troops demoralized.'

'No problem. Boss—'

'Yes?'

'Don't take it too much to heart. He was always a bent copper. We've always known it.'

Rosso decided not to respond to that.

'You're going off to the cemeteries now, aren't you?'

'Sure.'

'You know what to look for? What to ask?'

'Course.'

'Keep your heads down.'

Anil was walking away across the detectives' room with Boris, their feet crunching in the broken glass on the carpet, when Rosso called them back. The superintendent waited until they were both inside his office this time.

'No parties today, right?'

'Right, chief,' said Boris and glanced at Anil.

'None of that filthy weed. No drink, either. Hear me?'

'OK, boss. No problem.'

'I hope not. For your sakes. I'm relying on you. This is too important to fuck up. Right?'

'Right,' said Boris, standing crookedly on his false leg.

'Right,' said Anil. He lifted his right hand in salute, the hand with only one finger, his thumb.

Rosso felt he had done all he could. For now.

'I brought the gas,' said Flett, pulling the passenger door shut. The Yugo seemed to list under Flett's weight. 'Three jerrycans. I'm sorry I was late and missed the briefing.'

'That's OK,' said Rosso. 'Thanks for the extra petrol. It could make all the difference.'

'I had some problems.'

'I heard.'

'You did?'

'Sure. The military police locked you up in a civilian jail, remember?'

'I had no idea where the fuck I was. Who they were. They took my Rolex.' Flett spoke in an aggrieved voice, and looked away from Rosso, suddenly taking an interest in the view out of the passenger's side window. He was embarrassed, Rosso realized. 'Can't help you there I'm afraid. Not with the watch.'

Flett had no desire to pursue the subject of his latest public outrage, so he changed tack. He was lucky to be alive. Rosso tried not to seem to stare, but he could not help noticing that Flett's nose was badly swollen and there was a bruise ripening on one cheek, just below his left eye. He looked grey. That was probably the hangover.

'So what's the story?'

'That's for you to decide.'

'I meant to say what's the issue, what's going down?'

'It's a murder investigation.'

'So what,' Flett said flatly. 'There are stiffs all over the fucking place, what's special about this one?'

Selling Flett the bluff was possibly the most important part of Rosso's scheme. The reporter was irritable, his head hurt, his dignity and his nose smarting from the previous night's misadventures. Rosso modified his plan, resolving not to tell Flett everything, not all at once – instead just enough to keep him interested, enough to let him put the pieces Rosso had selected together.

They were turning onto Sniper's Alley.

'Why are we taking your car?' Flett frowned.

'Yours attracts too much attention.'

'Those guys up there on the hills aren't fooled.'

'I'm not talking about them,' Rosso said, jerking his head in the direction of the woods and the Serb gun positions, 'I'm talking about the place we're going.'

Rosso told Flett about the body, the way it was found in the bath, the manner of its disappearance, the state of the apartment, the dead woman's membership of the Serb committee, the detention, so far unconfirmed by the military, of Misic and his colleagues. He did not mention Vasic. He said nothing of Sabina's departure, nor the manner in which Luka had helped her on her way with a hard currency 'loan'. He omitted his own journey with Luka to the godowns and subsequently the front line at Ilidza and Stup the previous day, and decided to say nothing of his god-daughter's warning that the police force would be formally disbanded within a matter of hours.

It was deception, certainly.

A deal must have been struck.

Rosso did not know it, he assumed it.

The interior minister, responsible for law and order and to whom Rosso reported, wanted Luka's thugs off the streets. The defence minister, in charge of the external defence of the gradually shrinking territory of a sovereign Bosnia, had his reasons for wanting Luka brought to book: the Army's rank-and-file anger at blatant profiteering and lawlessness in their capital. The Army also wanted to get its hands on Luka's resources in the form of men and material.

How else could Rosso explain the military manoeuvres, the plea for Luka's men to move into the front lines, the assurance – without which Luka would not comply – that the civil police were to be disbanded and incorporated into the government army?

Rosso said none of this to Flett.

Luka was hungry for power. Luka saw great opportunities opening up to him. He wanted legitimacy. He demanded a place at the top table, above the salt. He wanted to call the shots.

His mistake had been killing Bukovac.

'So you really want to bring him down.'

'Who?'

'Luka. You want to clip the wings of the man who many people say effectively saved Sarajevo in '92. Do you really think you'll get away with it?'

'What sort of city will it be if we don't?'

Flett was silent for a moment.

'Have you lost the desire to live, Superintendent?'

'Not at all.'

'He has many friends.'

They glanced at one another, Flett hugging himself for warmth in the passenger seat, the policeman gripping the wheel, hunched forward to concentrate on the road. Rosso recognized in Flett's eye at that moment the same look he saw when Flett had crawled across the floor of his office; the glimmer of panic, the uncomprehending look of fright of an animal prodded up the ramp to the slaughterhouse.

'Have you gone crazy along with everyone else?'

'You have nothing to fear, Branston. You're an observer. You're doing your job. I don't ask any more of you.'

It was a lie, Rosso knew. He was asking much more.

'I thought you were so – sensible. Why are you doing this?'

Flett had his notebook open and was taking off the top of his pen. He was clenching his jaw. It was the way some people acted when they were afraid. They got angry.

But he wanted the story, as Rosso knew he would.

The chief of detectives thought carefully before replying. Rosso was fond of Flett. Again he experienced the sympathy, the triumphant this-hurts-me-more-than-it-hurts-you of the interrogations; at the point at which the detective finally breaks a suspect, gently pushing a typed statement in front of him or her, almost affectionately curling the exhausted prisoner's reluctant, frozen fingers around the pen and pointing to the place where he must sign. Always it was the same, the words said soothingly. Help yourself. Make it easy on yourself. Sign, and we'll bring you a hot meal. Sign, and you can see your children. Sign, and you can sleep. Sign, and we'll bring you a blanket. You take away whatever it is they need most, and then offer it back as a concession.

Now Rosso had Flett he must take care not to lose him.

'Branston,' Rosso said finally. 'You're an American. You know more about the rule of law than I do.'

It was turning into a perfectly lovely day, Tanja thought, one of winter majesty. Many people, gazing up at the sky, would not live to see the warmer weather still months off. But even they could turn away from their own dreary preoccupations and watch big, fluffy clouds scud across the hills. But what made today truly special for Sarajevans, peering cautiously from their windows and doors, was the immense quiet. It was still well below freezing, but it was going to be one of those days when mothers hate themselves for refusing to let their restive children play outside in the entrances of countless makeshift basement and garage shelters.

Someone once said, or wrote – and Tanja could not for the life of her remember who it was – that a man's dying is more the survivors' affair than his own. How true of Sarajevo, where burying the dead was a distinctively risky affair for the living, so much so that nowadays the dead were very often buried where they fell, in the gardens of their own homes, down some muddy alley, in a weed-filled plot where the corner shop had been. Tanja knew many such places. The graves were shallow, hastily scraped in the soggy, cold earth to reduce the risk of disease from corpses which, in the very first days of the war, had been left to rot where they lay because of the prevalence of snipers. Then the bodies were partially eaten by packs of stray dogs, turned out of their homes by people unable to feed them and soon maddened by the general hunger and terror of exploding artillery shells. Even now the cold, the rain, the ice, shifted, shrank or washed away the soil, revealing the gruesome remains and leaving over the vicinity of each anonymous burial site, that foetid smell of decomposition.

Tanja clambered uphill to Lion cemetery to perform her duties as a standby paramedic, and she overtook dozens of mourners, mostly wearing black, trudging slowly up the same way. Nobody spoke. It took too much effort. The graveyard had once been confined to a tranquil grassy slope, sheltered by the spreading branches of an oak copse at the north-eastern edge of town. In peacetime a more pleasant place to lay one's old bones could hardly be imagined. But by now it was gorged with dead, and the mute, subterranean army, perpetually on parade, had steadily advanced, rank by rank, until it had swelled beyond the confines of tall iron railings, bounded across the street and advanced inexorably once more, invading the Olympic football stadium as death's daily harvests steadily sought more real estate for its cold, stiff foot-soldiers corrupting in the deep clay. It was an uneven struggle. It was no sport. There was only ever one winner: death.

Over there, as Tanja entered by the top gate, was the corps

of Moslem martyrs, God rest them; neat rows of wooden, coffin-shaped grave-markers bearing the names of the dead, their birth dates and the dates on which they were cut down. Pensioners, widows, teenage brides and the little mounds that marked the remains of infants; they were all there. Entire families lay together (if together can be said to apply to a narrow hole 6 feet deep and 18 inches wide). To the right, as Tanja looked downhill, a division of Orthodox crosses, row upon row of Serbs, forming companies and divisions, households, streets, neighbourhoods; all brought low by their own so-called ethnic kin. Further up, closer to the young woman, almost under her feet, were the stark black crosses of the Roman Catholics, the city's Croats, swarming downhill in death's final charge.

Across all of it, the lingering, sweetish-sour smell.

It was wide open, bereft of cover. The grass, every available square foot, had been used for graves. The oaks and chestnuts had long been splintered by artillery attacks and finally uprooted to make way for new additions to the daily death lists. Tanja felt naked. Her instinct was to try and curl up behind the plinth on which the Lion itself rested, an old and ancient lump of statuary unrecognizable as any kind of animal. Instead she pushed into the crowd of mourners, feeling some comfort from the living, breathing flesh around her.

The gravediggers, elderly weather-beaten men with skin dark like leather, flat caps on their heads, shirtsleeves rolled up and sucking on their toothless gums, worked quickly with their long-handled spades, speaking urgently to the ulema – the Moslem priests – to hurry their prayers.

The living crowd squatted in the freezing mud, down on their haunches among the burial mounds and cupping their hands as supplicants, asking God to raise up the spirits of the newly dead. They moved their lips. The quick moan of prayer passed like a wind across the place and the dead, lying on wooden frames and covered in white shrouds, fine cotton like cheesecloth, were manhandled quickly over the heads of the mourners and clumsily pushed into the gaping holes. The gravediggers hardly paused, but tossed the first spadefuls of dirt onto the corpses, eight of them. Then they moved from one to the other, shovelling steadily, shovelling fast.

God is great, muttered the crowd, though for the life of her, Tanja couldn't see it.

Further up the hill a woman flung herself onto a Croat burial mound among the wilting flowers, shouting her daughter's name. White-faced and shaking, the dead girl's husband stared, face ashen, eyes blank. For his part, the girl's father cried, stricken by great heaving sobs that shook his grizzled cheeks. Tanja looked away. Somehow a grown man crying was always a terrible sight.

She was telling herself it was just a job, and that emotions were best left behind, when the first shell came over. It seemed to rattle like a pebble in a tin can before it fell out of the sky.

The blast knocked Tanja over.

One moment she was on her feet, the next she was down.

She fell on her side in the mud and immediately she scrambled up, her mind set on getting to the wounded as fast as possible to stop the bleeding with Misic's bandages, to keep them breathing. Something hit her low down on the right, like a vicious punch, spinning her round, making her grunt as the air was forced out of her. She was down again, on her face this time. She felt annoyed, irritated. It was like missing a bus, tripping over a pavement or failing to get a good table at a favourite restaurant.

It was embarrassing.

There was soil in her teeth and her tongue bled.

If there was any emotion it was one of being inconvenienced. She spat the filth from her mouth and pulled the sleeve of her jacket across her chin. Damn!

She felt as if she had been hit by a car. She managed to turn onto her back and looked for the wound.

I'm hit, fuck it.

Whatever it was had ripped open her clothes, tearing the cotton and wool away. There was no pain, no gush of lifeblood. She felt a sudden surge of adrenalin-fed well-being.

227

I'm all right. I'm OK. She wanted to laugh with delight. Black and blue but alive.

Tanja tried to get up. She heard what sounded like a long murmuring sound, an animal moan. She sought to focus on it, only to find it came from all around her. The crowd into which she had plunged for comfort, for shelter, now lay around her and she realized the strange, squeaky sound, like a leather cloth rubbing against glass, was composed of a hundred whimperings, a hundred groans and shrieks of pain and panic.

They needed her. She must get to them. That was why she had come here in the first place.

Help me. Help me. The words were those of a woman, repeated over and over again.

It took her some time – seconds probably, but to Tanja they felt like an age – before she realized they were her words. Shut up, she told herself. The tinny sound coming out of her mouth stopped. You fool. You don't need help. Get up. She struggled to get some control back, control over her breathing, over her trembling limbs. There was some sort of cloud like vapour in front of her eyes. She shook her head to clear her vision. In front of her she saw two men dragging a woman through the mud. They carried her by the legs and arms and her head hung back, her hair on the ground, her jaw slack. She looked like a gutted deer carried by poachers. It was like a silent black-and-white movie; not really real. It couldn't be.

There was a second impact. Tanja felt it rather than heard it. It made her teeth rattle in her skull. Mortar, Tanja thought. Fucking close. She could smell the explosive. It tore a huge column of earth skywards. She watched bits of things fly up, twisting and turning and start to drift back down, lazily. Pretty, she thought, until she realized they were human. Bits of people. Bits of people who had already died once, been buried. Bits too of the mourners who would shortly join their loved ones in the football ground. The dead and the dying.

Only now she saw the blood on her ski pants. Both legs were shiny, wet and warm with it.

God in heaven but there's a lot of it.

Must be somebody else's blood. Had to be.

There was no pain. Well, Tanja tl ought, I won't have to travel far for my funeral. Someone was bending down, his face close to hers, saying something. She tried to smile back. Why was the light fading, she wanted to know. The stranger said something to her, but she couldn't catch the words. She saw his lips moving. He was friendly enough. Their faces were almost touching. Did she know him? There was something familiar about the face but the thought slipped away from her, she couldn't hold it. Was this the way it all ended? Like this? So swiftly? Please, oh please, not yet. Was it an artery? Must stop the bleeding.

Why couldn't she hear what he was saying?

Tanja's face was contorted in a silent howl of terror, but she didn't know it.

14

'Only one step separates fanaticism from barbarism.'
DENIS DIDEROT

UP IN THE SKY ABOVE THE BATTLEFIELD, NOOR TURNED TO HER
father and, cupping her mouth with one hand, whispered into
his ear. Mahmud mumbled his reply yet was aware his visitors
might take offence. Every now and then the child would sit back
and peer at Flett, turning her face to him. It wasn't clear to the
newspaperman how much she could see. Perhaps he was no more
than a blur, although they sat only feet away.

'What are they saying?' Flett asked Rosso. The reporter and the
policeman sat side by side on a convenient concrete beam that ran
along the floor. Their hosts had thoughtfully spread a flattened
cardboard box across the top to protect the visitors' buttocks from
the cold and their clothes from the rough surface. Mahmud and his
daughter sat on something similar opposite them. The rudimentary
furniture reminded Flett of camping, the sense of being in a tent

emphasized by the wooden rafters and tiles reaching steeply up to form a peak above their heads. Here and there the sky could be seen where the roofing had been wrenched away by gunfire, letting misty shafts of light pierce the gloom.

'They're talking about you,' the detective replied. 'Noor is curious. She asks if you're a celebrity, like the film stars and footballers she hears about, and why all foreigners in Sarajevo seem rich. Mahmud is telling her you're not wealthy in your own country, only you seem rich here because the war has made all honest Bosnians poor, and your employers provide you foreigners with everything you need to do your work. Noor wants to know if you're good or bad and Mahmud says he doesn't know, but there must be some good in you to be here at all.'

Rosso grinned. Flett's neck and ears were pink with embarrassment.

'Now Noor is asking if you are married. She wants to know if you bleed like other people, if you die when you get hit.'

Flett looked aghast.

'When? Not if, but when? She asked that?'

'Sure. Mahmud is saying you're no different, human like the rest of us, except that you have better protection in an armoured car and in your body armour and helmet. He doesn't know if you're married but he doesn't think you are or you wouldn't be here. Your wife wouldn't let you.'

'I don't very much like being talked about.'

'Tough. People talk about you all the time. You're like something from outer space to them. You're healthy. You have unlimited cash. You eat a cooked meal every day. You have influence. You can get out any time you want. Maybe you should study Serbo-Croat properly and they would stop doing it in front of you, but you won't stop them doing it altogether. Anyway, Mahmud seems to take a rather charitable view of your vile nature, don't you agree?'

'I don't like it.'

'Don't be a prick. Try and be useful to somebody. At least you

231

can give them some entertainment in your otherwise short and brutish life.'

'Thanks a lot.'

'My pleasure.'

'Can I name the girl in my story?'

'No.'

'Can I say she's a blind girl?'

'No way.'

'What then?'

'Say it's a he for a start. A middle-aged he. Give your make-believe he a false name and a job and for God's sake make it realistic.'

'That's a lie.'

'Sure. You want to tell the truth? Then you'll have to lie a little to get to it. You have to protect these people.'

'I'm not sure I can do that.'

'You will. Otherwise I'll lock you up and throw away the key and you won't have this story or any others for quite a while. What is it you're always telling me: that a reporter is only as good as his last story? When was your last story, Branston? It certainly wasn't last night.'

Mahmud wanted to know what they were talking about this time. Rosso explained, and Mahmud chuckled at the notion of Rosso putting the famous American reporter away behind bars. They had to wait while he explained some of it to the girl. Noor got down off her seat then and came over to Flett, and put out a hand, and tentatively touched him. She traced his shoulder first, then solemnly felt his face, running her fingers down it, outlining his mouth and eyes. He was taken aback by the attention. How intuitive of the child, Rosso thought, to grasp that this reporter would be won over, when touched by a child. It was a calculated charm of a particularly feminine kind, and very effective.

'I can't see you clearly,' Noor told Flett in Serbo-Croat. 'But I know you wouldn't harm us. You won't hurt my daddy and me, will you?' Rosso translated and Flett asked, in a voice oddly strangled, that Rosso explain in turn to the father and daughter

232

that he would say and write nothing that would bring them into any more danger than they already faced by speaking out. Noor then wanted to know what was wrong with Flett's face, why it was swollen, but to Mahmud's obvious amusement Rosso would not translate that, or his reply.

'A night on the town, eh?' bellowed Mahmud, shaking with mirth to Flett's obvious distaste. For reasons that Rosso could not quite fathom, Flett seemed to want to create a good impression with the nine-year-old and her father.

Rosso had taken Flett to Block Six in the Alipasino Polje development. It was less exposed than the other towers and was unlikely to be closely watched by Luka's men. Would they too know the buildings were linked by passageways under the eaves where Mahmud waged his solitary war as a sniper? Probably, but it was worth trying. They had tramped up to the roof where Mahmud met them and led them by a circuitous route through breeze-block corridors and over dozens of water-pipes, squeezing past water tanks and chimney-stacks, clambering up and down ladders until eventually, begrimed and their throats dry, they arrived at Block Nine overlooking Serb lines – just so the American reporter could say in his report he'd been in, or rather on, the apartment block – the Monkey House – where the dentist had been murdered. Noor proudly made the guests coffee – begged, borrowed or stolen coffee – on her little stove and she told the American her story while he took notes and Mahmud watched and Rosso translated.

'There's one more thing,' Mahmud said.

'Yes?' Rosso was impatient to return to police headquarters, and kept looking at his watch.

'We didn't say anything before about it,' Mahmud continued, looking quickly at Noor. 'We weren't quite sure – we thought . . .' he added helplessly.

'It's OK,' said Rosso. 'Really. No problem.'

'It's something Noor found in the flat.'

They waited while Mahmud extracted two objects from a hiding place: inside the wheel-house above one of the lift shafts. No-one

233

went there any more because there was no power for the lifts. There was no need for maintenance. And whatever they were, one was well wrapped with black polythene and held together with broad elastic bands. Noor followed behind Mahmud, carrying the second object, an old tin, rusty and without a cover. It looked like one of those ribbed containers of powdered milk supplied by the UN agencies, but the picture of the red cow on a yellow field had long since worn off. The girl clutched it with both arms, hugging it to herself, as if the contents were precious.

'Where was it, Noor?' Rosso asked.

'The package was behind the lavatory. The tank—'

'She means the cistern,' said Mahmud. 'Taped to it.'

'Why did you look there?' Rosso pressed the girl.

'People often hide things there,' she said simply. This time it was Mahmud who looked sheepish, as if she had admitted to stealing valuables from empty homes and he had instructed her, trained her to seek out likely hiding-places.

'You went back?'

Noor nodded.

Mahmud was a sort of part-time Sarajevo Fagin, Flett decided. The sniper handed the dusty package to Rosso. They went back to their seats.

'Go on,' Mahmud said, nodding. 'Open it.'

Inside what turned out to be a voluminous bin-liner was another plastic bag, this one of clear cellophane. It had the consistency and weight of 2 kilos of sugar. The package had the same powdery, crunchy feel, but the contents were light brown in colour. Rosso turned it over in his hands, hefted it as if trying to gauge its weight.

'Brown sugar,' said Mahmud. 'Least, that's what we believed when we saw it. Noor thought it quite a prize. So did I, at first. That's why she brought it back.'

'It was wrapped like this?' Rosso wanted to know.

'Sure.'

'What happened then?'

234

'Well, I cut open a corner, licked a finger—'

'And?' Flett was fidgeting with impatience.

'They do call it brown sugar,' said Mahmud. 'But it's not the kind you put in your tea. It has a street value here in Sarajevo of maybe 6,000 marks. We really had no idea.'

'Morphine sulphate,' said Rosso.

'Right. Look, if we'd known . . .'

'Good thing Noor didn't try and eat it,' Rosso said mildly.

Flett put out his hands and Rosso carefully handed him the package. He weighed it, sniffed it, and handed it back.

'Penultimate stage in the process of reducing opium to heroin,' said Rosso. 'This is as far as anyone needs to go in terms of shipping it. It's down to one eleventh in volume. It's already high-grade, uncut heroin. To produce the fine white crystals that will be "cut" or adulterated by the dealers in Berlin or London takes one very simple step. A high-school chemistry student could do it.'

'Are you saying this is Luka's racket?'

'You got it in one, Branston,' Rosso said.

'Headed for where?'

'Western Europe, Zurich, Amsterdam, Brussels.'

'Holy shit.'

'Figure it out for yourself: the stuff for sale in Vienna or Hamburg is maybe 300 dollars an ounce, or 4,800 a pound.'

'That's 10,500 dollars a kilo,' cut in Flett.

'The two kilos I'm holding will be cut several times over – we're looking at maybe 100,000 dollars right here. Maybe a lot more.'

Mahmud whistled.

'Worth killing for,' grunted Flett.

'That's what they must have been looking for in the flat,' said Mahmud, 'but Noor got to it first.' He put an arm round her narrow shoulders, gave her a squeeze. 'My brave girl.'

Brave perhaps, foolhardy certainly, Rosso thought. Those thugs would have snuffed out her young life for a fraction of what was in that package. She was just lucky.

'It's called a bathtub factory,' said Rosso. 'All you need is a tub,

235

a few tubes and containers, cheesecloth and some clean water from somewhere. Rainwater would have been fine. I reckon Luka had several bathtub factories around town. He probably moved them from place to place, maybe even had a mobile bathtub factory or two on the back of a truck so he could take them wherever water could be found. Almost impossible to track down.'

'And the tin?' Flett wanted to know.

Noor brought it over to the two men. They glanced inside. It was full of hypodermic syringes, mostly cracked or broken, as well as discarded needles.

'We find them on the staircases,' said Mahmud. 'Particularly Block Nine. Also outside, on the ground. It's the kids, mostly, shooting up at night. We pick the syringes and needles up because they're dangerous lying about.'

Rosso shook the tin, put it down by his feet.

Noor sat on her father's knee and hugged him. 'Now you know why we're willing to talk,' said Mahmud. 'They're getting our young people hooked. To pay for their habit they're selling themselves – another Luka sideline – to the UN troops.'

Flett was turning the package over in his hands, as if looking for the corner where Mahmud had sampled it.

'Holy shit is right,' said Flett. 'Mind if I have a taste?'

Rosso stared at him.

'For research,' said Flett quickly. 'I need to know it's the genuine article.'

'Take my word for it,' Rosso said. 'It is.'

Waiters carried lunch from the hotel kitchens in two big aluminium tubs and with the help of three constables, they lifted them up onto the back of a battered pick-up truck reversed up to the back door. The uniformed policemen were there primarily to protect their colleagues' lunch by keeping at bay the crowd of beggars, lunatics and assorted shell-shocked who customarily gathered outside the hotel at mealtimes in the hope of scouring the dustbins for left-overs. The cauldrons were then driven without further incident to headquarters, down the ramp and into the gloom of the subterranean cavern that doubled as both parking area and basement shelter. Rosso sent his people down in shifts, four at a time, to pick up their food, ladled out into whatever they could find – a few chipped plates, plastic mugs, the odd army canteen, even a garish vase. Zlata fetched Rosso's portion – someone had found him a china soup bowl and a tin spoon. Everyone was given half a loaf of rather stale bread and two small, wizened apples. It was quite an occasion. Work stopped entirely, and officers gathered in small groups to eat together – some squatted on the stairs, others stood about in corridors or cleared their desktops. There was little talk. People were too intent on eating. A twist of newspaper containing salt and pepper was carefully passed from hand to hand. Flett stayed out of the limelight, refusing to eat – he had been reminded by Mahmud and his daughter that, unlike these people, he ate two meals every day, supplemented by all the goodies flown in by his editors at regular, fortnightly intervals. He did not want to appear greedy. In any case he still felt wretched from the previous night. Instead, he watched them wipe their plates scrupulously clean with bread, wolf down the apples, cores and all, and he saw their eyes light up when they smelt coffee. He helped Zlata and Samir distribute it. There weren't enough cups to go round, so those who finished first handed them back to be rinsed out for the next ration. As he moved about the detectives' room, Flett was gratified that no-one asked him about his face and his nose – although Anil gave him a sly, knowing look as the American handed the sergeant his cup.

Only one incident marred the festive atmosphere. Soon after the food arrived and the first detectives were already hungrily spooning the thick gravy and watery potato into their mouths, there was the sound of detonations, a brief rumble, then another, seemingly as harmless and commonplace as a distant summer thunderstorm. It seemed to come from the northern edge of town, but no-one said anything. Perhaps half a minute later they heard sirens and car horns blaring in the streets, a wailing that grew and then faded as the ambulances passed by, then swelled and receded again as they sped back to city hospitals minutes later. Flett saw Rosso's spoon pause, his chin lift, his eyes flicker across the room to the far side as if he was trying to see the incident itself through the walls and broken roofs of neighbouring buildings. Everyone else seemed to freeze, waiting, waiting, and when there were no more impacts the clink and clatter of feeding resumed, the tension evaporating as if nothing had happened. Not to us anyhow, their faces seemed to be saying.

Not here. Not yet.

When the mess was cleared away, Rosso stood before them again. Flett lounged in a far corner, back against the wall, knees drawn up, notebook and tape recorder at the ready. Everyone but Rosso and Flett seemed to be smoking furiously, those without cigarettes cadging them from those who had. Matches flared, were passed around, heads dipped and blue smoke rose to the broken ceiling panels and the fuzz of broken wiring. The idea that anyone should worry about the impact of smoking on his or her health was ludicrous. The only real hazard to health was out there, courtesy of the Cetniks.

'I promised you a progress report,' said Rosso. 'First, we seem to have located the remains of the woman Bukovac. They will be recovered, security permitting, later this afternoon. The body wasn't buried – just dumped – in a vacant plot. Someone tried to burn it, but they didn't use enough petrol or else they were disturbed and had to beat a hasty retreat.'

Rosso pushed himself upright, off the desk, his movement helping to keep their attention. With full bellies so early in the day, many would want to sleep.

'We've also located four hundred litres of acetic anhydride acid – the chemical used to refine opium.

'Most important of all, we have a statement from our witness. The statement has been taken down by hand and has been recorded on tape. It has been independently witnessed.' At this two or three

238

heads turned in Flett's direction. 'Furthermore, narcotics worth several thousand marks have been recovered from the scene of the crime.'

'What now?' It was young Murad again.

'I was coming to that. You've all done a great job. I'm proud of you. In any circumstances this would be regarded as a thoroughly professional investigation. Well done.' Rosso walked up to the first rank of police officers – Samir, Nenad, Andrei, Zlata, Boris and Anil – turned around, and went slowly back to his perch on the edge of the desk. He had their attention. There wasn't a sound.

'Thanks to you, we're on track. We've arrived at possibly the most critical phase.' Rosso wondered how many of them knew, or sensed, the next step. 'You will each be given new duties,' he went on. 'Some of you will be asked to get some rest and come back tonight. If so, you won't win any Brownie points for hanging about. If you're asked to get some rest it's because you can expect to work long hours later. So get your heads down, get some sleep. You hear me?'

They shuffled their feet, muttered to one another. It was an assent of sorts, Rosso decided.

'Samir and Anil have your new assignments. Don't argue with them. If you don't like it, see me. That's all, ladies and gentlemen. Good luck.'

They hardly spoke in Rosso's hatchback all the way there. Boris drove, Rosso sat next to him, Anil and Flett somehow managed to share the rear seat, squeezed in tight, knees up under their chins. They could only manage it if one sat forward and the other leant back. Flett was the only man without pistol and Kalashnikov, but his flak jacket with its heavy ceramic plates gave him the appearance and agility of a medieval man-at-arms. The reporter, putting fresh batteries in his tape recorder, thought he heard Rosso humming to himself as they hurtled downhill to Sniper's Alley and turned left, travelling east. Otherwise, he found his companions' uncharacteristic silence unnerving, and he had that

239

sense once again of being entirely in the hands of other people, his life very much at the whim of circumstance, chance. It was the sense of impending violence and the loss of control over his own fate that he disliked. He was getting used to it, but he didn't like it any the better for being familiar with it. It had somehow been assumed by all involved that he was there for the duration, that he would want to be in on it and he hadn't the heart to draw back now. He told himself he should have said something earlier to Rosso as they left the headquarters, as the police officers loaded their weapons, shoved spare ammunition clips into their pockets, primed grenades, slipped on makeshift body armour or protective vests 'liberated' from UN peacekeepers. One or two even shook hands. Anil and Boris, both wearing Bosnian army fatigues, hugged one another, slapping each other noisily on the back. It seemed to Flett to have some sort of awful finality about it.

Luka arrived at the presidency shortly after what most people would regard as the time of day known as lunch, only not many people in Sarajevo could say they had eaten anything resembling a meal so far that day. The tall young man was seen pulling himself awkwardly from his Mercedes and hobbling up the steps alone, shouting something over his shoulder and pushing himself along with his stick until he vanished into the interior, the doors held wide for him by two members of the presidential guard. Luka's manner was characteristically preoccupied and brusque, his movements impatient, almost as if he were punishing himself in the way that he pumped the stick, propelling his crooked frame forward. The guards, big men with shaved heads, nodded to Luka as he reached the top step. He said nothing in response. They were not obliged to salute him – he wore no uniform – and he did not spare them so much as a glance. He wouldn't have. They weren't his boys and in any case he hated to acknowledge anyone doing him a favour, even if it was merely holding a door open. Once he had passed them, the guards also withdrew, retreating backwards, facing the street, pulling the doors shut behind them.

Fifteen minutes or so passed. The temperature rose perceptibly, and the sky seemed to draw closer, to press down, somehow fastening itself to the hills around the city. The bodyguard who had accompanied Luka got out of the Mercedes, stretched, stamped his feet to get the blood moving, blew on his fingers and ambled over to the escort car, a black Opel. He shouted something, a rear door swung open, he got in with the others – four, all told, and the door shut behind him. They settled back for a long wait. They were used to it, and there were worse things on a wintry afternoon in Sarajevo than sitting together on real leather in a heated car, smoking, playing cards, talking politics or women, or both. They had the car radio on, tuned in to an Italian music station.

It was perhaps twenty minutes after Luka entered the presidency that the wooden doors opened again, making the four gunmen in the Opel sit up with a start, but they relaxed when they saw Bosnian soldiers emerge – not, as they feared, their leader, furiously waving his stick at them.

One of the soldiers, hands on hips, seemed to sniff the air, to study the sky, before walking stiffly down the steps and striding over to the Opel. His companions watched his leisurely progress as the first flakes of snow drifted down, and were whipped away, scattered, by a sudden gust of wind.

The Opel's interior was a fug of body heat and cigarette smoke. The occupants were aware of the steadily approaching uniform, but could not see much of the face below the beret. The soldier halted, rapped sharply on the driver's window with his knuckles, then straightened, taking a step away from the car and turning his back, waiting for them to lower the glass. His movements were diffident, his pistol was holstered, the holster itself fastened. He seemed in no hurry, and there was nothing about his manner that suggested he might pose a threat. As the window slid down, he turned and bent again. They thought he might want a cigarette, or pull rank by telling them to park away from the presidency, on the other side of the avenue. They were always doing that, the presidential detail, flexing their muscles, showing Luka's men who ran the place.

This one was friendly enough, though.

'Hey, boys,' he said, his eyes taking in the four, their weapons leaning against the seats. 'How are we today?' Before anyone could answer, the soldier had thrust a fist in the window, right in the face of the driver, not an inch from the man's nose. The fist held a grenade, the smooth roundness of an egg showing between his fingers, a shiny metallic grey with a hint of red lettering. His other hand, his left, flicked the safety pin, that had obviously been removed from the grenade, through the gap in the window, onto the driver's legs. The driver didn't move. The gesture of throwing in the pin was unambiguous: the soldier had only to open his fist for the live grenade to drop either to the floor of the car, next to the driver's feet, or into his lap. Then it would explode.

They all knew what it was, what it could do.

It was a modern fragmentation grenade: not the old 36 Pattern of World War II. That had been the stock-in-trade of infantrymen the world over for decades and was still widely used in the Balkans, but it was an imperfect tool. For a start it seldom fragmented properly. The most lethal part was the base plate, not the notched cast-iron casing that was more decorative than functional. However, this was an ingenious invention, a weapon of an entirely different order. It contained a tightly compressed stainless-steel spring, coiled up around the core of high explosive and comprising thousands of tiny, razor-sharp chips. Once the grenade detonated, the spring would literally burst in a cloud of tiny steel shards. This was designed to maim rather than kill, based on the cynical but entirely pragmatic premise that it took two able men to haul one injured man to safety, effectively taking three men out of the line. A dead man could be left where he was. Clever, nasty and at this range in the confined space of the Opel, it was abundantly obvious all four would die, lacerated to shreds. There would be no way the bleeding could be stopped, that they could crawl or hide away from the blast.

They would remember, later, that the stranger's voice was calm, assured, even relaxed. The soldier – if indeed that was what he was – smiled throughout.

'Four second fuse, lads, before it tears you a new arse-hole.' The soldier wore a sergeant's stripes. He had that sort of voice, too: paternal. He shook his right fist to make sure they understood that the fragmentation grenade was fitted with a four-second fuse. Four seconds was not much time to do anything very much. A seven-second fuse might have made the world of difference. A man in terror for his life could run a long way in seven seconds.

All the stranger in uniform would have to do to blow them to kingdom come was relax his fingers, let the grenade go. He could walk away from it, confident that the armour plate in the Opel would preserve him from the shower of steel blades.

'We want no trouble,' he said. 'We just want the car. No-one need get hurt. Do as I say and you'll all be home in no time.'

It was the kind of lie a man faced with his own death wants to believe. The soldier's two companions had come up to the car. One stood in front of the bonnet, facing the windscreen. He held his Kalashnikov across his chest, at high port. The third stood off to one side, to the rear of the Mercedes, his assault weapon at waist height, pointed at the back window.

The snow fell thick and fast, great bunches of white feathers, brushing the car, settling on the roof and the edge of the windscreen. It lay on the soldier's shoulders and found creases where his arm, holding the grenade, was bent at the elbow. He blew the snow out of his face but his look was unwavering, the smile still in place.

'You.' The soldier's eyes locked on the face of the youth in the far corner of the rear seat. 'Let me see your hands. Slowly. Good. Put them on the headrest in front of you. That's it. Now you. Good lad.' The eyes above the lip of the window swivelled to the front. 'Both of you. Hands on the dashboard. Slowly. That's it. Straighten your arms.'

The two other men in army uniform now pulled open the doors on the far side of the vehicle, pushing the muzzles of their weapons into the necks of Luka's men closest to them.

'Out, you two. Keep your hands where we can see them. On

your knees, that's it. Now face down. Spread your legs. Spread 'em!' The soldiers used their boots to kick the captives' legs apart, then bent over to search them.

Rosso was timing the operation.

When all four of Luka's men were spread-eagled on the ground, the superintendent sighed, seemed to relax. He had gambled – successfully as it turned out – that Luka would be too preoccupied when he arrived at the presidency, summoned to an emergency meeting of the ministers' war council, to notice there were no other cars out front, that the army details had been switched with policemen. There were cars and the usual retinue of drivers and bodyguards, but on Rosso's orders they had all been parked out of sight, their passengers shepherded to the rear. It was either that or risk having a shooting match right in the middle of the VIPs coming and going.

'Thirty-eight seconds,' said Rosso.

'Not bad,' said Anil.

'We had it down to twenty-two,' said Rosso.

'That was practice, chief. This is for real.' They were Anil's men, Anil had trained them.

'What now?' asked Flett.

'We'll search the vehicles,' said Rosso quietly. 'Put the weapons in the boot, let these boys run home after we get their ID—'

'Let them go?'

'Sure, unless we find something we shouldn't in the cars. Otherwise I've nothing to hold them on. They're just kids.'

'They'll tell everyone.'

'So what. It'll be all over town in an hour or two anyway.'

'Luka's got friends at court,' Flett said. 'They'll say you personally brought drugs into Sarajevo, that you planted them in the flat where the woman was found, that you fitted Luka up and that Vasic is the scapegoat.'

Rosso was silent.

Anil had a mobile telephone. He put it to his ear and muttered into it.

'Now it's our turn on stage,' Rosso said, opening the front passenger's door and pulling himself out. Anil clambered out over the front seat behind Boris.

'What about me?' Flett felt a stab of panic.

'You can stay here and watch with Boris. He'll take you back later with the others. Or you can come and meet Luka.'

Rosso was already walking away with Anil, moving down the cobbled lane to the edge of the little park opposite the presidency and then crossing the avenue to join the other policemen in their army fatigues.

'Well?' said Boris. 'What you wan', America? Huh? I'm getting cold. You stay – you go. No different for me. Just close fuckin' door. Quick.'

Flett hesitated. This would be too good to miss. He had to see Luka's face, record his reaction. He wondered if they would cuff Luka, if he would resist and whether they would beat him for the sheer pleasure of it. Hell, it was all good colour copy. Whatever happened.

He pushed his way out past Boris and ran, skidding on the wet cobblestones, the snow tickling his face.

'Fuckin' crazy foreign,' Boris laughed after him. 'You wan' die, no!'

Rosso sat in the driver's position, AK-47 next to him on the passenger seat of the Mercedes. Anil and Flett sat behind. The 'soldiers', having searched Luka's driver and bodyguards, marched the four away into the park across the street and made them squat under the trees, facing away from the presidency. Murad and Nenad took possession of the Opel. There was nothing for them to do but wait for Luka to reappear.

'What if he comes out the back?' Flett asked.

'He won't,' grunted Rosso. 'It's shut. We've taken care of it.' He was looking at all the footprints, the marks of scuffling, around the cars. It looked like a small battlefield. He hoped Luka wouldn't reappear before the snow had done its work in covering their tracks.

'How does the drugs thing work?' Flett inquired. He surreptitiously turned on his tape recorder.

'The stuff comes in through Split,' said Rosso, without taking his eyes off the presidency. 'It's been a big smuggling port for drugs for years, Europe's biggest entry port throughout the Tito era in fact. That's why there are so many addicts down there; sixteen thousand the local police estimate. That's why crime is so bad on the coast. We infected our own people.'

'You were there last week?'

'Yes.'

'So you weren't visiting your mother—'

'I did indeed visit her. I was also tying up loose ends on the coast with the Croatian police. They've a lot on Luka.'

'And what does Luka do with this brown sugar?'

'Sells it on.'

'To whom?'

'The Serbs.'

'Serbs!'

'It goes up the Danube.'

'But who does he deal with?'

'People like himself, only on the other side.'

'Where does he get the drugs?'

'The Fish Farm.'

'You mean the trout farm? Between Vitez and Gornji Vakuf?'

'Right.'

'The people we call the Fish Head Gang?'

'Right.'

'Are they Serbs?'

'They are everyone and anyone they need to be. Serbs. Moslems. Croats. It's called a war economy.'

'How does he get it into the country?'

'Same as he gets the cigarettes in. Croatia has signed an agreement with Bosnia that allows duties to be paid on entry to Croatia only. So it arrives in a container from Latakia or Karachi and goes straight into a bonded warehouse in Split and is then transferred without any further formalities to another just across the Bosnian frontier. Plain sailing all the way.'

A ringing sound came from Anil's phone.

'Boss,' said Anil. 'He's on his way.'

Rosso pulled the Kalashnikov towards him. Anil put his crippled hand on the door latch, ready to leap out. The big wooden doors were indeed opening and the two presidential guards reappeared – only they were Rosso's men in army uniform – standing to left and right. Behind them the crooked figure of Luka lurched into view; he hobbled out and without pausing negotiated his way carefully down the steps, now carpeted in snow. He would plant the stick, then drop his stiff and useless leg down behind it and finally shift his weight onto the useless limb. It was a slow process.

'He can't see us at all,' muttered Anil.

'Wouldn't his guys have gone to help him?' Flett asked.

No-one answered the reporter.

Rosso was leaning forward. He had not counted on the weather, but the snow undoubtedly helped. From where Luka was, moving towards them, the cars must have seemed entombed in white, their occupants invisible. The policeman pushed the door open, just a few inches. Anil followed him, using his foot to hold his door open a foot or two, as if Luka's gunmen had suddenly and belatedly become aware of their leader's presence.

'Go,' said Rosso.

Both Rosso and Anil were out of the car, standing upright.

In an instant, Anil was behind Luka, Rosso alongside him. The gangster's stick was kicked away. Flett saw it cartwheel in the carpet of snow. Luka was lifted and then forced against the car bonnet, thrown against it, held down. Anil pressed his weapon into Luka's ear, so that his misshapen face was pressed against the snow covering the grey paintwork. Luka's arms were pinned behind him. Handcuffs were snapped onto his wrists and from where Flett sat he could see a flicker of surprise register on Luka's face. Or was it pain?

Other hands – Rosso's – searched him swiftly, pulling a Beretta automatic from a holster inside Luka's jacket and tossing it into the back of the car. It fell on the seat next to Flett. A clasp-knife followed and finally, when Rosso squatted down on his heels, he took a small-calibre pistol from a leather anklet on Luka's stiff leg.

They seemed to know where to look, what to look for.

The two policemen half carried, half dragged Luka to the open door and pushed him into the front passenger seat. Anil placed his hand – the hand with the four missing fingers – on Luka's head to prevent the prisoner from hitting himself. Flett almost felt sorry for Luka and would have felt sorrier still had he not been in such close proximity to the thug. There was something pathetic about him, as if his status as captive had reduced him in size. He seemed to Flett to have literally shrunk in stature – he no longer, as the saying goes, filled his clothes. Rosso left Anil in charge of the prisoner for a moment, skidding around the front of the car and sitting behind the steering-wheel again, turning towards Luka, watching him. Anil slammed Luka's door and slipped in behind the prisoner. Flett made room, shifting over to the far side behind the driver's seat where Rosso sat.

Luka spoke for the first time.

'Fuck you,' he snarled.

Rosso read Luka his rights.

Flett could only recall ten words later – though he had taken a full and accurate note of Rosso's ritual remarks: '. . . for the unlawful and premeditated murder of the dentist Zjelko Bukovac . . .'

Anil sat forward, the muzzle of Luka's own pistol now pressed against his neck, just behind the left ear. Anil's face was a mask of furious concentration. Flett could see the hair plastered with sweat to Anil's forehead. The sergeant held the pistol in his left hand, forefinger tight around the trigger and his wrist supported by what was left of his right. Slowly – to the nervous Flett it seemed distressingly slowly – Rosso turned the Mercedes, the Opel slipping right behind, their wheels crunching and creaking through the new snow. As the two vehicles moved out onto Marsala Tito, Flett turned to see through the side window Luka's men stumbling out of the park, running from the trees, not looking back, not daring to look anywhere but ahead and no doubt not quite believing their luck in still being alive and even now expecting that final bullet in the spine. That was how things were done in their world, after all, a world Rosso was trying, here and now, to dismantle, before it crushed them all.

15

'Fate sucks, I swear.'
OCEAN OF LOVE

CANDLES – STUBS OF WAX MELTED DOWN IN BROKEN SAUCERS crammed with cigarette ends, night-lights floating in little tubs of water, Christmassy red candles, still festive in empty beer and vodka bottles, candles of devotion as rotund as their absentee bishop and taken from the cathedral's shell-shattered vestry – candles, in short, of every description, guttered and flared, making the detectives' room glow, casting huge flickering shadows on the walls and ceiling. It was late afternoon, and quite dark in this part of the city. It was also silent, save for the hissing of the snow against what was left of the windows, the odd murmur and snort from slumbering police officers, the weapons at their sides shining slick and oily in the uneven, unsteady light. Boots, bedrolls, blankets, piles of old newspapers, clothing – the little piles of personal possessions marking out the territory each man or woman had set aside for rest, for privacy and warmth. They had eaten, seen the prisoner brought in, watched him taken down to the basement, saw the leg-irons fitted, witnessed him chained to the wall of the cage they called The Tank and freely given of their advice to the first four officers who would guard the captive. Then they had drunk not one but several toasts to a successful day's labour, talked themselves hoarse and finally drifted away in search of dry floor space, away from windows and outer walls, each one to his or her own thoughts and, eventually, a restless sleep before it was time to be shaken awake for a turn keeping watch. As for their special prisoner below, he roughly demanded his orthopaedic stick and was told with equal force he wouldn't be needing it at the end of a rope. At that Luka cursed them, swore vengeance, then fell silent, squatting on his stained horsehair mattress, his back to his captors. He contemptuously ignored the food and water they brought him and eventually he slept, his face to the wall where one wrist was manacled to the bars and his feet and their leg-irons protruding from under a grey army blanket.

Upstairs, Rosso stalked restlessly, licking forefinger and thumb and extinguishing most of the little points of light, saving them up. Who could tell? They might be needed again. He stepped carefully over the sleepers, finally arriving at his office and flinging himself thankfully down in his chair. Anil sat opposite, chair tipped forward, his head on his forearms, forearms on the desk. A half bottle of maraskino – cherry brandy – stood between them. It was only 5 p.m. but in this sepulchral atmosphere and after all the frantic activity, it felt like midnight.

There was a new contraption among the mess of papers. Not so much new as strange, a wooden box with a hinged lid and containing what appeared to be a conventional telephone, only it was green with a handle protruding from the side and a thick connecting cable running from it to the floor and out of the door at the end of the room – a military landline, installed in the past hour by Bosnian army signallers and linked, so they said, to the local army exchange in what was left of the city's railway station.

'Now what,' mumbled Anil, his mouth muffled by the sleeve of his jacket.

'We wait,' said Rosso.

'For what?'

'Orders.'

'Fuck that. They won't make no soldier out of me. They had their chance to make me a hero.'

'You did well today, detective sergeant.'

'I did?'

Anil's head rose from the desk. He pushed his chair back and his hand moved from a breast pocket up to his face. A match flared, revealing the sergeant's features – the broad cheek-bones, flattened nose, tousled hair. Anil sucked on the cigarette, inhaling strongly, then blew the smoke in a stream at the ceiling. As he flicked the match away with his thumb, the darkness wrapped around him once more.

'Smoke, boss?'

'No thanks.'

Rosso heard Anil slop more brandy into his cup.

'Well, Anil. No regrets, no second thoughts? You knew Luka well. You were both among the first to take up arms. Didn't you feel just a little upset back there when we picked him up?'

'Not me, chief. He was a bloodsucker. He wasn't defending the city in April '92. He was defending his turf, his rackets. He was eating us alive – from within. We should've taken care of him two, three years ago.'

The box on the desk trilled twice, a high-pitched warble.

'Rosso.'

He waited while the local operator connected him with the minister's office.

'Superintendent?'

'Minister.'

'Our mutual friend is secure?'

'Very much so, Minister.'

'They won't take this lying down, Rosso.'

'They?'

'His people.'

'The *roulement* worked, Minister. We've shut down his head-quarters. All his boys have been distributed across the front lines. They'll be no trouble. By morning they'll be under army orders.'

'You found the murder victim?'

'What's left.'

'One of yours, I believe?'

'A snitch. An informer.'

'Did you know her?'

'Personally, no. I met her once. At the start.'

'She had a record?'

'No previous. She was selling small quantities of drugs to finance her own habit. Luka's people put the squeeze on her. My officers encouraged her to continue the relationship in return for immunity.'

'She had no choice, had she?'

'It's standard procedure.'

'It's a death sentence, Rosso.'

'It's police work, Minister. Luka found out she made up the lists of drugs needed by city hospitals and passed by the Serb committee to the United Nations. Luka needed chemicals to refine large quantities of heroin destined for European cities. His business was expanding. You could say there was a synergy there.'

'You went along with it.'

'The UN wouldn't touch it. Smelt a rat. We plugged the gap, provided the means, the necessary chemicals.'

'What went wrong?'

'Luka thought she was holding out on him.'

'Was she?'

'We think she got ambitious, yes.'

'So he killed her. You have him at the scene?'

'Yes.'

'You have your witness?'

'We took the statement today.'

'Anything else I should know?'

'We found heroin in the safe house where the woman Bukovac ran a bathtub factory, supplying local addicts.'

'You have a good case there, Rosso. But I wouldn't put any money on it coming to court while there's still a war on.'

'Question, Minister.'

'Go ahead.'

'Misic and his fellow Serbs – what happened?'

'Protective custody. I didn't want any retaliation against Misic or his co-religionists until Luka was put away. I believe they were freed by the Army this afternoon.'

'What happens to my people?'

'That's under review, Rosso. If the military does take over law and order, I see no reason why your team shouldn't stay together. I'll fight our corner, I assure you.'

'*Hvala*. Thank you.'

'*Nema na cemu*. My pleasure.'

Rosso replaced the receiver, closed the box. Anil gave his unequivocal verdict – a loud belch.

'Have a drink, Superintendent. You look like you need it.'

'I do, Anil.'

'You didn't mention Vasic.'

'Let's keep it in the family, shall we?'

'He betrayed the woman.'

Anil filled their cups. They raised them, looked at one another over the rims, tossed them back. The liquid seemed to set fire to Rosso's throat, burning all the way down to his stomach. Anil refilled the cups immediately and they repeated the ritual. It wasn't bad. After the third, Rosso thought, he wouldn't feel a thing. The wonderful anaesthetic feeling, the numbing fog, was already oozing into his brain.

'You knew Bukovac well?' Rosso asked.

'She was OK until she went to pieces. A kind soul. Brave. She did my teeth. Never charged me, neither. She did a lot of people's teeth for free. She must have saved the teeth of scores of kids. Until she got hold of the morphine there wasn't any anaesthetic. You can imagine. She used a hand tool and did it by candlelight on a kitchen chair. She had this way of tipping the chair back against the wall and then gripping your head under her arm so you couldn't struggle. She gave the children – the bad cases – crushed chalk as a placebo. Half a dispirin if they were very lucky.'

'Painful?'

'Bloody right it was,' Anil said. 'And you had to go back again and again because there weren't any fillings. You could buy temporary fillings for seventy-five marks a throw. Who has that kind of money I'd like to know. You know something? I think she was using the drugs money she earned on the side to buy them. Kinda odd, isn't it, helping to get people hooked and feeding their habit so you can buy fillings to save their fucking teeth? That's why she got killed – saving kids' teeth.' Anil laughed, shook his head in wonderment at human nature.

Murad put his head and shoulders through the door.

'A word, Sergeant?'

Anil excused himself, the two policemen joining a huddle near the stairway. It was too dark to make them out. Rosso leant back, stretched, shut his eyes.

'Boss?'

Anil was back, leaning across the desk, looking worried. The shapes of other officers hovered beyond Rosso's office, forming together, breaking apart.

The sergeant was holding out a piece of paper. Rosso took it and Anil moved the candle closer. Rosso had to hold the notepaper close to the flame to make out the writing, which he recognized as that of Misic.

My dear Superintendent. We were freed this morning. They dropped us all at the hospital when they heard the news of the attack on the cemetery. So far, by lunch-time, we have fourteen dead, twenty-three wounded. I fear some won't make it. Another bad day. I can hear you say there have been worse. You are right,

255

of course. As for ourselves, the soldiers looked after us pretty well, considering. Anyway, this is the first time since I got back to the hospital that I've had time to send you a message. I tried phoning. Useless. I know you're very busy. They told me. I hope you get this before long. It's Tanja. She's safe. Stable. But she was injured and I had to operate. Come to the hospital as soon as you can. I hate to be the bearer of yet more bad news.

Your good friend. Misic.

'Please thank whoever brought the note over,' said Rosso to no-one in particular.

'Chief—'

Rosso had stood up and was moving around his desk, stepping carefully over Anil's size-ten boots, then he was through the doorway and he could see the shapeless crowd of officers – just a shadow, darker, denser than the other shadows in the room – part at the far end of the room, split open as he approached, making way for him as he felt his way with his hands, fingertips tracing the edges and tops of the desks, heading for the faint rectangle of light. He could feel their eyes on him.

They knew.

'Boss—'

He walked through them, past them. He didn't take his coat, or his flak jacket. He hoped the place was too dark for them to see his face. Damn! It's only tiredness, he told himself, and the drink. What's another casualty? She'll live. Hadn't Misic said that? She'll live. She'd got a second chance, hadn't she? That was more than many got in this town. Stupid bitch. Hadn't he warned her? He pictured Bukovac, what was left of her, in the bathtub, the needle marks. Rosso shut his eyes, but the image of the blood-spattered bath in the Monkey House was still there. This time Bukovac had Tanja's face.

When he reached the street he paused, wiped his face with his sleeve and started downhill. He thought he heard foot-steps behind him and someone call his name. He did not turn. The hospital wasn't far, he told himself. He started to run.

Flett knew it was a good piece, one of his best, and the deputy foreign editor called him on the satphone within minutes of his having filed it to Washington, the Brooklyn accent bouncing up to the South Atlantic's geostationary communications satellite and zapping down to Flett's handset and still bubbling with effusive and false concern for Flett's well-being. He was consumed by envy, Flett knew. They all were.

That shit would like nothing better than for me to fuck up.

It would go on page one, no doubt about it, the man said, and probably above the fold if nothing happened to squeeze it out in later editions. He'll try damned hard to find something, Flett thought. Oh, yes. It was the metropolitan edition that mattered, Flett knew, the 234,000 copies that hit the streets in the early hours of the morning, Eastern Standard Time. Could he do a follow-up, something colourful, the deputy foreign editor asked, maybe an interview with a drug runner, or a gritty date-line somewhere along the drug route?

After the call, Flett's fingers traced the secondary roads on his 1:50,000 map: the Serb police checkpoint at Ilidza would take twenty minutes, maybe more if he had to drink with the blue-uniformed police while they examined his passport; the Visoko turn-off near the Canadian battalion's camp could be made in an hour if he was lucky, Kakanj with its coal-fired power plant and French garrison in another twenty minutes, then another half-hour or so until, turning left at the end of the bridge, where there was a Bosnian army checkpoint, before Zenica, finally the nastiest forty minutes – that flat, straight road through the fertile Lasva Valley to Vitez where the British were based.

Two and a half hours and it was already almost dark.

They'd say he was crazy driving at night, alone.

He thought about the rest of it on his way down to the car,

struggling down the hotel staircases with his bag, his laptop. From Vitez in the morning it would be fifteen minutes to the Travnik crossroads, bearing left – west – to Gornji Vakuf.

That stretch was by far the worst; the unpaved road cutting through the hills with a high embankment to the right, the river through the trees to the left. Thick undergrowth on both sides. An army could hide in there and probably did. The road was badly potholed. In summer the trees on either side were white with dust from the constant UN aid convoys, plying the route from the coast; in winter the road was a quagmire from the heavy-laden trucks. It was good ambush country, the Fish Farm itself just a forlorn collection of derelict buildings, the artificial ponds packed with trout no-one dared to venture close enough to catch. A man would have to leave his car at the side of the road, push through the trees and undergrowth, scramble down the bank to the river.

It was ideal territory for renegades trading in everything from petrol and cigarettes to drugs and people.

In the snow the condition of the roads would be atrocious. With luck he would be back at Vitez for lunch the next day and in Sarajevo by nightfall with plenty of time to file.

At Ilidza the Serbs took away his passport, searched his car and, as he had anticipated, they insisted he share a drink and accept a cigarette; the paramilitary Serb police sat him down in their bunker next to a makeshift gas fire (they'd run a pipe into one of the main gas lines; plenty of people had fried themselves that way) and filled a glass with *rakija*. Sitting there, feeling quite comfortable, smiling at his Serb hosts, he felt rather than heard the rumble of guns. They went outside to look. The night sky flickered red and they could feel it under their feet. Flett insisted on leaving then; he fretted that this was the big one they had all been waiting for and that he had missed it. He wouldn't know for sure one way or another until he reached Vitez and talked to the UN troops there.

'You wan' go back Sarajevo now, American?' one of the Serbs asked as he started his vehicle.

Flett shook his head, and the Serbs laughed.

It was as if the entire rebel army, the vast array of Serb guns, mortars and rocket launchers, had been waiting just for the moment Rosso stumbled out onto the snowy street and began his shambling run down the hill. The road curved down to the right where it met two more tributaries, then, a little further down the broader strip of tarmac ran through a small square on the side of a hill that in turn fell away and broke up into several alleys leading into the old souk of Bascarsija, now a pedestrian precinct (though few pedestrians were rash enough to use it). At first, to the policeman's immediate right as he slid downhill, were houses and shops, to the left a small and ancient Moslem graveyard, the *stecci* or carved stone grave-markers of the Bogomils sticking up above the snow like ghostly sentinels marking his erratic progress. Looming directly ahead and above him was the majestic and pale edifice of Mount Trebevic, the woods showing blackly against the white open rock and scree, its slopes emerging from rooftops across the bridge and vanishing into the low black cloud. If they had night-vision devices up there, and everyone said the Serbs had, they would be watching his clumsy descent through the Carsija quarter, probably even arguing over who should take the shot. Rosso kept going. There was no alternative. The first thing that happened was that the policeman became aware of bullets whipping past him, in front of him, mainly, at the level of his knees and thighs. They were rather like locusts. He couldn't really see them in the dark, but he certainly heard them – whup-whup-whup-wheee – followed by the distant thuds of the weapons firing.

They are shooting at me this time, for sure.

Bup-bup-bup.

Closer.

They were getting the range, probably firing from Mrakusa and Bistrik, on the far, Serb-held *obala* or riverbank.

He hugged the walls, anxious to move faster, but slipping and slithering on the uneven cobblestones. Tracer flew past, overhead, all around. It too was incoming, pumping out its lethal fireflies of steel fast and straight. And then very close, almost at his side, Rosso heard outgoing mortar fire; over the very next wall, in somebody's courtyard or garden plot. It was so close that he heard the firing mechanism strike the base of the mortar bombs as they were dropped one after the other into the tubes, a sort of metallic clink before the hollow *thock* of them firing, like a cork from a champagne bottle. Rosso reached the edge of the little square, a snowy expanse shining in the dark, the shops to his right falling away, the embankment and cemetery wall on the opposite side left behind. Only the brooding mass of Trebevic ahead of him rose like a wall, terrifying in its sheer size, so implacable. Rosso knew he stood out against the snow. There was nothing to do but go on. He could not go back. He could not stay where he was. If he followed the road it would sweep him through the square, taking him down and across the bridge into the Serb lines on the far bank. To his right, another lane converged on the square with its overhead tramlines and picturesque Ottoman ticket office and waiting-room in the centre, a black rectangle.

Rosso ran for this landmark, lunging out into the open in a flurry of snow, his shins cold from the wet, the snowdrifts over his ankles and soaking his shoes. His aim was to cross the square, plunge into the labyrinth of the old quarter and zigzag his way from wall to wall and house to house until he could find his way, gradually, to the hospital.

He saw, then heard, the mortar bombs impact on the other side of town, a pulsating orange glow and dull crashes in measured succession in the vicinity of Bostarici. As he reached the wooden building in the centre, the sky lit up in a series of ragged flashes of artillery that illuminated not only the crags of Trebevic but all the other mountains around the capital. They were backlit, as it were, most of the besieging Serb guns being on the reverse slopes. The very sky shivered electric blue and gold, dancing and shimmering like a display of northern lights as the Cetniks opened fire. For a fraction of an instant there was no sound at all and then only weird screeching, humming and fluttering above Rosso's head as the projectiles homed in on their target, coming in at all angles and trajectories, a ballistic free-for-all. The superintendent instinctively went down on one knee just as the world about him seemed to leap, erupting in massive spasms.

He was running, sucking in air through his open mouth, the smell of burning in his nostrils, bits and pieces of buildings falling around him, sizzling in the snow; a pattering of debris, of dust on his head and clothing. It was snowing again, but for once the weather seemed at the mercy of the war, not the other way around. Rosso had shed all caution, all attempt to use cover. What was the point? The streets were rivers of flame, boiling out into the night sky, bricks and plaster cascading down, windows and doorways alive with flickering tongues of fire. As he skidded and hopped diagonally across Marsala Tito Avenue he saw ahead of him an entire department store engulfed in its death throes. It seemed to have been hit by several rockets or shells simultaneously. A great rolling wave of flame, almost liquid in the way it curled up around the walls and roof, sprang from the interior. Rosso felt a hot wind on his back as the air was sucked into the hungry inferno. The great steel pylons and joists that had provided the frame of the building popped out like blazing matches – shooting out into the night sky. In a great shower of sparks, the entire building fell in on itself, pancaked floor upon floor, and Rosso's face was scorched by the heat of its implosion.

Rosso was close now, climbing, scrambling, sometimes on all fours then dancing crazily across intersections as bright as day in the detonations. This must be Hrgica, he told himself. There were gardens, individual homes set back from the street. The artillery was shifting its aim, stalking through the city, a moving curtain of destruction. He saw ahead of him a small house, a modest, alpine-style bungalow, a fenced plot before it and a man like himself, very like himself, snatch up a child; a boy by the look of it, aged perhaps seven or eight. They must have been clearing snow or tending their cold frames, then flung themselves down, hoping the inferno would pass and when it didn't they changed their minds and decided to make a bolt for it. The man held the child like a football against his body, his right arm wrapped around him and ran for the front door. It was open. A woman stood there on the threshold. She held both her arms open. She seemed to be beseeching them both to hurry, though Rosso could not hear her words for the roaring of the explosions and fires.

They reached her, the man and the boy.

Rosso thought he heard their voices.

'Hurry, darlings!'

'Mummy!'

They were on the steps, for an instant, the three of them together, united, and the woman drawing them in, her one arm around the man, the other cuddling the boy to her, when the shells or whatever they were reached them, blew the house apart, lifted it up, struck it with an immense flash like a wave striking a rock, covering it, shooting up and over it like spray, only the wave was white flame, incandescent, and the spray phosphorus plumes.

Rosso looked and looked, but the house had gone entirely and so had they.

The superintendent found himself in mid-air, his feet and arms paddling frantically. He was propelled some 200 metres along the street, as if by a giant hand, then dropped.

That was where an ambulance crew found him; on his hands and knees in the middle of the road and not 60 metres from the hospital gates, swinging his head from side to side, muttering and crying to himself, his scorched clothes hanging off him in ribbons, half his hair singed away, cuts and scratches on his face, arms and knees, but otherwise unhurt. The tarmac all around Rosso was melted into a small lake and the first thing they said when they brought him in – along with two badly burnt women and a child's foot (still in its trainer) which they found on a window-ledge – was that it was a miracle he hadn't got stuck in it, like an insect on fly-paper. Others, as they said, had not been so lucky but had burnt like torches when the firestorm reached them.

Rosso tried hard to keep his eyes off the stump of what was left of Tanja's left leg. It was very neatly bandaged, the clean white stretch cloth expertly wrapped around the end like a parcel. Instead of bows or string there was a shiny big safety pin holding it all in place. There was no blood seeping through. Misic had done a thorough job. Rosso found it difficult not to look at where the leg ended, above the knee. He had to force his eyes away from it. He thought it looked a bit like a leg of lamb wrapped in muslin. There was hope for the other leg, Misic said, prattling on in his best bedside manner. Rosso could see the surgeon was beyond exhaustion, he had that collapsed, unfocused look of deep fatigue. The danger was gangrene, Misic went on lightly, as if discussing the weather. The conditions they operated in. Well, he, Rosso, knew all that, had seen it before. No need to tell him, Misic said. And they had no X-rays so . . . here Misic paused . . . it was gas gangrene in particular. The biggest killer, the doctor added. After the Cetniks, chronic diarrhoea and perforated ulcers. Ho ho ho. Misic was trying to make light of it.

Rosso looked at her face. White, not a shred of colour in her, pale as the pillowcase. She smiled at him but was too weak to lift her head. He took her limp hand, and he felt a faint tug. 'Come closer,' she said. 'Closer.'

He was bending right over, his head turned.

'Are the Serbs trying to take the town?'

'I don't believe so. It's the usual punishment for being what we are. They have the fire-power but they don't have the men. We have the men but not the fire-power. So they try to destroy what they cannot have.'

'Didn't I say you men were like dangerous children?'

'You did.'

'And Luka's men?'

'In the front line, drafted into the Army.'

'So it was a trick, all those troops moving about. A trick to get Luka's men into the front line. You did well.'

'Musical chairs,' agreed Rosso. 'You played your part. Don't talk now. Rest,' he added.

'Tell me Sarajevo still lives,' she said. 'Tell me this isn't the end. That this isn't the price for bringing one gangster to justice.'

'Not even the beginning of the end,' Rosso said.

'Promise me one thing, then I will sleep,' she said.

'What?'

'Don't hate,' she said.

'I don't hate,' Rosso said, surprised.

'Not the Cetniks. Your father.'

'He's been dead for years.'

'You hated him alive and now you hate yourself for being his son. Make peace with yourself. Life's too short. Please. Will you do that?'

Rosso nodded.

'Two things. Promise me two things.'

'What's the second?'

'Kiss me. Gently. On the mouth.'

He did so. Her breath was dry, and smelt of disinfectant. As he pulled back she held onto his arm.

'I feel bad about Branston,' she said. 'We went out together, but I wasn't very nice to him. He was good company . . . I wanted to explain.'

'You didn't love him.'

'No. I didn't love him.'

'Then things started to happen,' said Rosso.

'He found out I was seeing Luka. His friends told him. He didn't believe them to start with. He was so loyal. Then they showed him a picture of us together on Hvar Island.'

'And Luka found out you were seeing Flett.'

'Yes.'

'You couldn't tell Branston you were seeing Luka because it was part of your work for me and you couldn't tell Luka you were seeing Branston because it was good cover.'

She nodded.

'What happened then?'

'Luka's people started watching Branston. He got scared. They searched his room. They stood around outside it and followed him in the street.'

'Go on.'

'Finally they blew up his car. Luka was insanely jealous.'

'Flett was frightened, it's true. He never told me they blew up his car, though.'

'Of course he wouldn't tell you. He started drinking heavily, took up with . . .'

'Tarts,' Rosso said.

'I'm sorry,' she said. 'It's my fault.'

'No. You did a wonderful job on Luka.'

'Did you know the woman?' Tanja's hand clung to Rosso's fingers now. Her grasp was almost painful.

'No.'

'I did. I knew her. She fixed my teeth.'

Tanja's hand relaxed. Her dark eyes could barely stay open. 'I'm all right,' she said. 'Really I am,' she whispered. 'So very sorry, must sleep now. Have to sleep.'

And she did, smiling – or so it seemed to him.

All the while the bombardment raged. It wasn't so much the noise, but the way the walls and floor reverberated with it, like a mild earthquake, a series of tremors. Everything that was loose, not screwed down, jumped and slithered, fell over, rattled. Glasses of water fell to the floor and shattered, bedpans clattered from cupboards, spoons danced along the floor and the very beds themselves squeaked and shook. It was like an invasion of poltergeists, or riding out a storm at sea. Orderlies held their hands out to catch the distemper yellow walls, they walked bow-legged, placing their feet carefully apart like sailors on a trawler pitching in a big swell.

Misic was still talking, sitting on the end of Tanja's bed and gazing for some reason past Rosso, staring into the gloom of the corridor. The patients, those not being operated on, were all in the corridors, lying head to toe in the dark, calling out, moaning, whimpering some of them, especially the children, crying for their parents, afraid of the dark, of the pain, of the terrible reverberating thunder of gunfire. It was a sea of limbs, constantly moving under the white, shroud-like sheets. It was safer here, away from the outside walls, Misic said. The less badly wounded were made comfortable on the floor because there weren't enough beds or stretchers to go round. The stench of blood and urine hung heavily in the humid air.

Tanja was lucky, Misic told him. Oh, yes. They found her dragging herself down the road from the cemetery – Kralja Tomislava – with one leg barely attached to her. She was clutching it to herself as if she had thought they could sew it back on. Well, if it was London or Paris they might have tried. Not here. No time. Covered in blood, she was. They put her in the back of a van along with others – all hopeless cases – but she kept raising her head and muttering the doctor's name. Misic. Misic. Then she would fall back again in her own blood. By the time they reached the hospital she was pronounced dead. She'd bled to death, they told Misic when he came out and saw her. He bent, put two fingers to her throat. She had no pulse at all. He could swear she had stopped breathing. But because she was one of the first to arrive and because an orderly had tugged him by his sleeve and told him a patient had just come in who'd called out his name, Misic had gone out to the forecourt, recognized her as she was dragged from the van, helped carry her in, straight to surgery and revived her, then gave her a massive blood transfusion. God knows, they needed blood. But he brought her back, he said. Cuts all over her head, literally dozens of bits of metal in her. If she'd come in two minutes later with the bulk of the casualties they would have made her comfortable as best they could, given her a shot to dull the pain a little and left her to die. You understand, he told the detective. Of course you do. Reverse triage, Misic said. I wouldn't have recognized her for the blood. He sighed. Yes, Superintendent, a matter of minutes and I would have let her die. Well, that's not exactly true because she was technically already dead. I would have left things the way they were. No choice, you see. He shrugged. He had left many to die today. As for the girl's leg, Misic had waited as long as possible before taking it off. But it was no use, he told Rosso, still staring into the dark passageway. No use. I had to, you see. I wanted to save it. As much of it as I could, dear boy. Rosso suddenly realized Misic was crying, tears pouring down his face. No use, the doctor repeated. Your Tanja needs to get proper attention. Overseas. She'll lose the other leg if she stays here. Misic took off his glasses, wiped them on the sleeve of his coat, the front of it stiff as a board with congealed blood. No use. The words seemed to hammer inside the superintendent's mind.

No use. No use.

DAY FOUR

16

'The last act is bloody, however fine the rest
of the play. They throw earth over your head
and it is finished forever.'
BLAISE PASCAL, *PENSÉES*

AN ARMOURED CAR, AN UGLY VEHICLE ON SIX HUGE RUBBER
wheels that reminded Rosso of a cockroach (notwithstanding
the white paint and pennant of a regiment of French colonial
infantry snapping from a radio aerial), carried him back the way
he had come four days earlier. Along Sniper's Alley it scuttled,
in front of the yellow, pock-marked front of the hotel, swerved
through the smoke and debris of the previous night's torment,
bounced across the tram tracks, past what had been Mahmud's
checkpoint – now a heap of smouldering ash – to the PTT building.
It was like watching a film on fast rewind. Comical, almost. Or like
those Chance cards in Monopoly. What did they say? Go to jail.
Do not pass Go. Do not collect two hundred.

The two French soldiers who fetched him that morning were patient, looking bored while Nenad, the earnest, bespectacled Nenad, woke him, and none too gently.

'*Nacelnik*! Supervisor!'

Nenad shook him roughly.

'*Nacelnik*!'

Rosso rolled out of his blankets on the floor of his office, sat up, groaned. He felt stiff all over. He peered at the face of his watch: 11 a.m. Two hours' sleep in twenty-four.

Being professional soldiers – he could see that by their shaved heads, their green uniforms bleached and threadbare from being washed so many times, their indifferent eyes, their nonchalant, unhurried manner – they were used to waiting. Soldiering is, after all, much a matter of learning to wait, interspersed with brief episodes of intense physical activity. Both must be undertaken without question, without resort to reason or justification. Rosso's father would have understood that odd physical quality of alertness coupled with passivity. When Rosso hauled himself up, holding onto his desk, then pronounced himself as ready as he was ever likely to be they gave him one of their flak jackets. It was the rule. And Rosso? He was wanted. By the general. Further inquiries from Rosso's fellow policemen were answered by a Gallic shrug, an offer of a cigarette. 'If we are in time,' one told Rosso. 'At least you will get a decent breakfast!'

Before leaving, Rosso staggered down to the basement to check on his prisoner; the superintendent found him sullen, silent. Luka sneered, his eyes and the set of his mouth oozing hostility. His guards said he had eaten, drunk a mug of weak coffee, accepted a cigarette. He had even grunted his thanks.

Minutes later the detective was clambering out of the Panhard's rear, directed up the steps, along the chicane of sandbags, through the PTT's heavy glass doors, past the French marines on guard, up the stairs.

Voilà! Breakfast – eggs, croissants, hot coffee.

He stood in line, stunned by the sight and smell of it all,

watching the others ahead of him in the queue to see how they helped themselves. How grubby our world must seem to these foreigners, Rosso thought. They must think we are animals, living in our own muck. It must be difficult to understand how quickly a combination of war, hunger and poverty can reduce a people, carry them back from the twentieth century with its video recorders, dishwashers, second cars and foreign holidays to Neanderthal man, living unwashed in a cave, ready and willing to bash his neighbour's brains in for a plate of beans.

'Better?' A figure in dark Nato battledress slid along the bench and sat opposite him. A red-haired giant of a man with blue eyes, who folded his hands – hands with reddish freckles all over them – around a mug of black coffee. It seemed to Rosso a gesture of enormous complacency and for an instant he felt unreasoning rage against the uniform.

'I'm Major—'

'Rosso.' Rosso couldn't really make out the other man's name. It was too foreign, too indistinct.

He should have stood, extended his hand, but it was not every day in Sarajevo he could eat so well. He had suddenly realized – while he shovelled eggs, sausages, tomatoes, freshly brewed coffee and hot rolls with little containers of butter and jam onto the tray, along with plastic knives and forks and the sachets of sugar and salt – just how hungry he was. How hungry they all were, all the time, like a constant itch.

Rosso was clumsy, trying frantically to manage the clutter, decide what to eat first and how to sort out the pile of food, the plastic and styrofoam tubs and tops. He kept knocking things over, spilling them onto the table and even the floor, as if someone might come along and take it all away from him or demand that he pay for it in a currency he could not afford. Rosso finally stuffed the remains of the last croissant in his mouth, wiping the jam off his fingers with a paper napkin and then, impatient with his own attempts at table manners, flinging the napkin down and licking them instead.

'Forgive me. I—' That wasn't what he really felt. He wasn't

sorry. He wasn't grateful. If the policeman felt anything at all, it was resentment at how these tourists lived.

'No problem, Superintendent.'

While Rosso picked at the crumbs on his plate and emptied his coffee cup, the major explained that he was a liaison officer. That meant he dealt with the local forces, in his case Bosnian Serb forces in the Sarajevo sector. Rosso was about to meet the UN commander, and he, the major, had been asked to brief Rosso before they met. Put him in the picture. Rosso said, gruffly, that to be perfectly frank he was less interested in the UN picture than he was in refilling his coffee mug. No offence, mind. None taken, came the reply.

'Do you know someone called Branston Flett?'

'Our resident American journalist,' Rosso said.

'You know him personally or simply by reputation?'

'Both, Major. I think you could say we are pretty much friends. We share a dislike and fear of violence.'

'Do you know where he is?'

'I saw him yesterday. He was leaving my office and going back to his hotel to file a story to his newspaper. Why?'

'He's been kidnapped,' the major said. 'Taken hostage.'

The general had a large head on a small body. His face was long, with enormous ears. His epaulettes were decorated with crossed batons and what looked like a crown.

'How good of you,' the general said, rising out of his chair and coming round his desk to shake Rosso by the hand. Good? Good? A frown passed across Rosso's face.

'It's Superintendent Rosso. Have I got that right? Do sit down. I don't think you'll refuse a cup of coffee or tea, will you? I understand you have had breakfast. It's not bad, is it? I particularly like the fresh fruit, don't you?' He seemed to ask another question before Rosso had managed to answer the previous one. To Rosso, the general's effusive welcome, his questions – none of which seemed to require an answer – were simply a smokescreen to conceal the ineffectual nature of his role, the bias of UN officers like himself

274

in favour of the organized, uniformed Serbs with their veneer of military punctiliousness.

'I'm told your mother's British, is that right?' This question was asked confidingly, the general leaning forward as if they shared the same Savile Row tailor.

Rosso nodded dumbly.

'Rather makes you one of us, doesn't it?' the major said brightly.

Like hell it did. Did they know about his father, too?

'How did you fare last night?'

Rosso opened his mouth, but the general was galloping furiously towards safer ground.

'Radios are saying eight dead. That's pretty light, considering the ferocity of the attack. Mind you, I suppose everyone was under some sort of cover. What do you think prompted it?'

'I—'

'We're frankly in a devil of a situation, Superintendent. It must be difficult for you fellows to appreciate. You see the suffering around you all the time. Ghastly! For our part, all we can do is observe, report. That's what we're doing. We're still waiting for our new mandate, while it seems no-one can agree on how to pay for our presence!' He smiled at Rosso as if it was a joke they could share, but Rosso had given up trying to respond and was being lulled into a comatose state by the combined effect of the monologue and the UN breakfast.

The major put a mug of coffee in front of Rosso, his third.

'Shall I show Superintendent Rosso the video now, sir?'

'Good idea,' said the general. 'Let's crack on.'

The major slid the cassette into the machine in the corner.

It was unmistakably Flett, sitting unnaturally upright, as if someone was poking him in the back. There was no sound. The kidnappers did not trust him to speak. Flett was holding up a copy of the previous day's edition of Sarajevo's *Oslobodenje* newspaper. He smiled briefly, crookedly. Blinked. One hand went up from his lap and brushed the hair back from his face. The captive's lips moved. It was 8mm video and the colours seemed to have run a little, particularly the red of the American's T-shirt. It must be a copy, no doubt one of several. They'd be looking at one in Washington, right now. Rosso thought Flett looked tired, but there was no visible sign of mistreatment. The screen went blank.

Rosso asked for it to be shown again.

'There is a statement, Superintendent.'

Rosso read the typed declaration. It was short. In exchange for Flett's freedom, his captors demanded the immediate release of Luka. There was a deadline at noon the next day, a vague threat – 'all responsibility for what happens to the American rests entirely with the war criminal Rosso, the so-called chief of detectives who planted evidence, falsified the charges and led the police informer, Mrs Bukovac, to her death.'

The major turned to Rosso.

'We went round to the hotel, checked through his things,' he said.

'You should have left that to us,' Rosso said. 'It's a civil matter.'

The major looked uncomfortable, turning to the general for support but he was gazing contemplatively out of the window.

'There is no question of releasing Luka,' Rosso said.

So now I'm a war criminal, not just the son of one.

'Oh, absolutely,' gushed the general in a voice that sounded far from convinced. 'But Washington is getting rather hot under the collar.'

'I hope you understand when I say that Washington's concerns, namely the life of one American, are hardly central to our struggle,' Rosso said carefully. 'You people will neither defend us nor allow us to do the job ourselves. You can't be surprised if we don't share your outrage at a single foreigner becoming a victim. And he isn't a victim. Not yet.'

'My dear chap, of course.' The general beamed at Rosso, but it was not a good-humoured smile. 'Your minister said very much the same thing to me. At some length, I must say.'

The major produced a piece of telex paper, a pink stripe down one side of it. 'Flett had a story on the front page of his paper this morning. SARAJEVO'S TOP COP TOPPLES MAFIA BOSS. The superintendent is mentioned. Want to read it?' Rosso shook his head. 'Apparently Flett was headed for Vitez last night, and indicated to his newspaper he was on his way past the Fish Farm to our base at Gornji Vakuf. None of our patrols has seen him. They were told to keep a watch.'

'His car?'

The major shook his head.

'And the video?'

'Delivered to our headquarters at Kiseljak this morning; somebody approached one of the Danish soldiers on duty at the main entrance. It was copied and brought over here immediately.'

'Who's got him?'

'Renegade elements.'

'That's UN doublespeak for Serb actions you can't, or won't, do anything about and that they won't admit to.'

The major gazed down at the surface of the general's desk as if suddenly fascinated by it.

'We think it was what the French troops call a *faux barrage*,' the general said cheerily, 'a false checkpoint, possibly even two. It's not unusual. You stop at the first one. They check your identity, see if you have an escort or are armed, then radio ahead to the next one with your vehicle registration number and once you open your door or lower your window to talk to them they pick you up without difficulty.'

'Only the separatists are that well organized,' said Rosso. He did not expect a response.

'What do you want me to do?'

The officers exchanged glances.

'We thought you might have an idea on how to tackle it,' the general said. 'So did your minister. This fellow was your friend, wasn't he?'

'What makes you think they'll take me?'

277

The general did not look at Rosso as he answered.

'Luka was really only useful to them when he was running the rackets here,' he said. 'His success was their success. Whether in jail or out of the city won't make much difference to them now. Either way, Luka is worthless to them. It's a matter of face-saving, I imagine. Honour among thieves and all that. As for Flett, they must be aware by now that they'll be leant on, hard, until they give him up. Even their Serbian masters in Belgrade won't want Washington breathing down their necks. Your friend Flett is hot property. Too hot.'

The general walked to the window.

Rosso knew the answer. But he wanted to hear it from them. The peacekeepers had done their homework, taken soundings. There was a Bosnian Serb liaison officer right there, in the building, a few steps up or down the stairs.

'They'll try and ransom you for some of their people held over here as criminals or prisoners of war,' the general said.

'They'll be disappointed at how few Serbs a Sarajevo Croat is worth,' said Rosso.

'I gather Rosso is a name that means something in these parts. Your father— ' The general hesitated, seeking a way around the awkwardness. He found none.

'There's that,' the general went on. 'The business of your father. That's all in the past. But you're also the senior police officer here. Capturing you gives them prestige. Maybe they'll hand you over to the Serbian authorities and try and take the credit. Earn a little respectability. Isn't that what all outlaws want? To be accepted?'

They must know what they are asking of me, Rosso thought. To the UN I'm just an administrative problem, or rather Flett is, and they've come up with the best way they can think of to solve it, close the file. Just as I would have done.

Serbia and Serb-held areas of Bosnia couldn't function without the black market, Rosso told himself. With factories and agriculture at a standstill and 60 per cent of the workforce idle, drugs were the most effective racket for anyone in need of hard currency to pay for smuggled fuel. A great deal of cash for a great deal of fuel – for tanks, planes and trucks, for heating and cooking. Luka's arrest would have cost them dearly. The general and his aide were looking at Rosso, waiting for his response.

'Do you have any hot water?' Rosso asked. 'I'd like a proper wash – possibly even a shower – while I think about it. Some clean clothes would be most welcome, too.'

Anil drove the superintendent. Rosso had wanted no UN escort or even a presence; indeed, he insisted on it and Anil volunteered to be the wheel man. The local ceasefire, mediated by the red-haired giant of a UN liaison officer, was agreed for 2 p.m. and would last thirty minutes. The exchange would take place on one of the bridges over the city's Maljacka River, just south of the old Ottoman quarter. They had chosen a bright, sunny day for it. A good day for skiing, Anil said. Perfect weather, Rosso agreed.

They had suddenly become shy with one another, keeping up the small talk as the Yugo bumped over the cobblestoned Saraci, passed the damaged pepper-pot dome of the Bascarsija mosque, then slowly along the deserted Asciluk Street, with its piles of masonry from artillery strikes barely concealed by snow. They were moving parallel to the river. There was no-one in sight. No cars, not a single pedestrian. Anil slowed right down to a walking pace now, and Rosso pointed to the high walls that hid the ruins of the once ostentatious town hall, pseudo-Moorish in style, at least it had been until until the Cetniks flattened it.

'Stop,' he said.

'Did you choose this place or did they?'

'They did,' Rosso said.

Anil grunted.

It was only yards to where the unfortunate Archduke Ferdinand stopped a bullet on a state visit to the city in 1914. A bomb had already been hurled at his motorcade. The route was changed, but the leading car took a wrong turn; the royal couple were driven into the sights of the assassin's revolver, precipitating the mobilization of armies that became World War I. It didn't look a particularly evil spot yet it was probably one of the most exposed and dangerous places in the entire city. Rosso knew there was a plaque where the Archduke was struck down; he himself had stood there as a youth, trying to picture the scene, putting his feet into the place where the Archduke had been, then where the assassin had stood, seeking to summon up the event from the dead pages of his school books.

It was just around the corner, one block down to the river. In a manner of speaking, he stood there now.

2.10. Five minutes to go. The policemen sat next to one another, waiting, the engine running, Anil smoking furiously.

'You don't have to do this,' said Anil, frowning. 'We can turn back. No-one will say anything or think the worse of you. We owe the Americans nothing.' He seemed tense, angry.

'It's not for the Americans, Anil.'

'What then?'

'It's for me. Tomorrow morning, when they take out the next medical evacuees on the Red Cross plane, Tanja will be there. So too will Mahmud and his daughter, Noor. I'd like you to be on hand with a couple of the lads to make sure they carry out their promise.'

'You're doing this for them?'

'And for Branston. I got him into this.'

'Flett? The son of a bitch got himself into it,' snarled Anil, his fury erupting. 'Bloody kid wants a fucking Pulitzer, only you won't be around to applaud when he collects.'

Rosso was patient.

'He's one of our witnesses, Anil. He can vouch for Noor's statement. Without him we won't have a case. Noor's statement wouldn't stand up in court alone. You know that.'

'There's Bukovac, what's left of her. There's the minister. Did I tell you? We even got one of Luka's prints in the flat.'

'The minister had other methods in mind.'

'You mean he wanted direct action, take Luka down?'

'I thought it would be too messy. He told me to gather evidence

280

on Luka's involvement in the drugs business. He made sure the winter troop rotation was something of an extravaganza, that Luka would be sure to part with his men, reduce his personal protection. Then he wanted to storm the place. When Bukovac was murdered, he extended my deadline by a couple of days. An unexpected bonus, you might say.'

'She died in a good cause, then.'

'She died in terror and pain. We did that to her.'

'She was a broken reed, chief.'

'My wife is an alcoholic, Anil. What's the difference between an alcoholic and a junkie? They were both victims, but my wife's spirit wasn't broken and I've no reason to suppose the dentist's had, either. She was hungry most of the time, scared stiff all the time and that stuff was just too much of a temptation. She got hooked and we turned the screw. I blame myself for what happened to both of them.'

'We didn't kill the informer; Luka did. And those motherfuckers—' Anil jerked his head towards the other side of the river, a furious scowl on his face.

Rosso turned to Anil.

'Time to go. When I get out of the car, reverse immediately along here and head straight back. Don't wait. If you hang about it'll only go badly for me. There's a lot of people out there who would like this to end badly.'

Three minutes.

'I'm sorry about your daughter—'

'God-daughter,' Rosso corrected him.

'Your god-daughter. She did well, getting close to Luka.'

'She didn't do it for us.'

'What do you mean?'

'She did it to protect me and my wife.'

'That's why he didn't come after you?'

Rosso nodded.

'She played a double game. Funny thing is, Anil, that this was the one thing Luka tried to do right. That's what got him in the end – his sense of how to behave right with Tanja.'

Anil didn't follow, didn't want to understand. Not now. He had taken on the job of driver because he wanted to persuade Rosso to give up the whole venture, but now he wasn't so sure. Getting Flett back was vital if the murder charge was to stick against Luka. The future well-being of Noor, Tanja and possibly Sabina all hinged on a successful exchange.

Rosso knew, as he had known all along, that Anil could not argue with that. The trade must go ahead.

'Oh, almost forgot,' said Anil. He played his trump card, knowing now it would not be enough. 'We found Vasic, or rather the UN people did. What's left of him. Out at Bacici, on the way to Stup. You know the bridge. Shot in the back of the head in the ditch at the side of the road. So was the wife.'

'How do we know it's them?'

'Fat guy. How many fat guys are there? Tyrolean hat. Police badge still in his pocket.'

'Poor man. They must have told him they were taking a different route to the airport . . .'

'Look on the bright side, boss. It means Luka's people don't have anyone else in our outfit or they would have taken better care of him. He must have been the only asset Luka had and now they've no further use for him.'

'That's one way to look at it,' said Rosso.

'It's the only way,' said Anil, triumphant. 'Look I've got a bottle here. Thought you might like one for the road—'

Anil was doing his best.

'No thanks.'

'Sure?'

'Sure.'

Two minutes. Rosso got out, pushed the door shut and ducked down, his face level with the open window.

'It was good working with you, Inspector,' he said.

'Inspector?'

'The minister asked me who was the best man for the job. My job. Just lay off the weed. If they ever get around to absorbing you lot into the military, it'll ensure they make you an officer.'

Rosso did not wait for a response but turned and started walking to the corner. He heard Anil put the car into reverse and start to move it back slowly, the engine revving.

It was not far and Rosso was shielded in part by the wall, though it was broken in places.

Think golf balls.

Only trouble was, he was the only green blade of grass out there on the fairway today and everyone knew it.

One minute.

There was not much left of the Eurasia Hotel, but a teenage Bosnian army soldier was waiting for him, wearing one of those Russian-style fur hats with ear flaps and beckoning him in through a huge gap in the rear wall, then leading him through the wrecked and dripping interior – it was some sort of nightclub or dining-room because of all the smoked-glass mirrors on the walls and ceiling – up a flight of stairs, along a passage, more steps, a door, another room, a passage. Mud everywhere, spent cartridge cases under his feet.

Through a third door and Rosso found himself in what appeared to be a spacious pantry, though a draughty one, and he could see the intersection before the Princip Bridge.

There were two more soldiers, one of them seated in a brown plastic car seat wedged into a corner and surrounded by sandbags, his back to the bridge but using a series of mirrors to watch the intersection, the bridge itself, and the open-air market now in insurgent hands.

The soldier got out of the chair, gestured to Rosso to take his place. Silently offered Rosso a cigarette. Rosso shook his head, smiled, and sat down.

A hole in the wall was buttressed by sandbags, and through this someone had stretched a mirror attached to metal tubing, so that it protruded out over the pavement at an angle. Sitting in the chair and watching the reflection on another, larger mirror right in front of him that looked as if it had come from someone's dressing-table, the superintendent had a full and complete view without exposing himself to enemy fire.

'How far?' he asked.

'Twenty metres to the bridge, to where you see the railings. Then it's another thirty-five across the bridge itself and maybe a further twenty until you're there.'

The soldiers watched him expectantly.

'Let's do it,' said Rosso, pushing himself up and out of the chair.

They took him to the side door.

He had never felt less like a hero.

'We'll be watching you. We'll talk you over to the bridge. Then you're on your own. Walk slowly, but steady. Don't run. Don't stop. Everyone gets nervous. If you see the other guy, don't stop to talk to him, don't say anything, keep going. He will have been told the same thing. You won't be doing yourselves any favours if you stop for a smoke and a chat, OK? We can hear and see everything. So can they.'

The soldier who was in charge touched Rosso's sleeve.

'Listen. There are lots of exchanges of prisoners and relatives on this bridge. Happens all the time. Mostly it works. You only hear about the ones that foul up. Remember, you've got lots of time. Take it easy out there.'

'Thanks.' They could see he was nervous. They must all look like that before a crossing. Poor devils.

2.15. It was time.

He stepped out awkwardly, almost twisting a knee, because the pavement was a bit of a drop down from the doorway. The snow was crisp, and his feet sank a couple of inches in it because no-one else had trodden there since the last snowfall.

'Haven't you got a white flag?'

It was one of the soldiers speaking to him.

'No,' he answered.

284

'Take off your shirt.'

'What?'

'Take off your fucking shirt.'

He stood there, let his jacket fall, dragged his pullover off, unbuttoned his shirt, removed his vest. The vest would do. It was white, clean the previous morning.

Oh, Christ. Had he messed up?

Rosso put everything else back on again.

His watch said 2.16.

'Now hold it up. Go on, raise your arm.'

He went out to the centre of the road, holding up the cotton vest in his left hand. He began to walk forward. There were beech and elm trees on either side of him, the blue sky showing through the branches. With the white snow all around him and the gurgle of water ahead, it seemed so beautiful. He yearned to stop and rest, sit on the bridge and watch the water go by, pretend not to see the war damage.

He had reached the railings and noted how the road under his feet began to rise very slightly as he mounted the bridge. He saw someone else at that moment, coming towards him, just his head and shoulders at first, then all of him came into view. It was Flett, carrying a makeshift flag, only his was a pillowcase tied by a single knot to a stick.

The American was also carrying a bag in the other hand, and over his shoulder Rosso could make out the rectangular black carrier he used for his laptop.

2.17. Rosso's shoulder ached. He switched his vest to his right hand.

The two men passed almost at the very centre of the bridge. Neither turned, not so much as a glance, they didn't dare, but each stared straight ahead, walking stiffly, like a slow march at someone's funeral. Rosso's funeral.

Neither spoke.

There'll be a show trial, the conviction and sentence a foregone conclusion.

It'll be the Rosso name on trial. Not me.

Rosso kept his eyes up, at the slopes of the hills before him, at the frosted firs, the white-capped houses, at the brilliant, impossibly blue sky. The air was so fresh, so cold against his cheeks. It feels great to be out, he told himself. It's just over there that I used to stop to eat *cevapcici* at one of those foodstalls – beef grilled over a fire. We were always ravenous when we were young. We never could have enough in those days. We were always eating.

2.18. Twelve minutes left.

Or maybe just a bullet, he thought. Without ceremony. Pushed onto his knees in the snow, feeling the wet through the thin material. Like Vasic. A cold muzzle pressed behind the ear and a quick glimpse of that Serb general watching from the warmth of his car, smoking a cigarette.

He would want to see a Rosso die.

Stop it.

At least one ceasefire is holding, he thought. Mine. This is my life. It's mine to give. They can't tell me how, or where, or when. It's the last thing, the only thing, finally, I have to give back. He saw the outline of people ahead, waiting for him, dark against the snow, hands in pockets and lounging in a doorway. They looked no different; scrawny, unshaven, stoop-shouldered, rifles slung over their shoulders, cigarettes in their mouths. Farm hands, reluctant soldiers. Waiting. Disinterested. Not caring if he died there and then.

He felt fear run through him. It was like swallowing ice. He had been frightened all along, from the very beginning, but he shivered with it when he saw the enemy in the flesh. Look up, he told himself. Don't look at your executioners. If you are going to die you can do so looking at this city, not their faces. This will still be here after we're all long gone, us and them. What does the Bible say about the sins of the forefathers? Rosso couldn't remember exactly but he was ending it here, now. For him there would be no seven generations, not of his father's kind. The buck stops here, as Flett would say.

The last sound in Rosso's ears as he reached the end of the bridge and began crossing the square was the steady, unhurried crunch of his own boots breaking the surface of the pristine snow. It was like cutting through the crust of bread so fresh it was still warm from the oven. He told himself there would never be a finer day for such a walk.